Chasing
My
Sister's
Shadow

Published in the United States by WordWings
Corvallis, Oregon

Chasing My Sister's Shadow

Copyright Linda S. Lingemann 2014
Cover art copyright Linda S. Lingemann 2014
Logo copyright Linda S. Lingemann 2013

ISBN 978-0-989-2559-5-0

Library of Congress Control Number: 2014905487

Chasing My Sister's Shadow

LENA LINGEMANN

For my mother, Emilie, and her sister, Erna

One does not become enlightened by imagining figures of light, but by making the darkness conscious.

—Carl Jung

PROLOGUE

Odd that my sister, of all people, would be the one to teach me about love.

When we were children, if I drew a mama, papa and two little girls under a brilliant sun, Ingrid would scribble in dark clouds and cover the family in bold strokes of rain.

"Why is Ingrid so gloomy?" I asked one night, as Mama tucked me in bed.

"Your sister sees the shadows." She gazed past the candle to eerie shapes dancing on the walls and ceiling. "You see the light."

Now, nearly thirty years later, I know that you need both to see clearly. And even then, just when you think something is in focus, the light shifts and the shadows change.

I have learned that looking closely at another person will reveal darkness as well as light, and your love must swell to encompass the whole human being instead of just the part that shines brightly. And always there is the danger of love stretching to the breaking point.

For love unbroken, my sister taught me, you must understand the shadows.

PART 1
GERMANY
1927–1928

CHAPTER 1
GERMAN GIRLS

When Papa announced that we would start a new life in America, his joy was a solo note against the chorus of Mama's tears. I was seven and Ingrid was eleven. August in Mannheim had just begun.

Within a few days, it was as if Papa's words had been written on paper and blown away by the summer breeze, as if Mama hadn't sobbed and pleaded with him to reconsider, as if he hadn't folded his arms and said, "I set sail for America in April, Senta. You and the girls will join me a few months later." What happened was, Mama closed her mind to the possibility of leaving our homeland. If anyone dared to mention Papa's plan, as Ingrid did, stomping her feet and demanding reassurance, Mama would say, "Hush. We will remain in Germany, where we belong."

Being a homebody, Mama took pride in our townhouse, even though it was owned by the factory where my papa, Andreas Varsten, worked as a machinist. The house was one of several lined up like encyclopedias, too close to the road for a front yard but with a backyard spacious enough for Mama's lovingly-tended garden and much-used clothesline. She had brightened up the interior with flowered wallpaper and curtains she sewed herself. Thus Papa's decision meant giving up not only her homeland, but the home she had made for her family within it. No wonder she resisted him.

Mama. Senta Varsten was petite, barely five feet tall, and when Papa called her "pleasingly plump," he intended it as a compliment. Mama would sigh in response. She was beautiful, with thick brown hair that fell into waves. When I pestered her to pose for Mr. Sholtz in town, who painted portraits in oils, she laughed and said, "That's for rich people, Katja. Mamas always look pretty to their little girls." I would meet girls who did not see their mothers in this rosy light, but at the time Mama's word was the final truth.

In those nine months before Papa departed for America, Mama made sure life was predictable, as if no changes loomed on the horizon. I went along with her, even though a nagging voice told me our lives could never go back to normal. Ingrid would have none of this make-believe and chose to confront Papa.

One sunny day at my favorite lake near the Rhein River, Ingrid said, "I will visit this lake for many years to come," to which Papa replied, "Next summer will be the last, but America has many beautiful lakes."

Mama turned her back on them and headed for the shoreline. As she spread out her towel, I waded into the water. Papa was a skilled swimmer and had taught me well. I looked over my shoulder and called to Ingrid, "Come on in, the water's fine." Like Mama, Ingrid was terrified of water (but enjoyed sunbathing). Though I never teased Mama, it was a treat to hold something over my sister since, as Papa said, Ingrid was "foolhardy as a billy goat, and more cantankerous."

It isn't easy to get along with a billy goat and Ingrid was my main companion. At home, we played house with an older boy who agreed to be the husband, though Mama said Peter only did this to get a meal, that his father "drank up all the family's money." Peter was gaunt and weary, but a decent husband. Ingrid played the wife and when I objected, she challenged me to do something about it. She was stocky, strong, and being four years older, easily able to bully me. I finally resorted to tears, which got me nowhere since she built it into my role as the spoiled child.

When I became frustrated as the daughter who got yelled at or spanked—I would have played the child willingly if Ingrid had been a nicer mother—I made a dramatic show of quitting and headed for the large chicken coop. There I plunked myself down on a rickety wooden stool to watch the hens go about their business. Their soft cluck-clucking seemed to slow my heart if it was beating too fast. They would have already forgotten their morning ordeal. Mama would grab each hen and feel the part that goes over the fence last; the hardness of an egg meant lost freedom for the day. The sounds uttered by the chickens during this manhandling made me cringe, for it was a shrieking, violated noise unlike their afternoon clucking.

Generally, though, I trusted that the chickens had good lives. Those who stopped laying eggs didn't think ahead to their fate as Sunday dinner nor did they brood over the loss of a lady friend. When I said as much to Ingrid, she grimaced. "Who cares whether those bird brains enjoy life or not? They're silly old things that scratch around in the dirt all day."

"It matters," I said, wishing, as I often did, that Ingrid would *understand*. "If they were miserable and then had their heads cut off, I don't see how I could eat them."

Ingrid scrunched her face into the hard lines that would become permanent. "Then you're the bird brain."

I look back on my German childhood as a happy one except for the pain inflicted by Ingrid's sharp tongue. When I asked myself why my own sister didn't like me, I couldn't find an answer. It took many years to realize that I wasn't asking the right question.

• • •

The leisurely days of summer were behind us all too soon, as our lives marched toward a departure date that Mama would not acknowledge. Fall meant school. My second grade teacher, like the first, was a stern older man who never laughed. I remember these teachers as the same person, but Mama said their features were as different as those of a pig and a bull. Early in the school year, I was punished for a classmate's crime. How a teacher could glance at quivery Katja, hiding behind hair the color of corrugated cardboard, and assume she would boldly whisper in class is a mystery. Yet one of those teachers who I couldn't tell apart growled *COT-yah* in a way that made my name sound repulsive, then ordered me to hold out my hand to receive lashes from a cane. When my tears gushed out like water from a shattered glass, a look of satisfaction crossed his face and that was when I had the fleeting thought—quickly chased away—that the teachers in America might be kinder.

It didn't occur to Ingrid to fear school but she was not one to skip gleefully out the door in the morning, either. Mama gave me the unpleasant task of rousing her. I learned to creep over to her bed, nudge her and run, for otherwise she would grab my arm and twist it. No matter what, she shouted, "Get out!" and sputtered bad words that only I could hear, reminding me of the neighbor's dog, a mongrel who would snap at a hand reaching to pat her head.

Once freed of my burden, I clattered downstairs and retrieved the pitcher from the cabinet. When Mrs. Gerber appeared pulling her cart loaded with a huge milk can, I raced outside to hold the pitcher while she poured milk into it. "Steady, honey," she crooned, her breath like milk just turning sour. We usually got a pint of milk and put some in our coffee, which was really chicory. After Mrs. Gerber had moved on to the next house, Papa patted his lap and said, "Hop up, little bunny." He cuddled me while I ate breakfast and I did feel like a baby rabbit cozy in a nest. It puzzled me that Ingrid didn't rush downstairs, too, but then I never saw Papa cuddle her. Perhaps this should have struck me as peculiar, but in truth I was pleased to have him all to myself.

The shortening days meant getting my sister up in darkness, which made her even more sluggish. I had to prod her repeatedly and she often made me late. When my classmates turned in their seats to stare, my neck and cheeks would tingle with heat. Being marked tardy wasn't entirely bad, though, since my punishment was to stay in for recess. The teacher would drop a book on my desk and command, "Read it!" as if giving me arsenic to swallow. I made sure to frown, for if he found out I loved reading he would choose a torture that was real.

It may seem strange, but my school clothes offered comfort during the teacher's outbursts. When he barked, "No slouching, sit up straight!" I would instantly comply, then rub the fabric of my dress between my fingers, picturing Mama's gentle hands sewing the seams, hearing her wren voice singing. Ingrid insisted our clothes looked homemade, trying to vex me, for she knew I hated standing out from others. To her, my weaknesses were like the bats in Grandfather's barn—she liked to poke and prod to get them fluttering.

Winter afforded Ingrid a worthier challenge than goading me. Railroad tracks ran near our house, and when the coal cars passed, people scrambled to gather pieces of coal that fell off. A group of rowdy boys had a bolder strategy, taunting the train attendants into throwing coal at them. Ingrid was the only girl; she wore boy's clothes, with her dark brown braids wrapped inside a cap. Some parents feigned ignorance of how the coal was procured; others threatened dire consequences. After swearing me to secrecy, Ingrid told Mama and Papa the coal was a gift from a boy. They accepted her explanation, never dreaming their daughter would engage in such an act, I suppose, though they had to wonder how someone as disagreeable as Ingrid could be receiving such a valuable gift.

Apart from the way it came to us, the extra fuel was a blessing. Our house had two stories plus an attic. Since the windows had no screens, the shutters were closed all day and the house lit with candles. The forced darkness made the cold worse, so cold that if Mama hung wash in the attic to dry, the clothes froze on the line. There they took on a life of sorts, their abrupt angles and flatness making them look like comic-book characters.

We spent our waking hours in the large kitchen on the ground floor, which was heated by a sizeable stove that drew us together. One day Papa tied a towel to a broomstick and strutted around the table waving it like a flag. Ingrid and I marched after him, laughing. The broomstick knocked over a pan of hot cocoa heating on a burner and spattered the contents on me. I screeched more in fear than anything else and everyone panicked. I can't recall feeling pain, nor did I suffer any scars. The memory is actually a fond one, for I was the center of my family's concern. Even my sister seemed to care about me.

Come nightfall, we tromped upstairs, where there was one bedroom for Mama and Papa, with twin beds pushed together, and another across the hall that Ingrid and I shared. I dove into my mushy feather bed like I did the lake in summer, getting the shock of coldness over with quickly. I waited for Mama to bring up bricks that had been heated in the oven and then wrapped in towels. She placed them at the foot of the beds, singing softly to herself. Forever after, I would associate Mama with a warmth that radiated from my toes upward. Did Ingrid feel this way, too? I couldn't tell, for I never saw her glow from the heat of our mother's love.

Always the high point of winter, Christmas was extra special that last year in Germany. Not only did my dolls get clothes to match my own, but Mama revealed a new talent: she could perform surgery. She gave my favorite doll, Lotti, eyes that opened and closed—imagine, new eyes—so they no longer stared zombie-like. I kept tipping Lotti up and down, mesmerized by the miracle Mama had performed.

"If you don't stop that," Ingrid said with exasperation, "I'll pull the eyes out and glue them to your shoes so you feel like someone is looking up your dress."

I stopped playing with Lotti when Ingrid was around and for weeks I carried her wherever I went. The day I forgot and left her in the bedroom, I approached tentatively, imagining two hollows where her eyes should be. But Ingrid had lost interest. I stared into Lottie's wide brown eyes with relief. Then I made her blink at me.

When spring arrived, Mama swung open the shutters to let in the light and flopped the feather beds from the windows to air out. The scent of fresh air on the beds was so strong that first night, I pictured myself sleeping under the stars. Spring would give us many gifts, like baby chicks and violets, but it would also take something away. Papa. Though I had heard the muffled arguments and the suitcases being dragged across the floor, I hadn't let myself attach meaning to the sounds. Ingrid was the opposite. If something ominous lurked in the shadows, she hunted it down and pulled it out of hiding. She never doubted that Papa would leave us.

CHAPTER 2
FAREWELL, PAPA

My parents tried to prepare me for Papa's departure. "You'll be my brave beauty, won't you?" Papa cupped his hands on my shoulders and locked his gaze into mine in a steady flow of light. His blue-grey eyes drooped at the corners, giving him a sleepy, wistful look. When he added, "No tears, right, Brave Beauty?" I nodded, sniffling, and vowed to be strong.

Mama's persuasion took a more practical bent. "You want your papa to remember you looking your best, don't you?" Again I nodded, desperate to be what they wanted me to be instead of the weepy Katja I was in real life.

Ingrid knew me best. "You're wasting your time," she advised Mama and Papa. "She'll bawl like a half-witted calf no matter what you say." In private, she warned, "If you snivel and embarrass me, I'll smack you when nobody's looking." It comes as no surprise that I wanted to obey my sister, too.

Of course wanting to be a certain way isn't always enough. When the awful April day came, I cried from the moment I sat on Papa's lap in the morning until we returned without him (though by evening my sobs were more like the barks of a sickly schnauzer). As the SS Arabic drifted from its port in Hamburg, headed for New York, I had to be dragged from the disappearing figure that was my father. His last view was of a puffy-faced daughter wailing and struggling to escape her mother's arms—hardly a brave beauty—while his other daughter stood at a distance, gazing toward the horizon as if she were a bystander rather than a member of the family.

After Papa went to America, Mama's younger brother moved into the attic bedroom. I feel guilty admitting this, but Uncle Albert proved to be a fine stand-in for Papa, though the men were distinct in appearance and temperament. Both were of medium height, but Papa was muscular, with dark blond hair and a touch of melancholy that compelled women to give him a second look. You could tell that Uncle Albert was Mama's brother, for he too was "pleasingly plump," his round face shiny with red dots on each cheek that seemed painted on. His thinning hair was black, his smile frequent and sweet.

I got whatever I wanted from Uncle Albert. He was much easier to sway than Papa. "Shameless," Mama would say, smiling as I secured yet another peppermint. "Disgusting," Ingrid would remark, nose in the air. *Jealous,* I would think, for Ingrid seldom got extra candy honestly.

Despite the indulgences of Uncle Albert, I missed Papa in wrenching waves. It was worst at night, when I was plagued by a reoccurring dream where Papa was swimming back across the ocean to me. I would be at the shore begging him to hurry, but the more furious his strokes, the wider the gap grew between us, as if his efforts propelled him backwards. At the point where he gave up, I watched him sink until only the tips of his fingers remained.

Jolted awake by my own screams, I scurried to Mama's bed, and as long as these visits were rare occurrences—she had been cautioned by a busybody neighbor not to spoil me—she welcomed them, probably because her bed was now a vast ocean on which she floated alone.

Even in the midst of my urgent need for Mama, I felt a sense of betrayal, for she had convinced me that Papa would remain in Germany. With time, I have come to judge her less harshly, for I believe she had convinced herself as well.

• • •

We spent the summer in Brühl with our grandparents. I know now that Mama worried we would never see them again. This visit was a treat for me, though Ingrid complained mightily. Being older, she would be put to work in the fields while I was permitted to play. Here was one instance where she did not want to be treated equal to a boy.

After riding the train from Mannheim to Brühl, we hiked through a wooded area toward the farm of Frank and Rosa Varsten. I picked violets for Grandma Rosa and admired the petals, drawn to things tiny and fragile. We crested a small hill and took in a panorama of the farm, nestled with others around a small village. In addition to tending livestock (small numbers of cattle, pigs and chickens) and a field of grass for hay, my grandparents had an apple orchard with trees lined up in rows like an audience watching a performance. Years later I would bite into an apple and see that vista, though the fruit never tasted as deliciously tart.

The farmhouse had one story and a huge attic sectioned into makeshift rooms. The only way to the privy was through a courtyard between the house and barn, an area guarded by a flock of vigilant geese. Ingrid could intimidate them, but they interpreted my "Scoot! Go away!" as a plea, not an order, and I had to run in zigzags to dodge their sharp pecks.

Once, when the huge gander chased me, I fell face down into a puddle and bawled like a toddler, my outrage not due to the goose himself, but goose droppings in the water. Grandma Rosa came running with the broom, though she needn't have brought it. The geese scattered, regarding her as the head goose, no doubt. She carried me to the house in her arms, soiling her black and white checked apron with the dreaded dung.

She plopped me into a tub of water and said, "This soap is a beluga that will turn you into a beautiful white whale like itself." Afterward, she patted my skin dry and carried me upstairs as if I weighed no more than a cloud that had taken beluga form. As I sunk into a feather bed on top of a straw mattress, she winked and said, "Goose feathers." When Ingrid poked her head in and called me a baby, I shrugged, sure I deserved the name but not caring.

My grandparents couldn't have been more different. Grandma Rosa's intense blue eyes gave off sparks of purple in the sunlight, reminding me of the violets I picked for her. Plush silver hair cushioned her face and made her ankle-length garments of dark fabric all the more jarring. She belonged in flowery dresses of crisp cotton, but only her aprons had color, and not much. I decided she wore black because living with Grandfather was enough to depress anyone's mood.

Frank Varsten was not *grandfatherly*, not one to read stories to a child on his lap. In fact, bedtime triggered nothing more than a "Get to bed!"—usually unnecessary because we scrambled upstairs early to avoid his raspy voice and the heavy-browed expression that went with it. But his disposition was nastiest at mealtime and could spoil the taste of Grandma Rosa's pot roast by making my stomach churn. One time, when the sweet-tempered spaniel Minchen got in his way under the table, he gave her a swift kick. I slipped her a bit of meat, trembling like the spaniel for fear of being caught. To Grandfather, supper offered the perfect opportunity to address what Mama called his "beehive of complaints" because of their sting, mostly having to do with how each of us fell short of his expectations. We were lucky he often lingered at the tavern and came home late, falling into bed with a thud.

To my surprise, the atmosphere in my grandparents' home improved in Papa's absence. Only then did I realize how much he and Grandfather had quarreled. "Regardless of what their fight appears to be about," Grandma Rosa said, "if you dig deep enough you will find the same worms. Your grandfather values farming above all else and your Papa detests it." At age fourteen, Papa quit school and left home to study the machinist's trade, which Grandfather took as a rejection of all he revered.

The only people bold enough to talk back to Grandfather were Ingrid and Papa. Ingrid received spankings as a result, and one time a searing slap across the face. I knew that Papa had endured worse at her age, being a boy. His older brother Gerhard had left the family as a teenager to make his fortune in America, or so everyone was told; Mama said the real reason was to escape the beatings that followed any wrongdoing, no matter how small.

The only time I sought out Grandfather was when he cut hay, for I was allowed to slide down the huge pile before it was tossed on the wagon with pitchforks. Once loaded, the wagon was pulled to the barn by oxen, with me on top like a queen on her bristly throne. Papa started this practice (even with his job, he helped out on the farm) and though Grandfather muttered that "Haying is not playtime," he came to view it as a necessary evil, like a heifer kicking up her heels in the meadow instead of acting like a proper cow. Given Papa's delight in such acts, I suspect he disliked farming because Grandfather wrung every bit of pleasure from it.

Grandfather's influence in the kitchen was a fire that burned dirty, but Grandma Rosa made raisin bread, my favorite, with enough love to dissolve the unpleasant residue. Bread making was best if Ingrid was off working in the fields, for otherwise she would pick raisins from the loaf and stuff them in her mouth, boasting later that she had spit them out. I hoped she was lying, for I couldn't bear the thought of my sister throwing away food to keep me from enjoying it.

Grandma Rosa made loaves of rye bread so big we had to cart them to the baker's cavernous oven. If it was just the two of us, we sang on the trip up and back. Eventually bread making was scheduled during Ingrid's farm duties, perhaps because of the raisin theft but more likely because no one was inspired to sing in my sister's company.

Grandma Rosa used lard from the butchered pigs to make the bread. The notion of devouring the living, breathing, animals I had come to know upset me, but she was matter-of-fact. "It's perfectly all right to eat a pig," she said, "as long as we waste nothing of the animal." When Grandfather prepared for the butchering, I raced to the far end of the property to mute out screams that made me shudder even at that distance. Ingrid stayed to help. It wasn't that she was so coldhearted as to be untouched by suffering, but she believed that enduring the slaughter would make her stronger. "The more fears you meet head-on," she told me, "the better able you are to face life's problems."

Sometimes I grew stronger in spite of myself. Grandma Rosa was a self-taught nurse and midwife and she let me tag along on her routine calls. Ingrid couldn't fathom why I would "seek out the company of sick people" and she had no interest in my descriptions of deathly ill patients coming back to life under Grandma Rosa's care, nor in the infants she delivered. I did get queasy in the midst of the blood and pain of birth, but it was nothing compared to my enchantment with babies brand-new to the world. Grandma Rosa recorded each visit neatly in the pages of her journal and asked for my observations. I would dictate comments like *Baby Anna has blond curls, sweet angel,* and *Baby Emil squeals like a puppy.*

Birth and death were woven into my German childhood. On Sundays I walked with Mama, Grandma Rosa, and Ingrid to the cemetery at the other end of Brühl. Sometimes Uncle Albert joined us for the day.

The cemetery was a source of pride to the community. Families were buried in common plots set off by low brick borders that formed a raised garden. A large tombstone guarded all whose names were engraved upon it. Some people visited daily, taking hoes and spades to cultivate flowers, but Sunday was most popular.

I loved the flowers, my favorite being pansies because they looked like little faces turned toward the sun. But if there is a flower that blooms at night, this would be Ingrid's choice. With ghoulish glee, she declared that the bodies beneath the earth were skeletons and described how they got that way. I put my hands over my ears, but Ingrid, always stronger, peeled them back and shouted first in one ear, then the other, "Worms and maggots eat away the flesh." My mind draws pictures to go with words and these made me shriek as if it were my own body in the grave. Grandma Rosa stalked over to Ingrid, hauled her behind the garden shed, and gave her a sound whipping. I heard my sister's growly yelps with satisfaction and so did many of the adults gathered at the cemetery.

"That girl is so willful," Grandma Rosa said when she rejoined us.

I nodded emphatically.

Uncle Albert said, "Youngsters at Ingrid's age are trying to understand death. It frightens them, and so they talk back to it like a dachshund yapping at a snorting bull."

He was defending her!

Mama pursed her lips and let out a puff of air. "Ingrid needn't overcome her fears by terrifying her sister."

I shot Uncle Albert an injured look, but he only glanced at me without apologizing. "I'm not excusing what Ingrid did," he told Mama, "but Katja needs to realize that sometimes people act the way they do for reasons having nothing to do with her." He looked at me. "Remember, too, that when you get hysterical, it only encourages Ingrid."

I snubbed him the rest of the day.

Sundays weren't usually this controversial. Rarely were visits to the cemetery about death or those who died, unless it was to share some juicy tidbit about the person and that was only acceptable after a period of time (dead people were saints for at least two years). Most often Sundays were social gatherings where people tended flowers, exchanged gardening tips, and gossiped, and so I came to associate death with flowers and people chatting in the sunshine. As usual, Ingrid saw the clouds rolling in long before I did.

I still get embarrassed recalling our last week in Brühl. Grandma Rosa wanted to give Ingrid and me earrings to remember her by, so she took us to a jeweler to select a pair and have our ears pierced. How I yearned for the pearl earrings with their smooth sheen—not only was it grown-up to have pierced ears, but I intended to wear the earrings every day to keep Grandma Rosa close. Yet the needle that pricked Ingrid's ear lobe was an ice pick to me (though she didn't so much as flinch) and the image of it stabbing my ear propelled me out the shop door and down the street. No one could catch me.

When I slunk home, I learned that Grandma Rosa had purchased the earrings anyway. I cried in her arms, ashamed that I couldn't wear her gift. "Keep the earrings for a braver girl," I insisted. "I don't deserve them."

She pulled the velvet box from the pocket of her apron and flipped it open. "They don't have to decorate your ears. You can look at them and think of me."

I turned the earrings in the candlelight to admire their rich creaminess. When I went to return them to the box, I noticed the satin pillow upon which they rested. "How pretty," I said. "Just the right size for a little doll."

Grandma Rosa's eyes crinkled at the corners. "Go ahead and take the pillow for Ada. I have something else to cushion your pearls." She pulled open her dresser drawer and took out a small hankie. "My own grandmother embroidered this and now it's yours." The hankie had an intricate pattern of flowers—pansies! She folded it and placed it in the box, nestling the earrings on top.

Grandma Rosa bought the earrings certain I would get my ears pierced someday, but I never did. It wasn't fear of the pain, for that faded with time. I think I needed to punish myself for letting her down. And after the need to punish died, it seemed too late.

CHAPTER 3
LAND AND SEA

Ingrid seemed anxious for Grandma Rosa's farewell hug to end; I wanted mine to last forever. But as the train to Mannheim pulled up to the station, Grandma Rosa eased away from me and turned toward Mama. The two women stood on the platform facing each other. No words were exchanged, at least none that I could hear, but they seemed to be talking without words. Finally, Grandma Rosa kissed Mama on each cheek, and Mama reciprocated. Then Mama guided Ingrid and me up the railcar steps, her face taut with grief. Mama's parents had died when she was a young girl and Grandma Rosa had become a mother rather than a mother-in-law to her. It was after this good-bye that Mama seemed to accept that she would be leaving Germany.

Getting ready for a trip to another country was a full time job for Mama. Not only did she have to dismantle her household, but she sewed traveling clothes for us, which included knitted undershirts of tan worsted wool with green trim, garments built up at the shoulders and buttoned down in back to the waist. Like everything she sewed they were made to last, which was a curse in this case, since the undershirts were so itchy she may as well have sewn scouring pads together. And we would never be free of them. When Ingrid outgrew hers, they would go to me, and when I outgrew them, Mama would use the wool for mittens and scarves.

As the time to leave drew closer, we didn't make it easy on Mama. Ingrid declared that she wasn't going, that she was a German girl who belonged in Germany.

My mouth dropped open. "But what about Papa? Don't you want to see him again?"

"If he wants to see me, he can come back to Germany."

"But he's making a new life for us. We'll own a house with a lawn in front and garden beds in back." This was Mama's dream. She had shared it so often that I could see the perfectly straight sidewalk leading to a welcoming front porch with lilacs on either side of the steps. "Papa said he will work less but make more money in America," I continued. "He won't change his mind."

"Then I won't see him again, because I'm staying here." Her brown eyes looked black. When I started to cry her eyes brightened, sunshine piercing through clouds. "That would make you sad?"

I nodded. "I couldn't live without Papa."

A violent swoop of her arm and I was knocked to the ground. Ingrid loomed over me. "That's all you care about, your precious Papa." She spit "Papa" out like something foul on her tongue.

A whirlwind of Mama tore into us, bending Ingrid over her knees and spanking her hard. When Mama let her up, Ingrid bounded off like a wolf released from a trap.

"Why is she so hateful?" I whimpered from the shelter of Mama's arms.

She kissed my face. "Ingrid was born with a kernel of meanness inside. The best we can do is keep it from growing."

But part of me felt bad for Ingrid. She had thought my tears were for her.

• • •

We could only bring what we were able to carry, which eliminated treasured keepsakes and furnishings. In the weeks before our departure, Grandfather's gangly twin sisters took a sudden interest in visiting us. They could never wave goodbye on their way out because their long arms were loaded with dishes and knickknacks or extended to carry a table. As we filled our trunks with clothes and rolled up our feather beds tightly for use on the ship, we tried not to get sentimental about what must be left behind.

We had to go to the dentist before embarking on our journey. In the waiting room, I remember hearing the child ahead of me screaming. But that's all I remember. I learned later that I had two decayed molars pulled. And my baby teeth. I would never get to wiggle them like my schoolmates in America. Mama explained that we could be turned away at the hint of a medical problem. I have no idea how the dentist kept me in the chair while he pried open my mouth. Mama said it took three people to hold me down and that she had to be escorted from the room. I suppose my mind covered up the experience in the same way I pulled a quilt over my eyes to hide from monsters in the night.

Our last afternoon in Mannheim, I stood in the empty chicken coop missing the cluck-clucking. The hens had disappeared one by one, reappearing as meals on the table, except for the best layers, which had gone to Grandma Rosa. A new family was set to move into our townhouse; in fact some of their furniture had already invaded the premises. We had permission to use these items, but I wouldn't even sit at the kitchen table. The house seemed alien and I asked Mama to let me sleep outside. She refused.

"You would rap on the door at the first hoot of an owl," Ingrid said with a laugh, and we all knew she was right.

I got up before the sun the next morning, earlier than I needed to but unable to sleep. Cupboard doors slammed below as Mama fixed breakfast and the floor creaked above as Uncle Albert dressed. He would accompany us only as far as the dock, although Mama hoped to convince him to make the journey later on.

Ingrid lay in bed staring at the ceiling. I dressed without a word, since Mama had said to ignore her. Then I trudged down the stairs to take my place at the new people's detested table, wise enough not to make an issue of it that morning. Uncle Albert followed in short order, ruffling my hair before settling next to me.

"Ingrid, breakfast," Mama called.

I stared at the gruel in front of me, which was runny and had a sour smell.

"Eat!"

I willed myself to hold it down.

Mama ate in silence, shoveling huge spoonfuls into her mouth as if the bowl were something to be excavated.

After washing and drying her dishes and telling me and Uncle Albert to do the same, she clumped upstairs.

Though I expected it, I jumped when she yelled at Ingrid. "I'd be happy to leave you behind if I could find someone to put up with you!"

I heard no reply from Ingrid.

Uncle Albert patted his mouth with a napkin and said, "Excuse me." I watched him ascend the staircase in an unhurried fashion. When he disappeared into Ingrid's room, Mama appeared on the landing like magic.

She took each step as if she had walked a hundred miles, then flopped onto the kitchen chair and said, "I'm sorry." When I started to protest she held up a hand wearily. "There are better ways to handle your sister."

This turned out to be true. Whatever Uncle Albert said to Ingrid got her downstairs, though she sat at the table with her hands in her lap, her thoughts closed off from the rest of us.

● ● ●

We took a train to the bustling port of Hamburg again and boarded a fairly new ship, the Hamburg America Rhein. It was a good one, Mama said. As it pulled away from our beloved Germany, the band played a common folk song, *Muss I Denn*. "Must I then, must I then," Mama sang, in a voice deeper than you would expect in such a small woman, "leave the village, leave the village and you, my dear, remain here?" The first time I heard the American song *Wooden Heart*, my own heart nearly stopped, for the melody was the same. Though it was many years later, I was instantly back on the ship, teetering with its sway. I heard the seagulls call and I inhaled the damp air. In my memories, I could even smell the salt.

We traveled second class, sharing a room and a pair of bunk beds with two young women. They were ideal roommates. Not only did they entertain us, chattering about how they would search for husbands in America, but they also knew some English. In the evening, as we prepared for bed, they would repeat words and phrases to us, some useful ("Where is the toilet?), a few not ("I am unmarried"). We would have plenty of instructors, Mama said. Papa had been learning the language and our aunt and uncle had been speaking English for years.

The accommodations on the ship meant that Ingrid and I were allotted one bed. She slept like someone hunted in her dreams, flailing her arms and legs so that I took a battering. The first night, I climbed down to Mama and flattened myself against the wall to take up less space. For the next twelve nights, I started out with Ingrid—my way of telling Mama I would try—but switched beds after a few minutes.

We spent our days outside. Mama rented deck chairs, but we didn't sit much because we were usually slumped at the rail heaving our meager meals overboard. The October wind shoved the ship back and forth like a bully taunting a child. When the rain pelted us, I imagined this bully as America spitting on us so we would go back to Germany.

One morning a huge wave slurped over the deck and soaked Mama. Her hair dried stiff as a scrub brush from the salt water, so the next day she went to the beauty parlor on board. I thought this was an indulgence only rich people could afford and I felt a shiver of happiness when a young girl washed Mama's hair as a servant would do. The shampoo made her hair soft enough to pat and poof with my hands, and when I snuggled up to Mama that night in bed, I was lulled to sleep by the faint scent of lilacs. To my mind, we had thumbed our noses at the bully. The trip didn't seem as frightening after that and my stomach settled.

Our first glimpse of land was a dim light in the distance; all the passengers crowded on deck to cheer as New York Harbor came into view. We made a stop in Lower New York Bay, where doctors boarded to check us for diseases. "They act like we're foreign livestock that will infect their prized heifers," Ingrid grumbled. "I hope I gave that mealy white-coat my cold."

It's true that there were no smiles or handshakes for the immigrants. When we disembarked at New York Harbor, no one greeted us with baskets of fruit and bread, as we would welcome newcomers to Mannheim. Instead, we were herded into lines for another physical examination. "America does not welcome sick people," Mama said, "but at least we've been spared the humiliation of Ellis Island." Had we arrived a few years earlier, she explained, doctors would have tested us to determine if we were stupid as well as sick, chalking an X on the shoulder or back of anyone who didn't pass. In that case I would have failed every test, struck dumb with fear. Ingrid must have had the same thought, for when I undressed for bed that evening I discovered an X drawn on the back of my blouse. Hurtful, but evidence that Ingrid was herself again.

We had to spend the night in a huge hall crammed with people. We were given two cots and a crib and when I realized the crib was for me, I raised a fuss. Mama's efforts to shush me only made me shriek louder, and her cheeks reddened. To my amazement, Ingrid offered to sleep in the crib, "to shut me up." I felt guilty seeing her lying on her back in the baby bed, legs hanging over the lowered rails, but not enough to change my mind. Mama kissed her on the forehead, but Ingrid turned away and gazed through the bars without expression.

From New York we took a train to Chicago. I was too excited to sleep, but it would have been impossible anyway, what with the jerking and pulling of the car, the old men hacking, and the young mothers yelling at unruly children in a language that was new to me. I tried to peer through the dirty yellow windows, but gave up. The scenes of factories and dingy snow with brown patches and bare trees made me ache inside, though I held out hope that the windows made the landscape seem worse than it really was. But that wasn't so.

We switched trains in Chicago to get to our destination, Milwaukee, in the state of Wisconsin. Weeks at sea had given us time to pour over a map of the United States and get our bearings while exclaiming over the size of the country in comparison to our homeland.

I had barely stepped from the car at the Milwaukee Road Depot when I spotted him.

"Papa!" I leapt into his arms before anyone else could. When he lifted me up, I said, "I'll give you one hundred kisses." I pecked at his face wildly.

"Bunny busses." He was laughing.

I tilted my head at him.

"*Buss* is another word for *kiss*," he said, his eyes enlivening his tired face. I inspected him. Could a person get wrinkles in only a few months? The lines creasing either side of Papa's mouth and his forehead were like new streets added to a familiar neighborhood.

"What's wrong?" I said, but he was stretching to kiss Mama, drawing her in as he shifted me to one side. I was engrossed in the power of their embrace when Ingrid disrupted it.

"HI, PAPA."

Mama jumped to the side, startled. I rested my head on Papa's shoulder and watched.

Ingrid stood about five feet away but her fury made her seem closer. "Aren't you glad to see me?" It was a demand, not a question.

Instead of getting mad as he typically did at such an outburst, Papa set me down gently, keeping hold of my hand. He held out his other hand to Ingrid. "Of course I'm glad to see you. Come here."

She shook her head furiously and crossed her arms so tight she seemed to be hugging herself. "No, because I'm not glad to see *you*. We were happy without you."

Mama swung forward and slapped Ingrid across the face, a slap that came from her whole body. Any other child would have fallen, but Ingrid staggered and regained her balance. They glared at each other.

"Apologize to your father."

"No."

Mama lunged and Ingrid flung her arms up in self-defense.

I took in a sharp breath. Ingrid, afraid?

Papa pulled Mama back, his jaws tense. "Enough, both of you."

And so began our life in America.

PART 2
AMERICA

1928–1937

CHAPTER 4
SETTLERS

Papa had fetched us by horse and wagon. We would spend the winter months with Uncle Gerhard and Aunt Elsa, who lived on a farm outside of Milwaukee. We clattered along behind a shaggy draft horse whose body was caked with mud. Dust clogged the air, making my eyes water and my throat shudder with rat-tat-tat coughing spells. The flat terrain was as gray as the overcast sky, with snow like moldy cottage cheese.

How did Mama keep from crying out when she saw the old farmhouse? We had left a tidy white townhouse with red shutters to come to this haunted house with its three stories of peeling greenish paint and shutters flapping every which way like frantic ravens. We soon learned there was no inside plumbing and the first time I opened the outhouse door a rat dashed over my foot. I ran screaming into Mama's arms while my cousins laughed uproariously.

Uncle Gerhard was an elusive figure who talked in jumbled sentences and wobbled when he walked. Mama said he drank too much liquor. His children included a daughter and three bratty sons. The boys mimicked the way we talked, as if their broken English were superior. Mama said to turn the other cheek, that they were teased for the way *they* talked. But these tyrants were hard to ignore, for they concocted ways to torment us and I got to skittering around the yard like a mouse harassed by barn cats. They especially liked to hide in trees and throw rocks...until the day one hit Ingrid and caused blood to trickle down her face.

She was a sight, scrambling up a huge oak after her chunky teenage assailant. When she grabbed Hendrik's leg, he screeched like a squirrel caught in a badger's jaws and his fingers made scrabbly sounds against the bark as she yanked him down. He tumbled backwards and she shifted to the side so he wouldn't fall on her, then lit into him with her fists.

The other boys had clambered down from their trees and stood open-mouthed, arms dangling. I ran and got Papa. He pulled Ingrid off Hendrik, then dressed her down something fierce. I tried to explain that Hendrik had hit her with a rock, but he shouted at me to be quiet and said there was no excuse for a girl beating up a boy. And that is what Ingrid had done, for Hendrik had a black eye and bruises of various sizes. Except for the cut on her head, Ingrid was unharmed and clearly the victor. Had she been a boy, she would have received a hearty slap on the back. I didn't understand Papa's anger, particularly since Ingrid's actions put a stop to the rock-throwing.

● ● ●

During that first month in America, my only respite came from the Montgomery Ward catalogue I found in the outhouse. I ripped out pages and took them to the basement room Ingrid and I shared. There I painstakingly cut out models and pasted them on cardboard to create a paper doll family. For the younger daughter, I selected the prettiest girl my age in the catalogue. Her hair was the color of a newly hatched chick and fell into comely waves rather than coarse brown curls like mine. She stood confidently instead of slouching to look smaller. I picked a strong-looking brother to protect her and a smiling teenage sister to hear her secrets.

Our girl cousin was Ingrid's age but more interested in me because I did what she wanted. She loved to play school and I was an eager student who steered her to teach me English. In this way I prepared for the American classroom on the horizon. I had already picked up many words, since Uncle Gerhard required his family to speak English. This was true for most of the German families in Wisconsin. The Wendts were the only ones we knew who continued to speak German.

The Wendts lived on a parcel of land a couple of farms down, and shortly after our arrival, Mrs. Wendt invited Mama for tea, adding, "bring your girls along to meet my daughter." Their farmhouse perched on a slight rise. It had a gabled roof and wraparound porch, and had been newly painted a soft yellow with white window trim. The expansive lawn was bordered by well-tended flower gardens. After our first visit, more invitations were extended, probably because Mrs. Wendt was one to enjoy praise. I think Mama accepted because it gave her a few hours in the house of her dreams, filled with furniture from the home country.

The Wendts acted as if their hilltop home made them special. Ingrid and I dreaded our visits, since we were obliged to sit perfectly still while the adults talked. I couldn't help sliding down the high-backed leather sofa and had to struggle to right myself, which prompted Mrs. Wendt to remark, "My goodness, Senta, your youngest is fidgety." I doubt she knew our names, for with the exception of her daughter, Mrs. Wendt didn't seem to have a high regard for children. To make matters worse, Mama would reprimand me, intimidated by this woman's wealth and attitude of superiority.

The Wendt girl was held to a different standard. She did not have to imitate a statue and was free to do as she pleased. At some point during our visit, she would interrupt my misery to inflict one of her own. Bouncing up and down in her dirndl dress, she would beg her mother to let me play with her. Permission was immediately granted, prompting the Wendt girl to skip down the hall with me following as if I were going to have tangles combed from my hair, which I would have preferred. Once she had me trapped in her princess room, she presented crisp new dresses, colorful books, and pre-printed paper dolls with extensive wardrobes, each time asking if I owned any as nice. She knew I didn't, but she seemed to require reminders of her good fortune.

On one occasion Ingrid was summoned to join us, I suppose to expand the audience. The first item offered for our admiration was a tortoiseshell comb.

"Ooh," Ingrid gushed, with a flutter of her hands, "isn't that just too lovely?" The Wendt girl glowed as my sister turned to smile at me. "It's nearly as nice as the smallest comb in that set Papa gave us. Of course ours are skillfully carved, with hand-painted decorations, not plain like this one." She blinked her eyes at the Wendt girl. "I'm sure your comb would keep the hair out of your eyes. You really should wear it. How can you see through that frizz?"

Though the Wendt girl's spirits were dampened, she continued to bring out items only to have Ingrid describe finer examples in our possession.

I knew Ingrid's dishonesty was wrong, but it meant the end of invitations from the Wendt girl. She quickly learned that one sister came with the other and I benefited from that rare alliance. Still, my relief was blunted by guilt. "Mama says being nice is the only proper way to behave," I told Ingrid, "even when other people are not nice."

She shrugged. "That braggart needed to be taken down a peg or two."

• • •

Papa was away most of the winter working at a factory in Milwaukee that made parts for machines. He stayed at the apartment of a co-worker and spent his time off searching for a place of our own. One March evening, when we were gathered for supper with our relatives, Papa announced that he had rented a house in the city. At this news, I felt light enough to flitter about the room like a pixie.

Papa avoided my eyes. "Don't raise your hopes too high, Katja. Until I can save more money, we must take what we can get."

Ingrid's chair made a grating sound as she slid back from the table. "Don't tell me it's a dump like this."

"Ingrid." Mama's face was crimson. She glanced at Aunt Elsa, then Uncle Gerhard. "I apologize for my daughter's bad manners."

Aunt Elsa nodded curtly. Uncle Gerhard's face was dead-looking, as if he had passed away angry.

"Leave the table," Papa told Ingrid.

"No," she said quietly. "I'm not finished eating."

All three boys stopped gorging themselves with pork sausage to stare at her, their fingertips glistening with fat.

"Ingrid…" Mama's voice had a pleading tone.

I had never known any child who would defy her parents in this way.

Uncle Gerhard stood up and unbuckled his belt. He whipped it through the loops and held it out to Papa. "Use this."

"No one asked for your advice." Papa did not respect Uncle Gerhard because of Aunt Elsa, whom he considered slovenly, nor was he one to raise a hand in anger.

"This is my house," Uncle Gerhard said.

I trembled in my chair and looked across the table at the smug face of my sister.

• • •

My aunt and uncle left us in Milwaukee with handshakes and vows to visit soon, though everyone knew they wouldn't and this was fine with us. I heard the creaking of their wagon as it made its way back up the dirt road, but I was too overcome by the condition of our new home to glance over my shoulder. Lacking Ingrid's insight for disaster, I had assumed nothing could be as bad as the ratty farmhouse. I was wrong.

Even brand-new—which I couldn't picture— the house must have been shabby and cheap. It had a thrown-together feel, as if the builder didn't care that boards met crookedly or paint dripped willy-nilly. Nor had it improved with age. Its paint was the color of soiled straw and the only bright spots in the yard spurted up as crabgrass and dandelions. Stepping through the front door, I wrinkled my nose at the musty odor and looked up to see water stains on the ceiling. Yet Mama was able to enthuse over the pump in the kitchen, which was hardly a lavish feature. She would still have to heat water for cleaning, but at least she was spared the toil of lugging pails of water from outdoors. She also laughed along with Papa when he said the outhouse didn't have rats, "only mice, so we're moving up in the world."

Senta Varsten was trying to make the best of things. She hated the house as much as Ingrid and I did, but she didn't complain. A good wife wouldn't cast doubt on her husband's ability to properly provide for his family.

The neighborhood matched the house. When we hung laundry in the yard, we had to keep an eye out so no one stole our faded and mended clothing. But unlike the rest of my family, I had a gilded path leading out of the darkness. School. I was placed in third grade again, which was playtime, for the work had been much harder in Germany. We attended a Catholic parochial school with nuns in black habits. My teacher loved to sweep me up in her fleshy arms, but Ingrid was not so fortunate.

Ingrid arrived in America wearing her thick hair in braids, but before school started, she demanded that Mama cut it short so she looked less like a foreigner. Always at odds with Ingrid, I wanted to let my short hair grow long. Mama couldn't be bothered and didn't trust me to use a comb regularly. Hair styles didn't make the difference, anyway, because I was easily accepted while

Ingrid was not. Her struggles with English worsened in the presence of a grouchy, strict teacher and Ingrid's temperament didn't help. Each day she stomped home from school, slammed her books on the table, and went to her room.

I started the next year in fifth grade with children my age, while Ingrid stayed back to repeat eighth grade. She wasn't dumb—no one was more cunning than my sister—but Mama said the older you are, the harder it is to adapt to change. And the changes would be many.

CHAPTER 5
SHARP TURNS

One chilly October afternoon in 1929, Papa came home from work early. He looked like a stranger. His skin was the color of meat marked down at the market and his face quivered the way a horse's flank will when bothered by flies.

"What is it?" I said, his fear igniting the same in me.

He patted my head distractedly and murmured, "Senta." I tore upstairs to get her.

"Mama." My breath came in gulps.

Her heavenly eyes were huge. "Tell me."

Hiccups strangled my words, but when I stammered out, "Papa," she clattered downstairs. I moved to follow, but Ingrid pulled me next to her on the step. I met her eyes and read fear there, too. If the strong people in my family were scared, the world must be coming to an end. I started to speak, but Ingrid put her finger to her lips. "Hush."

The murmur of voices in the kitchen became distinct.

"So you still have your job?" Mama said.

"I do, but many do not." A long pause. "I saw men weeping in the streets. Some lost more than their jobs, their savings are gone, too."

"Savings?" The word came out shrill as a whistle. "Tell me our money is safe!"

I couldn't hear Papa's reply, but Mama's voice was clear. "That money is for a house. It's our money. I'll go to the bank and demand they pay up."

Again, I couldn't hear Papa, only Mama. "I refuse to lower my voice. If we lose our savings the girls will know soon enough. I'll track down that bank manager—" Her voice collapsed under the weight of emotion. "I won't live this shanty life forever."

Papa tried to boost her spirits, but how could he succeed when his were so low? I didn't understand *Black Tuesday*, though it was a perfect name for this day. Ingrid's explanation was that businessmen gambled with other people's money and got carried away. "Like Gus next door and his endless card games," she said. "He bets and loses, then takes the money Vera has saved to bet some more, confident he will have the winning hand. People bet on companies that failed and lost money. Then everybody else panicked and tried to pull their savings from the banks."

We were blessed for a while because Papa was employed. But love of the automobile was his undoing. He so admired the Ford Model T owned by his boss that he often stayed late to help crank it. One day he slipped and the crank spun down and broke his arm. The doctor bills were hardship enough, but when Papa was let go because he couldn't perform his job, Mama's storehouse of bitterness swelled. "You give that sleazy Goebel a helping hand and this is how he repays you?"

Papa could have accepted this, but as Mama was apt to do now, she went a step further. "And you, kissing the feet of such a man because you covet some foul machine. It's revolting."

Papa would lash out at Ingrid in anger, even me at times, but never Mama. He seemed to shrink under her disapproval. And he knew there was truth in what she said, that his lust for a car had jeopardized his family's welfare. After this, Mama's singing and Papa's jokes became joys of the past and I lost myself more in books.

It was due to Ingrid that we came together at all. Though she did nothing to improve her grades, she arranged to get the daily newspaper when our neighbors had finished with it so she could read the comics. And because she asked for help with the words, our family was able to laugh at Blondie and Dagwood and others. It was an odd turn of events that Ingrid was the source of our only fun, although naturally that wasn't her intention.

• • •

By the summer of 1930, our world was as bleak as that of the men Papa had seen sobbing. He had been unable to find a job and though no one in our family gambled, our savings were lost. During the hottest, most humid months in Wisconsin, we earned small change by picking raspberries. A farmer drove up to a street corner before sunrise each day to collect those who wanted work and brought us home after darkness fell. We rode crammed in the bed of his truck, standing for the thirty-minute ride and trying not to fall into the bodies of other people who were already sweating. In fields of gnats and chiggers, I gorged on berries and scratched at bug bites until I developed horrible rashes. It was worth the pain to have Mama dote on me with hugs and kisses like she used to.

To everyone's relief, autumn brought a turnaround in our fortunes. Papa was hired to manage a four-story apartment building in a better part of town, though it would be more correct to say that he and Mama got the job. The sturdy red brick building had stores on the first floor, with efficiency and one- and two-bedroom apartments on the upper floors. I was happy to leave our gloomy house, and because I had been destined to get Ingrid's teacher the next year, I didn't mind changing schools, either. When I said as much, Ingrid replied, "She would have been sweety-sweety to you, bootlicker that you are."

Mama was quick to jump in. "Katja doesn't snarl when she talks, and she knows how to read, so Sister Royale would have treated her well."

I had become a rock one of them grabbed to hurl at the other.

As manager of the Cherry Street Apartments, Papa was given the only unit on the first floor, located in a back corner of the building. We had four rooms plus our own bathroom. And running water. Sometimes I turned the faucet on to remind myself of this luxury.

The grocery store in the building was a godsend, Mama said, as we had no way to keep food cold for long. I loved going to the store with her. When she told Mr. Jolitz what she wanted, he retrieved the items from behind the counter. Because Mama was frugal and always paid in cash, Mr. Jolitz never had to open his notebook for her, which was where he recorded a person's name and what was owed, due on payday or at the end of the month. Some people would "forget" to come in and shop elsewhere, taking advantage of another merchant. Mama said Mr. Jolitz's willingness to put names on the books during these trying times showed that he was a man of good character.

I hoped that in this more agreeable setting my parents would resume their carefree ways, but as Ingrid said, "Everything good comes with a price." Papa took care of the furnace and hot water heater, which was coal-fired, and saw to any handyman jobs that arose, but Mama did the bulk of the work. She had to sweep and mop three flights of steep stairs and three porches running front and back, as well as clean apartments that frequently became vacant, since tenants sometimes departed in the wee hours of the morning. Ingrid and I were expected to help after school and on weekends. The first day we followed Mama out the door, Papa peered over the newspaper from his customary spot on the faded sofa, his feet—in darned socks—propped up on the coffee table.

Mama waved to him. "See you in a few hours."

When we stepped into the hallway, Ingrid was fuming. "How can he let you do all the work?" Her tone accused Mama as well as Papa.

"German men do not touch a broom or a mop," Mama said. "They consider it woman's work."

"Why?"

I looked at Ingrid as if she were simple-minded. "For the same reason girls don't fight fires or build houses."

She folded her arms. "And what reason is that?"

"Well...men are stronger, so they do the jobs that need muscle."

"You're saying Mama has it easy?"

"No—"

"You think it's fair that Papa sits on his behind while Mama does the work?"

I could see that Ingrid was trying to trick me, confuse me. "It's the way things are, that's all." I crossed my arms to match hers.

A faint smile eased the stiffness in Mama's face. "Come along." She led us to the closet where the cleaning materials were stored, then handed me a broom and Ingrid, a mop. "You're both right. It's not fair, but it's the way things are."

"It's the way men decided things should be." Ingrid let the mop fall to the floor.

Mama sighed. "You're going to have a hard life if you constantly challenge the rules."

She snorted. "The suffragists knew all about hard times and challenging unjust rules. If it were up to you and Katja, women wouldn't have the vote."

Eyes flashing, Mama said, "No more back talk. And pick up your mop."

I resolved to ask Ingrid more about the suffragists.

● ● ●

We settled into day-to-day living. Mama still dreamed of buying a house, but she had to start over building a nest egg. Once, when I happened upon her in the bedroom stuffing money into a box of holiday decorations, she became agitated and grabbed my shoulders with such force I cried out. She said, "Never, ever, tell Papa you saw me putting money away. Do you understand?"

I was shocked by her roughness and harsh tone. "Keep a secret from Papa?" She may as well have ordered me to lie to God.

"Yes." She shook me while chanting hysterically, "Keep this secret from Papa, keep this secret from Papa."

Whimpers came out of me instead of words. She let go and fell back on the bed, arms and legs stiff as those of a bisque doll.

"I'm sorry." She sat up again, her gaze suddenly tender. "It's just that for you the world is black and white. To be loyal means to have no secrets." She looked at me hopefully, as if I would deny her words, but I didn't. She smoothed the fabric on her flowered dress, one from Germany that had seen many washings. "What about your loyalty to me?"

"You're my mama." I knew where this was leading.

"You must keep my secret from everyone."

I nodded.

"Papa especially."

"But why?"

She worked a worn section of her dress with her finger until she made a hole. "He would spend the money. In dribs and drabs, he would spend it. He would buy me a fancy hat, or you a new doll, because he's comfortable with the way things are. He doesn't care about owning a house, in fact, I think he would rather not."

"I will keep your secret," I whispered, for at that moment I understood that my desire for a house burned as hotly as hers.

She pulled me to her in a hug. Then she massaged my shoulders, trying to remove the ache she had put there.

● ● ●

Mama's hidden money was one more brick added to the wall forming between her and Papa. Beer was another.

During prohibition people could get the ingredients needed to brew their own beer, although they couldn't buy them all in one place and the ingredients were labeled for some other purpose. Papa got himself an oak barrel for a keg and kept it in a shed behind the apartment building, along with his beer-making supplies. I associated beer with the sloppiness of Uncle Gerhard, but that wasn't the reason I shook my head when Papa asked if I wanted to lend a hand. It was the set of Mama's jaw any time he talked about his "brewery."

Papa was left with one possible assistant and Ingrid was an eager volunteer. Brewing beer was one of the few activities she and Papa did together. As she stirred water heating on the stove, he added ingredients that included malt, hops and sugar. They poured this mixture into the keg and let it ferment for a few days.

When the mixture was ready, it was Ingrid's job to clean the bottles. I couldn't resist saying, "I see the suffragette has lowered herself to bottle washing." She reacted swiftly, pouring the contents of a soapy bottle over my head. Mama wanted to forbid her from helping Papa after this, but he let Ingrid off easy with no dessert for a week.

To fill bottles from the keg, Papa used a hose for a siphon, sucking on one end to start the flow of beer and then stopping it with his finger. He positioned the hose at the bottle's opening and released the liquid. Ingrid stood by with a special gadget to cap the bottle before it overflowed. Papa and Ingrid then loaded the bottles into wooden apple crates from the grocery store and carried the crates to the shed. They worked as a team, which I should have applauded, but I had a sense of uneasiness I couldn't shake.

In the days that followed, it was Ingrid's job to check on the brew. One morning she burst from the shed yelling that a bottle blew. Mama rushed outside with mop in hand and admonished her to keep her voice down. Ingrid immediately apologized, then thoroughly cleaned the area of broken glass and sticky beer so Mama wouldn't complain about flies.

Papa brewed beer for himself at first, but eventually he gave some away. Gifts to family and friends led to requests with a few dollars added. I woke up to arguments in the middle of the night. Papa quietly maintained that his brewing did no harm and meant extra change for the cookie jar. Mama shouted that it wasn't worth the risk and called him a bootlegger.

Ingrid put an end to the argument.

• • •

It was a snappish fall afternoon in Wisconsin, not pretty as it had been a few weeks earlier when the trees flaunted pom-poms of orange and red. Now their leaves were dull and scattered about like discarded party favors. My friend Doree and I sat on the front steps of the apartment building, buckling roller skates over our shoes. The junior high school we attended had let out for the day and I had an hour of free time before chores.

I stood up and helped Doree to her feet.

"Thanks." She squinted down the sidewalk. "Isn't that your sister?"

"Oh, yes." I started to skate in the opposite direction.

"Why is she walking so funny?"

With reluctance, I swerved to look.

Ingrid shuffled toward us singing *With a Song in My Heart,* loud and off-key, then stopped abruptly to pick something up. "A penny," she chirped. "I knew this was my lucky-ducky day." She jumped at me, shoving her face into mine. "Boo!"

I backed off, smelling beer.

Doree grimaced. "You stink."

Ingrid straightened up in an exaggerated manner. "The queen did not come here to be insulted by her subjects." She broke into giggles. "Off with your heads."

I glanced around. "You can't let Mama and Papa see you like this."

"Like what? I've never felt so good in my life. They'll be bowled over by my smiling face." She pulled a bottle from her book bag. "They should drink more beer. Keep 'em from getting so crabby." She fumbled in her pocket and extracted a bottle opener.

"Don't!" When I went to grab the bottle, it flipped in the air like a juggler's club and shattered on the pavement.

Ingrid's dopey sunniness vanished. "You little goody-goody, I'll make you sorry you did that!" She landed a blow that knocked me down. I screeched when I hit the glass and cut my hands trying to get up. Ingrid was on me like the beast I envisioned lurking under my bed.

Then Papa was there, pulling her off. Mama came running up with Doree, who must have gone to get them. I expected yelling, but the silence was worse. Papa held onto Ingrid as if she were something foul. Mama's hatred flowed from Ingrid to Papa and back to Ingrid. I knew there was no hatred on my face, only sorrow, for as much as Ingrid upset me, underneath it all I loved her. I could not say the same for my parents.

The effect of this incident on Ingrid was to make her edges sharper. She had pilfered bottles the whole time she and Papa were making beer, she told me that night in our room. It was her only motivation for helping him. "Did you think I did it for his company?" She looked askance at me. "I was born because he did something dirty—it's not like he wanted me."

If only I could let Ingrid's words careen into the air without trying to catch them. But I was a foolish dog clamping my jaws over a hornet. "What do you mean, dirty?"

Ingrid raised an eyebrow. "He had sex."

That word instantly made me think of the call girls in our building, and a conversation I had overheard between my parents. Mama had been appalled to learn we had tenants who "entertained men," but Papa convinced her to hold back her judgment. He pointed out that unlike many tenants, the call girls were quiet and regularly paid their rent, a higher amount because they preferred furnished apartments. Later, when I asked Mama if *entertaining* meant the girls held parties, she said it was something less nice than that, something I would understand when I was older. But I wanted to understand now.

"Does entertaining men have something to do with sex?" I asked Ingrid.

She snickered—"You bet it does"—and went on to explain sex to me, relishing how I squirmed and wrung my hands at each prurient detail. "So, your mama entertains your papa like a call girl," she said, "the only difference being that she doesn't demand payment. At least not in the form of a wad of bills smacked into the palm of her hand." When I looked at her in confusion, she added, "Never mind. I was making a joke. She's not really like a call girl."

I was shaken by the tone Ingrid had used in talking about our parents and I didn't want to believe they would perform such a disgusting act. Yet I didn't doubt Ingrid's facts. Her meanness always sprung from some hidden truth.

"What about me?" I said. "Did Mama and Papa only have me because of...you know?"

"Sex. God, you're a prissy thing." I could see that Ingrid was calculating how much to hurt me. Finally she said, "They wanted sex first, but then when you were born, Mama said, 'Why, Andreas, will you look at those dimples and that smiling face? She's such a cute and happy baby,' and Papa replied, 'Oh, yes, I'm so pleased we have her. I'll call her my Bunny-Boo.'" Ingrid's voice was mocking, but her face showed a sad resignation.

"I'm sure they had the same feelings when you were born." My intent was to comfort her, but as was often the case, I had misjudged my sister.

"You wicked little troll—you know they never wanted me." She thought this was obvious, but the idea had only just been born in me, so slippery-new I couldn't grasp onto it, for in my young mind it was impossible for parents to dislike their own child.

• • •

Ingrid had the power to tip the seesaw, launching our family into light or plunging us into darkness.

Her drunkenness was a smear on the Varsten name, but the damage went beyond that. She had also been, in Mama's words, following in Papa's footsteps. A boy tattled to the principal that Ingrid had been selling beer to classmates. Her month-long suspension from school was hardly a punishment to Ingrid; the ramifications for our family were far worse.

I trembled in my room as Mama went outside and methodically smashed the keg with a hammer. The yard smelled like beer for weeks. For me, the smell never left, though of course it couldn't remain in the ground year after year. Mama got what she wanted through Ingrid—the end of Papa's brewing—and at the time I sided with her. Looking back, I could make sense of my father's reasoning.

"It's my hobby," Papa told her, "and it's such a small operation. Only people I'm acquainted with. The money they give me barely pays for the ingredients. If you read the newspaper, you would know that Prohibition can't last." Papa wasn't a big drinker. He didn't get wobbly like his brother or cruel like his father, though perhaps Mama feared he would. His connections with the men who bought his beer were embedded in friendship; he sat on the porch on Saturday nights, talking and joking with them. Most lived in the building.

After Papa's brewing ceased, he went to a man across the vacant lot who was a real bootlegger. This man in a dark overcoat acquired liquor from different sources and met buyers next to the garbage cans. The way I know this is through Ingrid, who hid behind some bushes to snoop. When a customer showed up for hard liquor, the bootlegger would get the bottle (a pint or a quart, depending on the thickness of a man's wallet and the degree of his thirst) and pour a shot or two, then hide the bottle. He held his hand out for money, not a hand-shake. When visits to this man began, the laughter on our porch ended. And Papa lost another bit of sparkle, like a Christmas ornament that sheds glitter each year.

And Ingrid? Never one to sparkle, she was a silver bell becoming more tarnished with time.

CHAPTER 6
SPARE TIME

In 1931, we weren't well-to-do, but we didn't view ourselves as poor, either. Besides the rent-free living quarters, my parents received thirty-five dollars a month for managing the apartment building. Even so, Mama accepted clothing as gifts, being by nature not only gracious, but practical. One of the call girls, Charlotte, was young and pretty and donated garments for Ingrid and me. (Mama had come to accept the call girls in the same way she had accepted Ingrid's coal for the stove—by ignoring what she didn't wish to see.) Charlotte's generosity had its drawbacks, since we weren't allowed to turn anything down and though the clothing wasn't risqué, it often wasn't what girls our age wore. And they definitely didn't wear fur coats. The one Charlotte gave me for Christmas—her smile gleaming scarlet—had close-cropped plush fur that triggered a clammy sweat when I put it on. Forced by Mama to wear it, I took obscure routes to school and entered the building with the coat balled up in the bend of my arm, no easy task with such a bulky garment. Doree only asked about it once and when I held up the coat she nodded in sympathy.

To my relief, Mama deemed the fur coat "good clothes" and I wore a wool jacket on the weekends when I headed for the skating rink, which was a pond frozen over. I kept track on the calendar and I went skating forty-one times that year, including days when the temperature was below zero, though I was no stranger to the warming house. As soon as we arrived, I plunked myself down on the bench to lace up my skates. Ingrid joined a group of older kids, the boys sullen and the girls brash with rouge and loud voices. They skated to the back of a small island where the teenagers were rumored to smoke and neck. I didn't see my sister again until closing.

My favorite skating partner was a Jewish boy who looked like Mickey Rooney. Max was a speed skater who displayed endless patience in teaching me to skate backwards. He wasn't my boyfriend, but we liked each other. His religion made him mysterious, though we never discussed it. I didn't know what to ask and he kept his faith clasped to his heart. We only met at the ice rink.

When the weather warmed enough to turn the ice to slush but not enough to put my wool coat in storage, I spent my free time at the library. There I pushed my paper racehorse across many finish lines by reading increasing numbers of books. After the walls of my side of the bedroom became plastered with certificates, Mama suggested we combine them into a book. She sat me down at the kitchen table and made much of designing a cover with the title *Katja Reads for Success*. (I liked *Billions of Books* better, but Mama said it had an element of bragging.)

"I wish we could make a book for your sister," Mama said when Ingrid came in to pour herself a glass of water, "but there aren't any books with no pages. Such a shame the library doesn't give credit for reading the comics." Ingrid gulped down her drink, wiped her hand across her mouth, and left the room. Mama followed after her.

To witness such taunting made me miserable. What would cause Mama to act this way? And then I saw the answer in the form of our report cards on the countertop. I was aware of Ingrid's failing mark in English because she had asked me to read her the teacher's note.

I pulled the card from its cardboard holder and re-read the scathing words conveyed in beautiful script, like poison ivy clothed in sunburst colors: *Your daughter has a terrible attitude. She makes no effort to read her assignments. When given a second chance to catch up in study hall last week, she looked right at me and pulled out a comic book, one stolen from another student (who was disciplined for bringing it to school). Such blatant disrespect for adult authority suggests lax discipline at home. If you fail to correct this situation, your daughter is in danger of being put back another grade. I cannot emphasize too strongly the importance of instilling the correct values in children, as your daughter's questionable moral character does not bode well for her future.*

Ingrid did pass ninth grade. I heard Mama tell Papa that the teachers probably didn't want to suffer through another year with her. No matter; the pressure that had been building in the Varsten family was released. School was out for the summer and we were carefree, at least for the time being.

We regularly walked the three blocks to the swimming pool and bathhouse. For a nickel we could rent bathing suits that were probably ten years old, with long skirts, built up shoulders, and holes in various places. Though I shudder to think of them now, I wasn't bothered then, probably because we didn't rent them for long. On the day Mama went with us, she looked aghast at the suits and within a week had made us new ones.

I swam the whole time we were at the pool, while Ingrid reclined in a lounge chair or dangled her feet in the water. We stayed until the manager chased us out, then lingered in the showers if it was the right day (girls on Wednesdays, boys on Fridays). Like most families, we had a bathtub but no shower at home, so the bathhouse with its steaming burst of water was a treat, and we loved the tangy scent of the soap that was provided.

Our leisure activities expanded the day Papa brought home an automobile. Mama said the fact that the old Ford had many previous owners should have been a warning sign. If it was so grand, she argued, deflating Papa's excitement as she was wont to do now, why did people keep giving the car up? He muttered that they probably moved on to newer or more expensive models. "If you would let lose the purse strings," he added, "we could buy a better automobile."

Mama picked up an empty bottle of beer he had left on the coffee table and rubbed vigorously with a rag at the ring of moisture remaining there. "I don't want one at all. If my legs can't carry me where I need to go, the bus will do just fine."

But she did ride in the old Ford and although she would never admit it, she enjoyed our excursions to Devil's Lake. As soon as the car rolled to a stop under a spreading elm tree, Ingrid and I burst from the back seat. We shed our clothes down to our swimming suits and dashed through the grassy picnic area to a beach so smooth it seemed to be made of tiny pearls instead of sand. The lake was clear and warm and I waded off to the side, away from my family, and stood stock-still, waiting for the minnows that had scattered to return. I loved the tickle of tiny mouths on my ankles, like being kissed by Lilliputians. If I ventured out far enough, the minnows would be replaced by sunfish, which were shaped like small pancakes. They darted out of reach but when curiosity got the better of them, they glided back and weaved around my legs.

One time, through what Mama referred to as a lesson in patience, she and I were able to catch a sunfish. We lay on our stomachs on the pier and I held a large jar in the water, arms aching, until she had gently herded the fish inside it. When I lifted the jar to the light, the sunfish's scales glinted and shimmered like jewels. I cradled the jar in my lap on the ride home and kept the sunfish alive in the apartment for months, but later I felt bad condemning him to such a life. At first he would challenge his reflection in the glass, but unlike the goldfish I had owned, he soon tired of that. He probably died of boredom, if such a thing is possible. Ingrid said, "It's not like a fish reads magazines or anything. What is there for it to miss?" *The company of other sunfish,* I could have replied. *Rippling water teaming with life. Swimming in a straight line.* But at the time it was a feeling without words attached. I never wanted to catch a fish again.

During each visit to Devil's Lake, Papa and I would exhaust ourselves in the water, then spread out towels and sunbathe side by side until our suits were dry. Mama and Ingrid would already be on the beach, though separated by a large expanse of sand. When Mama clapped her hands and said, "Time to go," Ingrid and I scrambled to the car. Whoever arrived first got to pull down the window shades to make a dressing room. After Mama and Papa changed clothes, it was our turn. At sixteen, Ingrid had a woman's body and I would sneak peeks, trying to quiet my anxiety about growing up. The day she caught me and called me "perverted," I was so mortified that for the rest of the summer I waited outside the car and let her get dressed first.

That summer of '31 my own body had begun changing. Blond fuzz appeared on my upper lip and I worried about becoming one of those women with a dark moustache or a mole sprouting black hair. And then there were the bumps on my chest that were supposed to be breasts but looked pointy instead of round. I asked Mama for a brassiere, without realizing that Ingrid had hung around to listen. After erupting into gales of laughter, Ingrid said, "Stick to your little girl undershirts, Katja, and by the way, a smaller size will do."

"Stop your nastiness," Mama said. "At twelve, you asked for a brassiere."

"But I had reason to."

"Do you have reason to be this spiteful?"

I stared at the embroidery on the tablecloth, knowing my request would be forgotten. These battles might start with me, but they were never really about me. It was as if Mama and Ingrid needed an excuse to shriek at each other like hawks over a rabbit. Their anger seemed unnatural, for I had assumed love between mother and child to be automatic. If this wasn't true for Ingrid and Mama, it meant something was wrong with both of them. I could accept a defect in my sister—I thought she must have been born screaming with rage—but shouldn't a mother love her baby, even a baby scream-ing with rage?

What I couldn't reconcile was that something was wrong with Mama.

CHAPTER 7
REAL LIFE

Real life seemed to start in 1932, the year I turned thirteen. The time before belonged to an innocent girl who once was me. The events of that year are ever-present, as if they happened a moment ago. They drape a black veil over my life, marking the period when our family disintegrated. Not all at once, but piece by piece. I tried to save us without knowing I was powerless to do so. I was patching a hole in the wall of a house, unaware that the foundation had rotted and the whole structure would cave in, that the one wall I had worked on would be smooth and not matter.

It began on a March day. I came home from school and hesitated in the doorway, tempted to escape to Doree's flat, or the ballpark, anywhere far from Ingrid's yelling. But I stayed.

"I'm going home to Germany!"

"Don't be ridiculous." Mama's voice was calm, which meant the argument had just started. "You're not going anywhere." Water gushed from the faucet, dishes rattled in the sink.

"I'm sixteen and I can do what I want!"

"Not without money you can't."

"I have a job as a salesgirl. I quit school."

Silence. Not the lovely quiet of the library, but the foreboding absence of sound before the avalanche gives way, the tornado snatches a house, or the torrent of water bursts a dam. There was no stopping what was coming. I thought I should get Papa, but I was frozen in place.

"You did what?" Mama's voice sizzled like oil on a griddle.

"You heard me."

"Tell me again. Surely you can't say something so stupid twice."

There was that silence again, but no...I could hear a low rumbling. The rocks, the gales, the floods. Coming.

"I hate school and I quit and you can't make me go back. I start at Gimbels on Monday. I'll earn the money for my fare to Germany and that's the smartest move I'll ever make."

I peered cautiously around the doorway to see their faces, though if I had clomped into the room they wouldn't have noticed. There was a sound like a punctured tire releasing air. It was Mama letting her breath out through pursed lips. She said, "This is my thanks for raising someone else's child as my own."

I grabbed the door jam, which became my guide as I slid to the floor.

Instead of being shocked and hurt, Ingrid stood taller. "I know you're not my mother. Grandfather Frank told me. He didn't need to, though, so don't congratulate yourself for raising me like your own, because you didn't. You'd have to love me to do that."

Mama's face crumpled. "You knew? I'm sorry, Ingrid, very sorry." Her features took on a hopeful cast. "But then you also know that Andreas Varsten is your true father."

"He had sex that made a baby," Ingrid scoffed, "but he's no father. He snatched me from my real mother and forced me to live with you. As soon as I have enough money, I'll find her."

Mama turned away from Ingrid. I could tell that she wanted to say more but was restraining herself. She started. "Oh, Katja. You shouldn't be hearing this."

"Why not?" Ingrid said. "The princess should know she has a bastard half sister."

"Stop," Mama said.

I couldn't grasp hold of this. "But how—"

"You know the facts of life, thanks to me," Ingrid said. "Papa screwed another woman besides your dear mama, and lo and behold, a bastard was born."

"Shut your mouth!" Mama's power had returned and Ingrid knew it, but that wasn't what stopped her. I saw in her face that whatever sister—half sister—bond there was between us made her think better of wounding me when Mama was her target.

"Sit down." Mama thumped the table.

We obeyed, probably because we didn't know what else to do.

She sat across from us. "After your father and I became engaged, his friends threw him a bachelor party. Remember that all I know about this comes from Andreas. He had too many mugs of beer, he told me, which clouded his thinking. He went to the back room with this woman, who later bore a child. She couldn't keep the baby. He begged my forgiveness, at the same time asking me as a new bride to raise the infant as my own. It was hard for me, too." She searched Ingrid's eyes, but they were unreadable. "I did the best I could." She patted my hand, still looking at Ingrid, as if imploring her to understand and forgive.

"My real mother wanted me," Ingrid declared. "Grandfather said you tricked her into giving up her child, stole her baby because you were afraid you couldn't have one of your own."

Mama stood up. "I'll hear no more lies. Whatever else you care to learn about your history must come from your father."

Ingrid rose to face her. "I don't want anything from him."

Mama sucked her emotions into somewhere deep within herself and left the table. I heard the padding of her feet as she went to her bedroom and the click of the door closing.

Ingrid's face lost some of its toughness and she sounded forlorn rather than accusing when she said, "What are you staring at?"

"My sister," I replied.

• • •

Months passed and our family remained splintered but at least the rift didn't widen. Mama and Ingrid no longer screamed at each other. Mama and Papa seldom argued. There was little conversation between any of them. Everybody talked to me, and at times the weight of my family's desperation hunched my shoulders, for I couldn't fill each person's need for the other. Yet the absence of shouts and curses created a stillness that seemed healing to us all.

Our life developed a new pattern. On weekdays, Ingrid rose at six-thirty. By then Mama had been cleaning the building for an hour or so and would return to make sandwiches. At first Ingrid refused these offerings, but one day she shrugged and said, "If you insist on preparing my lunch, I may as well eat it," though she never thanked Mama, who also kept supper warm for her. When I suggested pushing suppertime back so we could all eat together, Mama explained that routine was important to German men and Papa must eat at five.

Each morning I watched the clock until Ingrid left to catch the bus, for she seemed to pack the tension into her handbag when she headed out the door. Papa would venture to the table then and join me for breakfast. It was just the two of us, since Mama had resumed her housekeeping duties. He would ask what was in store for me at school and offer guidance if I needed it. I came to rely on his undivided attention to start the day right.

Typically my hours at school sailed by untroubled, but there was one exception, near the end of the year. I had to speak in front of the class and when my name was called to present a report that Papa had pronounced "inspiring," I claimed illness and was sent to the nurse. I *was* ill. Even so, before the last bell rang, the teacher insisted that I give my speech and I hurried through it in a monotone. Weeks of studying Gertrude Ederle, first woman to swim the English Channel (so daring, so unlike me), resulted in a *D* for presentation and an *A* for content; my first *C* ever in English.

Despite my mediocre showing, I skipped to Doree's house when school let out, relieved to have survived my ordeal. We kept a secret stash of romance magazines in her basement, issues I found behind the apartment building, neatly stacked in cardboard boxes by the call girls, I assumed (I never said a word, nor did they). We liked to pore over each issue, particularly those from *True Confessions* and *True Story;* the covers were much the same from month to month—a man and woman in a clench—and the inside was steamy with stories of passion and betrayal.

A book, *Bad Girl,* had been stuck among the magazines and Doree invited some of our friends over to read excerpts. She and I knew the ending: the main character gave birth to a baby outside of wedlock, which made her a bad girl. In one scene, as the couple necked feverously, the girl said, "Oh, Eddie, I want more." Doree and I twirled in circles, hands on our hearts, crooning, "Oh, Eddie, I want more." No one understood when I abruptly stopped laughing and fled to the bathroom—I'd made the connection between Papa and Ingrid's mother. I told my friends it was a dizzy spell.

We had to hide the magazines because our mothers forbade us from reading "trash." I only felt a little guilty because I knew Mama had nothing to worry about. I loved good books too much to be corrupted by bad ones. I devoured Pearl S. Buck's *The Good Earth* and was inspired by the *Collected Poems* of Robert Frost.

The world was opening up to me in many ways, with one avenue leading to another. Doree and I discovered the picture show and a handsome actor named Clark Gable (I was even able to giggle when Doree said, "Oh, Clark, I want more"). Due to the beauty of the actresses we saw on screen, we became obsessed with our appearance.

Ingrid, who had been nicer since her outburst with Mama, took Doree and me to the beauty school downtown, where we had finger waves done free of charge. Mama's lips formed a straight line when I came home with these tight waves—the height of style for older girls—but she made no comment. Ingrid and I taught ourselves to do the waves on each other, though it took all day for our thick hair to dry.

A month later, Mama surprised the family with a new hairstyle of her own: a bob. She met Papa's fury head-on, saying she wanted a modern look and besides, the short haircut was cooler in the heat of summer. It was their first real quarrel in months and remarkable because it had nothing to do with Ingrid. Though Papa called her a flapper and barely spoke to her for days, Mama said she would never again wear long hair wound into a pug. The bob was here to stay.

Although the new hairdo made her seem less motherly, I glowed with pride when heads turned to admire Senta Varsten. I loved doing her hair in pin curls or finger waves and dreamed aloud of working at a beauty salon. Mama was adamant. "No, Katja. You must do more with your education. Setting hair is fun when the patrons are your mother and sister, but doing it all day for women who are vain and difficult to please would bore you and wear down your spirit." At thirteen, I was willing to disagree with Mama but in this case I suspected she was right and I didn't give the idea a second thought.

• • •

Just when life had settled down, Ingrid stirred it up again.

"You've got school smarts," she said, after we had perched ourselves on stools at the soda fountain. I had been expecting her to ask for a favor; if she offered to treat me, there had to be a catch. Not only was Ingrid stingy, but a trip to the soda fountain was an extravagance during the depression and only possible because our family had a small but steady income.

"I need your help in locating my real mother," she continued, "so I can be reunited with her in Germany. I've been saving what I earn from Gimbels—"

I raised an eyebrow. Ingrid brought home a new dress or sweater every month. This was one of many ways she hurt Mama, who still sewed clothes for me and would have done the same for her. It also meant Ingrid had less money to contribute to the household.

She rolled her eyes. "I can't save every penny. A girl's got to look nice when she works in the fashion industry. Besides, my mother will send money once she realizes I'm looking for her. That's where you come in. I need you to play detective."

Something inside of me was hardening, what it might feel like to be lost in a snowstorm and slowly freezing to death. "I won't help you leave our family."

Ingrid snorted. "I've never been a part of this family."

"How can you say that? We grew up together."

Ingrid leaned back on one elbow. "You don't understand what it's like to be unloved."

I thought about that and had to agree. "But you *are* loved," I said.

She was shaking her head.

"I love you," I said in a small voice.

She laughed. "You don't matter."

I wasn't frozen any more. I was melting, my heart liquefied and running out of my body in tears. I slid off the stool just as the soda jerk set a root beer float in front of me. He was a gangly boy with hair sticking up in thatches, but his face was kind. "What's wrong?" he asked.

"She's a cry baby," I heard Ingrid say as I stared at the floor. "It's none of your business anyway, so scram."

I met his eyes then. "She's mean and I apologize for her rudeness. Thank you for showing concern."

He nodded and backed away uncertainly.

"Listen," Ingrid said, taking hold of my arm, "that came out wrong. Think of it like this, if I loved you, but Mama and Papa didn't, you wouldn't want to stay in the family either."

"Maybe not," I said, stuck on *"if* I loved you" and wondering whether my sister did love me and thinking probably she didn't. In that case, I should let her go. "What do you want me to do?"

"Get my mother's name and address from Grandma Rosa."

The thought of my grandmother was soothing. I climbed back on the stool and took a sip of root beer. "Why don't you write to your precious Grandfather Frank?"

Ingrid grinned. "You *can* be sarcastic, there's hope for you yet." Her smile faded. "He can't read and write and you know it. Even if he could, he wouldn't respond because he doesn't care one iota for me. He only blabbed about Papa and my mother to get me to cry when his beatings didn't work. And of course he can't miss a chance to criticize Andreas and Senta Varsten."

"But what made you believe him?"

Ingrid stirred her soda listlessly. "I always knew they didn't want me." She straightened, then swiveled to face me. "I have to find out if my mother wants me. Please help."

Over her shoulder I met the eyes of the soda jerk and read his expression: *Maybe this is the reason she's so mean.* I smiled at him. "I'll write to Grandma Rosa tonight."

My intentions were good, but fate broke more than my promise.

CHAPTER 8

MAMA

"My head is pounding worse than usual," Mama whispered.

I hovered over her in the darkened bedroom. "Does the cool cloth help?"

She moaned softly. "Oh, yes."

"I'll be right back." It was Saturday and Mama hadn't cooked supper. While Papa waited at the table, I hastened to heat leftover casserole and Ingrid chopped vegetables for filler. I hoped she wouldn't complain about Papa's inactivity, for it wouldn't take much to set him off. Someone who swears by routine would need it most when he was anxious, wouldn't he?

"Thank you, girls," Papa said, when food was on the table. "We must do whatever we can to help your mama."

"You're welcome," Ingrid murmured.

Fighting would have been better. Now I knew how worried they were.

We ate in silence until Papa's overly-cheerful statement, said almost to himself. "Senta will feel better after resting."

"If she doesn't," Ingrid said, "we must call Dr. Perry."

He frowned. "You mama only has a headache. She would give me a piece of her mind if I used household funds for a doctor's visit."

Ingrid stood up. "You'll grab a fistful of dollars and release them to the outstretched hands of a bootlegger, so I think you can spend some on Mama—"

"Since when do you care about Mama? I thought you hated us both."

"Only you," she said, eyes reduced to tiny slits.

Anger makes people blurt out words raw. I have come to regard emotions as paint on a palette, with love and hate mixing until it's impossible to determine where one ends and the other begins. On that day, Ingrid painted Mama the color of love and Papa the color of hate.

"Let me look in the cookie jar for that wad of bills you're guarding." Ingrid went to the counter, removed the head of the smiling ceramic pig, and pulled out a few coins. Papa's face turned paler than it was already. "It's not just that you don't want to spend the money," Ingrid said. "There's no money to spend. I'll pay for the doctor. After all, I've got a job." She spun round and disappeared into Mama's room.

Papa was gripping the edge of the table. "I earn money as an apartment manager."

"Yes," I said, knowing that money in Papa's hands disappeared through his fingers.

"Your mama wouldn't approve of me calling the doctor for a simple headache."

"Sometimes we need to do things Mama wouldn't approve of." I carried a stack of dirty dishes to the sink and set them down with a clatter. Who was I to criticize? I refused to use money from her secret house fund in defiance of her wishes.

Papa's hands hit the table and rattled the silverware. I turned to see him stomp out the door, which wasn't unexpected. This was what he did when Mama shouted at him for procrastinating on some repair or chastised him for dipping into the cookie jar on a whim. He would reappear hours later as if there had been no problem and because Mama's anger would have faded into resignation by then.

Though tempted to leave dishes in the sink, I hurriedly washed and dried them before tiptoeing to the bedroom. I stopped in the doorway. Ingrid was sitting on the bed, holding Mama's hand and looking toward the ceiling, her eyes beseeching in the manner of someone praying, though she denied believing in God. When she looked at me, I saw that tears had formed in her eyes.

A drip of perspiration meandered down my left side.

"Who's that?" Mama asked in a garbled voice.

I crept to the bed. "It's me, Mama." I brushed damp hair from her cheek.

"Who's she?" Mama asked Ingrid.

Ingrid looked at me in confusion.

"It's Katja." I struggled to keep my voice from screeching out of control.

"Pleased to meet you." She flicked the washcloth from her forehead and closed her eyes. In seconds she was sleeping.

Ingrid steered me from the room. "Let her rest."

"But what's wrong?"

"I don't know. Maybe it's some type of fever, though she doesn't feel hot."

"What should we do?"

"Let's ask Papa," she said.

"He left. I don't know where he went." I couldn't defend him. My papa had lost his way.

She didn't react outwardly to this information; I think she decided there was no time to be mad. "Then it's up to us. You stay with Mama while I get the doctor."

• • •

I dragged a chair in from the kitchen and sat next to Mama, feeling helpless. She was lying on her back and as I watched her sleep, it dawned on me that she would care what she looked like when the doctor arrived. I cracked the door open so light would stream in, though I made sure it didn't strike her eyes. Then I found her favorite comb, the one hand painted with lilies of the valley, and gently ran it through her hair. Taking strands from each side of her face, I wound them around my fingers to help guide the waves. Yes, that was better.

When I lifted the covers, I saw that Mama was wearing her oldest, shabbiest housedress. Dr. Perry wouldn't care, but Mama would be mortified to be seen like this. I slowly rolled her to one side, unbuttoned the back, and painstakingly worked the dress from her other side. It hurt me to see her white cotton undergarments, threadbare and mended. Anger at Papa rose like phlegm in my throat. After slipping one of Mama's nicest flowered dresses on so she was wearing two garments at once, I turned her and removed the rest of the old dress to replace with the new, proud that I accomplished all of this without waking her. She would be so pleased with me.

I went to the bathroom to run a comb through my own hair and use the toilet. Then I began straightening up the apartment, also important to Mama. Papa tended to leave newspapers and clothes tossed about, which aggravated her to no end. I emptied the ashtrays, for Papa did like his cigarettes. I was surveying the results when she appeared in the doorway.

"Mama," I cried out. "What are you doing up?"

She smiled wanly. "Thank you for doing such a nice job, my darling. I can always count on you. But let me help." She took a step forward, swayed, and grabbed for the door jams.

I rushed to her side.

"Oh, my…" She gasped and shifted her weight onto me so I lost my balance. Noticing that I strained to support her, she tried to stand on her own but nearly fell. "I'm sorry," she said, and her embarrassment made my heart ache. Suddenly her face contorted in pain, then panic. She looked into my eyes and spoke frantically, as if she were on a train pulling from the station. "I love you, Katja. Tell your father I love him. And Ingrid, tell Ingrid, convince her. My sweet children. My sweet—"

She was down, we went down together. Even years later I would curse myself for not being able to bear her weight. Perhaps it was hitting the floor that killed her. Dr. Perry would say *no*, he would diagnose a brain hemorrhage and tell me there was absolutely nothing I could do. But to let her fall. How could I have let Mama fall?

Her eyes had life inside and then the life left. I remember the instant her spirit floated from her body and how I wanted to grasp onto it, though I can't describe what I would take hold of. All I know is that those same eyes once alive were now staring and not seeing and it was then that I felt the limpness of her body. My lips parted to scream, but no sound came out; they opened and closed like a fish thrown on a pier and I imagined what my screams should sound like. I couldn't bear looking into the eyes that had allowed Mama's spirit to float from her body. Somehow—somehow—I closed Mama's eyelids as I had seen Grandma Rosa do to a woman who died in childbirth, and that calmed me as it had the woman's husband. I could pretend Mama was sleeping.

I couldn't lift her and wouldn't drag her, so I put a pillow under her head and fixed her curls to make her look pretty. I smoothed her dress and moved her arms, which were heavy, not like they should be, and her oddly ponderous legs, to make her presentable. I couldn't leave her, so I didn't seek help. I got another pillow for myself, then a blanket for us both, as if we were resting together. Deep inside I knew there was no help. Mama had left us.

Papa arrived before anyone else. I could smell beer and I can't explain what that scent does to me now, other than to say that it brings back the echo of my own whimpering.

"Oh my god," he said. "What's happened?"

I giggled and the remembrance brings a pang of shame, but Mama's death was unreal and my laughter was actually a kind of sputtering. "You're speech sounds funny," I told Papa, "like Mama's did."

He started to come to me first, I suppose because I was making noise and Mama was so very quiet. So very still and quiet was Mama. But then he fell to his knees and pulled her to him, her arms dangling as he held her, and he was whimpering, too.

CHAPTER 9

MOTHER LOVE

People clucked over us for a few weeks, but then it seemed as if they expected us to go on with our lives. Go on without Mama? But that's what I did, like a robot, for it didn't occur to me to neglect my duties at the apartment building. I only missed a day of housekeeping and that was for Mama's funeral, and now I was one person doing the work of three. Papa implored Ingrid to quit Gimbels, but she refused, though she promised to clean for an hour before she went to work and another hour when she came home. She told Papa to help me himself or hire someone to do it.

"I can't afford that," he said. "We barely make ends meet as it is."

"Then get a job."

His response was a sullen silence.

I lived in a world without sunshine. Tenants complained that the apartments weren't clean enough and Papa dressed me down in front of them for doing inferior work. He was a stranger to me, for there was a hollowness where his will to look after his daughters—and himself—should be. Our breakfasts together ended. And there was no Mama.

A month or so after the funeral, Ingrid asked if I had written to Grandma Rosa. In fact I was the one who informed her of Mama's death. Papa said he couldn't do it and suggested we let her continue to believe Mama was alive. When he added, "What's the harm?" I felt a hammering inside, as if multiple drums were thumping to different beats. "Do you expect me to pretend Mama still kisses me goodnight and makes me breakfast in the morning?" I screamed at him. "Act like she didn't leave me with a selfish sister and a father who wallows in his grief and shuns his daughters?" This was not normal Katja Varsten behavior. I was never one to yell and certainly not at my beloved Papa, but it felt as if he had died, too.

I received a letter back right away, but I didn't tell Ingrid.

Though Grandma Rosa's words were swollen with tears, there was joy inherent in her memories of Mama—*the tilt of her head when she smiled, her habit of cradling your hand as if it were fine porcelain, her rich singing voice.* I would reread this part many times. The rest of the letter I read only once, for my stomach clenched tighter with each sentence:

Andreas has always depended on strong women; first his mother, then his wife. If he descends into helplessness, harness Ingrid's strength to pull him out. Which reminds me, your grandfather lied to Ingrid. Her mother, Nadine Oberlin, tried to abort the baby she was carrying. I know, because I was called in to treat her following a botched attempt with caustic fluid. Nadine declared that if she couldn't destroy the infant in her womb, she would leave it on the doorstep of an orphanage. At my urging, Andreas offered to take the child. My grandchild. I don't know how he got his wife-to-be to go along with this arrangement, but it is to Senta's credit that she accepted the infant as her own.

Today Nadine dances in a beer hall, a painted woman. She looks much older than her years. When informed that her daughter dreamed of reuniting with her, she laughed and told me to send Ingrid a photograph of a proper lady and label it as her deceased mother.

How you will share this information with Ingrid, I cannot tell you. She has Nadine's hardness, so perhaps she will simply accept it.

Poor, poor Ingrid. Both mothers gone, just like that.

• • •

I couldn't let Ingrid go to Germany expecting to run into the open arms of a loving mother. But how to stop her? The letter was too hurtful to share. If she realized that her real mother didn't *ever* want her—not before she was born, not now—would Ingrid fall into darkness so profound she would be lost to us forever? These questions badgered me as I trudged down from the third floor of the apartment building, my back aching and my hands raw from scrubbing.

My thoughts veered to my own plight. It would be impossible to do all of Mama's chores in addition to my own and earn the grades needed to graduate from high school, yet getting a diploma was Mama's dream for me. After that I was to marry an American man or a German who was Americanized. Ingrid would be surprised to learn that Mama viewed the role of women in German culture to be too narrowly defined.

I opened the door of our apartment to the usual scene of Papa smoking, with his feet on the coffee table, too lazy to take off his shoes. He was unshaven and newspapers were strewn about. A faint glimmer of light came into his eyes when he saw me. "Katja," he said warmly.

My expression must have been the same as Mama's when he aggravated yet endeared himself to her.

His eyes dulled. "What's wrong?"

"I start eighth grade next week. I won't be able to keep up with the housekeeping and my homework."

"Quit school. In a few years you will marry and have children anyway."

A tiny Ingrid hopped on my shoulder and shouted in my ear. I voiced her opinions, but in my own words. "No, Papa. I want to be independent before I marry. I won't go from cleaning other people's homes to cleaning for my husband. I need help with the work of the apartments. I will not quit school." I sucked in a mouthful of air and prepared for his tirade.

I needn't have worried. Papa had no driving force in him anymore. He rested his head on the back of the sofa. "Then I don't know what you'll do."

I wanted to shake him, douse him with water, whatever it took to make him care about something besides his own pain. "Do you want to ruin my life and Ingrid's, too?"

His head jerked up. "You're talking nonsense. Such a question."

"Then you can't give up."

I expected outrage at my suggestion, but he was straightforward. "How will I go on without Senta?"

"You need to care about what *she* cared about. Her children and her home."

"I'll try," he said without conviction.

"We have to meet as a family and decide how to run the apartment building together, so you do work that suits you and Ingrid keeps her job and I finish school. If we can't figure it out, maybe we need to move and you can find another job."

Papa turned his wedding band round and round his finger. "I'll never leave the place where Senta died." When his eyes met mine, his features softened. "But we can discuss what to do."

It was a start. "Another thing—" I handed him Grandma Rosa's letter, aware that she didn't mince words where he was concerned but but lacking the strength to protect him. I missed Mama so badly and had no one to hold me up. Papa must face his own demons.

He read slowly and then folded the letter. "She's right about everything, about Nadine and me, and especially about Senta."

"Ingrid has to be told the truth; most of it, anyway, not that her mother tried to keep her from being born, of course. You must convince her that Grandfather lied about Nadine's desire to raise her child." My boldness amazed me but always in my mind was what Mama would want me to do.

"Ingrid never listens to me."

"Don't think of it as fighting Ingrid, but as weakening Grandfather's power." Yes, that was what Papa needed to do.

After pondering this point, he gave me a look with a trace of resolve in it. I left him then and laid on my bed to talk with Mama, which brought me no comfort because my words seemed to bounce back to me. Mama wasn't there.

• • •

Papa did not procrastinate. The next day, after I cleared the breakfast dishes, he asked us to remain at the table. I sat across from Ingrid, my stomach doing flip-flops. Earlier, while she been sleeping in (her Sunday morning ritual), Papa and I had coffee together and he divulged more about Ingrid's mother. Having this knowledge made me nervous that he would say too much.

Ingrid yawned without bothering to cover her mouth. "How long will this take?"

Papa chuckled. "That depends on how interested you are in Nadine Oberlin, your real mother."

I've never seen Ingrid so alert. If she were a German shepherd, her ears would have been pricked forward, her neck arched, her legs and back taunt. Papa spoke fondly of Nadine. (From what he told me, he had only the faintest recollection of her, didn't know the color of her eyes and not because he had forgotten, but because he never noticed.) Smoothing the truth like a saxophone playing through a mute, he conjured up a young and impetuous woman who searched her soul and concluded that she lacked the skills to be a proper mother. When she talked of giving her baby to an orphanage, Papa said he became alarmed.

If Papa made Nadine seem nicer than she was, he also exaggerated his fatherly interest, describing how he pleaded with her to give him the child, as if all he wanted was to have Ingrid for his own. I knew this wasn't true and I expected Ingrid to challenge him. But I have come to understand in the years since then that people often hear what they want to hear and I thank God this was the case for Ingrid. The power of her mother's rejection was defeated by the power of her father's love. When Papa paused in his story, Ingrid said, "Don't you think my mother would want to meet me, to see how I turned out?"

"Not now," he said, "though perhaps someday the three of us can travel to Germany—"

"When? Can we go this year?"

He was shaking his head. "Visiting at a time when Germans are being ordered to boycott Jews would be difficult, possibly dangerous. Nadine Oberlin, you see, is Jewish."

He hadn't revealed this to me.

In Germany, they were burning books by Jews. But surely no one in Mannheim would set fire to a book or persecute people like my skating partner, Max. I let myself grow excited at the prospect of a trip to the Germany I remembered, though I had a nagging suspicion Papa only intended to pacify Ingrid, nothing more.

She was staring at him. "Are you saying that my mother didn't want me and my country doesn't, either?"

"Your father wants you," I said, "and so does your sister."

For the next couple of hours, Papa answered whatever questions he could about Nadine, and some that he couldn't, with Ingrid none the wiser. Papa and I understood that her calmness might be short-lived, that she could swirl into a funnel cloud without warning, but for the time being we breathed easier. And I learned that it was possible to lessen my sister's throbbing pain.

• • •

The upkeep of the apartment building was not discussed during our family meeting, and in the weeks after school started, I waited for Papa to bring it up. He did not. I continued to sweep, scour and polish before school and then came home to cook supper, followed by hours of cleaning. I began my homework after Papa and Ingrid went to bed and woke up each morning sagging like an overloaded pack mule.

Ingrid helped with the apartments in the morning, but she no longer did chores late in the day, her time consumed by her job—and, astonishing to Papa and me—her beau. Not only had she found someone willing to put up with her temperamental nature, but this someone was unexpectedly ordinary. I had imagined her living in sin with a flamboyant American, an artist or musician with a rebellious streak like hers; instead Ingrid kept company with a staid German in his twenties who had lines in his face and hair already thinning.

Henry Spengler frequently took Ingrid out after work and always on weekends. The first time he came to the door, Ingrid was obliged to introduce us, since I made myself an obstacle to her departure. Henry was dressed in a three-piece navy suit that made him appear even older and he clutched a fedora in his hands. I smiled and received a barely visible nod in return, accompanied by a slight uptake at one corner of his small lips. Ingrid said, "We'd best be on our way," and put her arm through his, which seemed to unnerve him. After that first time, Ingrid would wait outside for Henry to pull up and he would emerge from the car to open the door and guide her inside. I held out hope that there was more to Henry Spengler than my first impression.

September brought improved spirits to Papa. He began to care about his appearance and asked my advice on the selection of his wardrobe before going out in the evening. He said that meeting with friends helped stave off loneliness. Since I went to bed before he got home, I don't know whether he had alcohol on his breath. I didn't want to know.

Even for me the shroud of Mama's death lifted once in a while, offering a glimpse of the colors of life. But only a glimpse. Doree persuaded me to attend Saturday matinees, where we got in for half-price, a nickel each. One of my favorite movies was *Dr. Jekyll and Mr. Hyde.* I closed my eyes during the scary parts and Doree filled me in on what was happening, though I had a good idea from having read the book. But the price of escape amounted to more than five cents. I left the theatre bursting to tell Mama about a man who was good and evil at the same time, only to remind myself that Mama was gone. Being fooled into thinking she existed outside of my heart meant I experienced the pain of losing her again.

Yet sometimes I *tried* to fool myself. Mama and I used to sing duets to lessen the drudgery of housework. *Me and My Shadow* was one of our favorites and she took to calling me *My Little Shadow.* Now, when I tackled the same jobs alone and sang the song, I sometimes heard her voice chime in with mine. The spike of elation was immediately crushed by reality, so most of the time

I pushed thoughts of Mama away. Grief was a predator that never stopped pursuing me.

• • •

Papa announced that he was taking us to the park for Oktoberfest, a fall celebration with German food, dancing and music. I clapped my hands in delight. Ingrid added to the festive mood by asking if Henry could join us.

"Yes," Papa said, "I think it's time to meet your young man." (The day I was introduced to Henry, Papa had been asleep in his bedroom.) "We'll try to behave, won't we, Katja?" And he winked. When had Papa last been playful? I couldn't recall.

Henry picked us up in a Buick sedan as enormous as a circus wagon, though given Henry's solemn demeanor, the atmosphere inside was anything but gleeful.

I climbed in the backseat with Papa, whose jaw tightened when Ingrid slid close to Henry. He was prudish where his daughters were concerned.

After miles of silence, Papa said, "This automobile is a beauty. Where did you get it?"

"I bought it used, from a friend," Henry said.

"How does it handle?" Papa asked.

"Fine," Henry said, ushering in the silence again.

"He must be shy," I whispered.

Papa muttered that he needed to get over that or we would have a boring celebration.

The day was warm, with clouds like feather beds. Indian summer, they called it. As we walked to the picnic area, Henry remarked that he overheated easily and would prefer a table in the shade. I rolled my eyes at Papa, who stifled a snicker.

Papa had insisted that we splurge and buy frankfurters and Polish sausage at the festival, but to save money I had packed side dishes in a picnic basket. It was hard to keep a straight face as Ingrid played the part of housewife by spreading out the red and white checked tablecloth and setting the table. When I opened the basket, she elbowed me aside with the warning glance I recognized from childhood. She smiled coyly at Henry. "I hope you like my German potato salad."

My mouth fell open. Papa nudged me and said softly, "Say nothing. Let her pretend." When I started to object, he said, "It will be entertaining to watch."

I assumed Ingrid would rather die than behave like the weaker sex, a term she ridiculed, but she did a satisfactory imitation, being solicitous to Henry's every need. When he brushed away debris that had fallen onto his clothing from above, she was adamant about exchanging places with him.

"The chestnut tree spreads over the whole table," I pointed out.

"It's shedding more here," Ingrid said.

"They're just *leaves*."

"That's enough," Papa said. "Ingrid is trying to be considerate of Henry."

Of course Papa would approve of such behavior.

Henry caught my eye. "Maybe I should reconsider. If the leaves fall fortuitously, I'll end up with a natural toupee."

I nearly fell off the bench. Henry Spengler had made a joke. Papa was laughing and Ingrid's face had lost its tension. I realized she wanted us to like him.

After that it was easy to rally round her. Our compliments and praise were like cheers helping her gain height on a trampoline. And Ingrid began to look almost pretty. At first I thought it was love that brought about this transformation, but watching her with Henry changed my mind. Though she focused on him, her actions were a tad too bright and dramatic. I had the uneasy feeling she was playacting. The sparkle in her eyes seemed to come from knowing we were on her side, or because she had an admirer, for if she wasn't in love, Henry certainly appeared to be.

"Henry works for the railroad," Ingrid said.

"Really?" Papa spooned potato salad on his plate. "What job do you do?"

I found myself observing Henry rather than listening to his answer. He was not an animated man and when he did gesture it was as if bands were attached to his hands to keep them from stretching too far. He spoke precisely—possibly trying to hide his German accent—but his voice lacked fullness, like a guitar missing the thick bass strings. His wry sense of humor made us laugh. He was in a way his own straight man, his features so solemn you thought he was serious, which made the fact that he was joking funnier somehow. When he smiled, dots of red appeared, but they were too small to call his cheeks rosy. His lips pursed like a doll's and imparted a sweetness to his face, but everything was constricted, tight. When Ingrid slapped him on the knee in laughter, he recoiled. Such an odd combination they made.

We finished lunch and strolled the grounds. When a loose dog raced at us, tongue lolling, with a huffing boy in pursuit, we scattered, joining up again at the pumpkin-carving contest. Papa took second, and we moved on to the relay races. Ingrid couldn't convince Henry to enter the three-legged race so I offered to be her partner. I should have known better. She wanted to win with her usual fervor and yanked me along until I fell and skinned my knee. I yelped, but she pulled me up by my arm and kept going. When we came in next to last, she said it was due to my laziness.

Henry complimented our form, though I couldn't picture what good form would be in a three-legged race and even if there was such a thing I knew we didn't have it.

In Henry's presence Ingrid turned into a nice person and said, "We gave it a valiant try."

I was about to mention her poor sportsmanship when I noticed Papa engaged in conversation with a woman. I had to look twice, because I thought the woman was Mama. Ingrid must have made the same mistake, for she stopped speaking mid-sentence.

"Who is that with Papa?" I asked, my throat dry.

Ingrid was already moving in their direction. "I intend to find out."

As we drew closer, I was embarrassed to have confused this person with Mama. Though she was short in stature, with light brown hair cut in a bob, she had a mouth that was too big and eyes that were too small. And I didn't like her familiar manner with Papa.

"Here's my girls." With his simpleton grin and jerky movements, Papa reminded me of a marionette on a string. "Sally," he said, "meet my youngest daughter, Katja."

Mama had taught me to be polite regardless of the situation, but I could barely manage a smile.

Sally clasped my hand firmly and shook it too hard, saying, "Pleased to meet you." I was relieved when she let go. "Andy's told me so much about you."

"*Andy?*" Ingrid said. Mama had taught my sister manners, but she was polite only when it suited her. And it didn't suit her now.

Papa laughed nervously. "This is Ingrid, my older daughter. She's one to speak her mind, which will be obvious as you get to know her better."

"What do you mean, get to know me?" Ingrid scowled at him. "Will this Sally person be hanging around?"

Sally stepped forward and came face to face with Ingrid. "You bet I'll be around. Me and your Papa are engaged to be married."

"Oh, Sal, it's too soon to tell them…" Papa's eyes were on me.

"Your eldest needs to hear it, so we can come to an understanding."

Ingrid was saying something in reply, but I didn't hear what because I was running away.

I had no idea where I was going, just far from the cruel woman who masqueraded as Mama and then removed her mask to reveal an ugly caricature. I ran in zigzags so no one could follow me. When my leg cramped, I hobbled across a school playground and collapsed on the wooden border of a sandbox.

Papa approached, panting. I wanted to be anywhere but near this man who dishonored Mama's memory. As soon as he sat down, I slid to the other side of the box and looked away. I vigorously massaged my leg, which made it ache more.

"I'm sorry you had to learn of my engagement so abruptly. Sally is as hot-tempered as your sister." Papa's dry laugh ended in a sigh. "I can't be alone, Katja. I missed your mother so much I didn't know how to go on. When I went to do a repair at one of the apartments and Sally opened the door, I thought my eyes were playing tricks on me. Senta's ghost, I told myself."

"She doesn't look like Mama." I broke into sobs. "She's nothing like Mama at all."

"No, she's not your mama, but she bears a resemblance to her and that consoles me. And she likes to go out and have fun. Your mama was more of a homebody."

"The way a mama should be."

"The way a mama should be," he agreed, then added under his breath, "but not a wife."

"Go away. I'm an orphan. I have no Mama or Papa. Go away and find someone who will listen to you talk badly of Mama."

He slid over and pulled me close. He was crying in big slushy sobs. "I need a wife. I loved your mama more than life itself and that's the problem. Sally will be a suitable wife." I struggled to escape his grasp and finally gave up.

"I know you can't see any good in this now," Papa said, "but you will have more time for your studies." He wiped my eyes with a red kerchief and then did the same to his. "Sally is eager to help manage the apartment building. You won't have to do all the cleaning yourself."

I hate to admit that I brightened at this news. I vowed to apologize to Mama later.

"Shall we walk back, bunny-boo?"

I took the hand he offered with a feeling of foreboding lodged in the pit of my stomach. I couldn't forget the look that had passed between Sally and Ingrid.

CHAPTER 10
PRETENSES

Sally's real name was Berta Kubek. A few months after we met her, Ingrid snooped in her purse and discovered a card with that name on it.

Ingrid picked her moment. Sally was sifting flour into a bowl, making a cake in our kitchen. She had instructed us to sit at the table to watch. She liked giving us cooking lessons.

Ingrid said, "Hey, Berta."

"Yes?" Sally turned and pushed her hair back, leaving a white swatch on her forehead. Her face colored. "Why did you call me that?"

Ingrid grinned. "Why did you answer to it?"

"Tell me how you found out my other name." Sally spoke in measured tones while tapping the sifter and dislodging flour in puffs.

"One of the salesgirls told me she saw my papa with Berta Kubek and I said, 'You mean Sally Kubek, don't you?' and she said no, the woman with him was definitely Berta. So unless you have a sister, I'm willing to bet she meant you."

Sally glanced at Papa, who was playing solitaire at the end of the table, then addressed Ingrid again. "What was this girl's name?"

"Mary. I didn't catch her last name and she doesn't work at Gimbels anymore." Ingrid filed her nails, humming.

"*Berta* is too German-sounding," Sally told Papa, who was peering at her over his reading glasses. "I want to be viewed as an American. That's what I am, after all, an American."

Papa went back to studying his cards.

"Ashamed of your German heritage, are you?" Ingrid asked.

"You need to learn some manners, young lady." Sally rapped the wooden spoon against the counter. "Andreas!"

His expression was vacant. "Ingrid, you're not to use that tone with Sally."

"Okay, I'll only use it with Berta." Ingrid stalked out of the room.

Papa and I jumped when Sally slammed the bowl on the floor with a shattering thunk—Mama's bowl reduced to shards and flour smoke. Sally glared at Papa. "Are you going to stand by and allow her to taunt me?"

He rubbed his forehead. "I'll talk to her."

"Talk to her? That nasty snip should be punished."

"She'll be eighteen in May. What would you have me do? Take her over my knee and spank her? The two of you must figure out how to get along."

• • •

Sally lived in one of the nicer apartments on the third floor. She came over almost daily with a casserole for supper, occasionally stollen for breakfast. Ingrid and I grudgingly accepted these offerings, for she was a good cook. Mostly her dishes were American, which we liked more than Papa did, so she made sure to prepare German meals on a weekly basis.

Ingrid said Papa's visits to Sally's apartment had tongues wagging, that bringing his tool box along wasn't fooling anyone. On Saturday nights, they went dancing. Papa would sleep late the next day and emerge in his robe, red-eyed and groggy. Sally must have been in the same state, for she never appeared at our door with stollen on Sunday mornings.

Papa seemed happier and although I had no feelings for Sally I tried to keep an open mind for his sake. My life got easier in some ways, not only because I was relieved of the cooking, but because Sally took over the bookkeeping when tenants came and went. She also did some light housekeeping. The tasks requiring elbow grease were left to me because she had back problems to watch out for, but she promised that once she and Papa were married, she would persuade the owner of the building to hire a maid.

In other ways, life was harder, for another female walked in places that were Mama's places, doing jobs Mama should be doing. It was like catching someone robbing your house and then letting the thief live with you. And I rarely had Papa to myself. He was often gone, and when he was home, Sally came over and demanded his attention.

As for Ingrid, it was sad that just when she and Papa might have become closer, other people pulled them apart. Papa didn't actively dislike Henry, as Ingrid did Sally, instead he dismissed him as "levelheaded, dependable, and thoroughly boring," which seemed worse. Sally was quick to list Henry's virtues. "Ingrid would do well to marry such a man," I overheard her tell Papa. "He has steady employment and a trustworthy temperament. Exactly what she needs."

Papa replied that she was too young for marriage and that as decent a man as Henry was, he did not match up well with Ingrid. "They'll aggravate each other to no end," he said.

"She needs someone to settle her down," Sally said, in a tone signaling the end of the discussion.

Henry was a frequent guest and I wondered if Sally invited him to subdue Ingrid, since in his presence she was the model of what a young German woman should be. Sally and Henry seemed to have an unspoken pact, for they supported each other in any family disagreement. An example of this occurred one morning when Sally observed that Ingrid's skirt was too short.

"No one asked for your opinion," Ingrid snapped. "Henry, I need some air."

"Yes, all right." He motioned for me to come along.

I followed them outside, pulling a wool scarf around my neck in the crisp autumn air.

"Sally is trying to give you a mother's guidance," Henry told Ingrid. "Look at it from her standpoint. Think how hard it would be to win acceptance from sisters who lost their mother."

"Sisters who lost their mother *three months ago,*" Ingrid said with the bluntness she usually spared him. "Only an insensitive woman—or worse—would chase after a widower this soon. It's selfish of Sally to push herself on us."

"Maybe your papa is the selfish one."

"How dare you criticize Papa. He's a grieving widower, easy prey for a shrewd gold digger like Sally, I mean Berta."

You tell him, I thought. *He has no right.*

Henry's face was purplish-red. "What gold is there for her to dig? Your father sits on his posterior and accomplishes nothing. Sally certainly could do better, so count yourself lucky that she cares for Andreas. Not only that, she provides a model of what a good wife should be. You and Katja have much to learn from her."

Ingrid's face had the puffiness of an over-inflated tire and I expected her to take him to task. Instead she replied, "Papa lacks ambition, that's true. You're the opposite and I respect you for it. And Sally does have admirable traits. But she's rushing a closeness before we're ready." Henry started to reply, but she talked over him. "I'd rather be alone to collect my thoughts. Please take Katja home."

Henry's color had faded to its customary white, with a faint purple tint. "I only want you to be realistic about your father and appreciate what Sally has to offer."

"Yes, yes," Ingrid said impatiently.

"Come along, Katja," Henry said.

The last thing I wanted was be alone with this pompous man. "Couldn't I walk with you?" I asked Ingrid.

She frowned, but when I mouthed *Please,* she relented. "Let Katja do as she likes," she said, with a dismissive wave of her hand. "We won't be gone long."

Henry gave me a stony look, then transferred that look to Ingrid. "See that you return in time for dinner." He checked his watch. "That's in fifteen minutes."

"We'll be back." There was the slightest roughness to her voice, like sandpaper on wood. I waited for her to add "when we're good and ready," but she started walking.

When we had advanced half a block, I swung in front of her, hands on my hips, forcing her to stop. "Why did you let him talk that way about Papa?"

Ingrid shrugged. "He has a point. Papa is lazy. He lets the women work while he lolls about on the sofa."

Papa was not lazy. Sadness was a bully holding him down so he couldn't move. "Mama said that's the way German men were raised to act."

"We aren't in Germany."

"What about Sally? You think she's the model of a good wife, do you?"

Ingrid's reply was matter-of-fact. "Of course not. She's a bitch. I was just pacifying Henry."

"But why?" Here was something I could not fathom. Where did my fiery sister go when Henry Spengler entered the room?

She kicked at a pebble on the sidewalk and missed. "Because I may need him."

I chill ran through me that had nothing to do with the temperature. I blew on my hands to warm them. "What do you mean?"

She sighed. "Let's walk."

I matched my stride to hers.

After a while she said, "I'm not pretty—don't argue, just listen—I'm not pretty or especially smart. I don't even get the booby prize awarded to plain girls, 'she's got a great personality.' Men won't flock to me, and the way the world operates, a woman has to have a man. So if I decide I need one, Henry will do."

"But you do love him?"

She laughed. "It would be hard to love such a stiff flag pole, wouldn't it?"

"You would marry a man you don't love?" I felt like I was forcing down something rancid.

"Katja, Katja, get your nose out of your book of fairy tales. Can't you see that your beloved Papa is set to marry someone he doesn't love?"

As so often happened with Ingrid, I wanted to cover my ears, but it was too late. Even as I said, "But he does love Sally," I knew it wasn't true. "Why would he marry her if he doesn't love her?"

"Papa can't bear to be alone, and we don't count. So you see that for a change I'm no worse than he is. I play a game with Henry like Papa does with Sally, but for different reasons. I don't mind being alone—I prefer it—but I'd rather not work at a menial job for a living. I intend to devote my time to woman's rights and I need a man for a paycheck. Who's the worse for this setup? I let Henry believe I love him and he's happy. If I pretend to obey him we get along fine."

I stared at the sidewalk, where paw prints were preserved in concrete. "You would have a child with a man you don't love?"

"What makes you think I want children?"

I took in a sharp breath. "Every woman wants children."

"Is that so? If I must have them to keep a husband, I will, but I'd be content childless."

I hadn't imagined another life for a woman besides wife and mother. Women had careers, but that was only when they were young or after they had raised a family. Some held out for the right man, and then there were the spinsters, but they didn't chose that fate, nor was Ingrid choosing it.

"Can you really picture me as a mother?" Ingrid offered a misshapen smile.

"Yes." I avoided her eyes. I could picture it, but not without thinking *poor baby.*

She kept her eyes on me. "What else is on your mind that you're not saying?"

I was glad my face was red from the cold, so she couldn't tell I was blushing.

"What?" she asked again.

"When you go to bed at night…" I hoped she would take my meaning from that.

"Yes? When I go to bed, the first thing I do is plump up my pillow."

Her teasing made me too mad to say anything else.

"Katja's asking about sex, isn't she?"

I shoved my hands in my pockets.

"Henry won't be the first, so I'll know how to pleasure him."

"Then you're what Sally calls a whore," I blurted out.

Ingrid's laughter became a twisted growl. "And you're a simple-minded little girl who knows nothing, full of other people's *shoulds* with no ideas of your own. You wouldn't dare question what an adult tells you. An empty-headed doll, that's Katja Varsten."

I was crying.

"This is what simple-minded girls do when they're upset. Cry. That's your answer to anything that threatens your small world. Don't weigh what I've said, don't try to improve yourself. Just cry." She spun round. "Come on. We mustn't be late for supper."

● ● ●

We endured what Ingrid called the Counterfeit Christmas of 1932. Everyone tried to be cheery, which in Ingrid's case meant not losing her temper. We opened presents on Christmas Eve as is the German custom. Sally was buoyant, an exaggerated version of herself, offering extravagant gifts from "me and your papa," that were plainly her selections. There was a red sweater and black wool skirt for Ingrid, a Chesterfield overcoat for Henry, a lovely winter parka with rabbit fur trim for me, and a white dinner jacket for Papa, who looked handsome but ill at ease wearing it. How Sally acquired the money for these purchases was a mystery, but the effect was as if Santa Claus had visited the Varstens.

Ingrid and I bought a gold-plated case filled with cigarettes for Sally, whose smoking we considered exotic, and a shirt and matching tie for Papa. Ingrid got her discount at Gimbels and everything was also marked down because of minor flaws (a break in the hinge of the case that Ingrid fixed; a spot on the back of the tie that Papa would never notice; a missing button on the shirt, which I replaced). Only Henry's gift—a black derby hat—was flawless, but Ingrid felt upstaged by Sally. I told her the gifts made him look sophisticated, though in reality it was a strange juxtaposition, Henry's stern face emerging from a black velvet collar and topped by the sweep of an elegant hat.

Sally had chosen Henry's gift for Ingrid, though I kept quiet about this fact. Ingrid should have known her beau didn't have it in him to select a ruby necklace, but she told herself otherwise. That night, when we lay in bed chattering like the sisters I yearned for us to be, she said, "What a fella, my Henry, decking me out like royalty. He's more romantic than I thought."

"Uh huh."

"Sally's gifts were generous, too, however she paid for them, and she was fun tonight. She seems to be trying. Maybe I was wrong about her."

How I wish Ingrid had been wrong about Sally.

• • •

I slipped out of bed on Christmas morning before Ingrid. She was snoring, which made me smile. Tying the terry cloth sash on my robe, I padded into to the kitchen.

My stomach crumpled in on itself. Dirty dishes filled the sink, beer bottles (courtesy of Sally's bootlegger friend) littered the counter, and cigarette butts soiled one of Mama's delicate saucers. I was well aware that Papa and Sally had stayed up late to make this mess, since their voices and laughter kept me awake long after Ingrid said goodnight and fell into slumber.

I sat down, woozy, hit hard by this truth: *Mama is gone forever.* On every other Christmas in my life, she rose in the wee hours of the morning, lit the little candles on the tree, and sang carols as she fixed a hearty breakfast for her family.

The kitchen was sickening in this state. I lifted the bottles as if they were contaminated, placed them under the sink, and shut the metal cabinet door like a prison gate. I emptied the saucer and scrubbed it to eliminate every trace of ash, then kissed it as if soothing an injured child. Next I washed and dried the dishes. When the kitchen was spick-and-span by Mama's standards, I mixed batter for pancakes. I retrieved the bacon from outside, where it had been stored to keep cold. Though its bargain price guaranteed it was mostly fat, the bacon would smell good cooking and add a festive touch. I left it next to the bowl of batter, ready for when Ingrid and Papa awakened.

I went to the living room, flicked on the light, and lit the candles on our tabletop tree, all we could afford this Christmas. I picked up my luxurious parka and buried my face in the soft fur. But suddenly I was cuddling a dead rabbit. Mama would never have spent so much money; she was always saving for a house and even if not, her gifts were handcrafted. I let the parka fall into a mound on the floor.

I slumped into our old worn chair and stared at the tree. "Mama," I said, "this is all wrong. Maybe Ingrid and I should return to Germany and live with Grandma Rosa."

"Maybe you should." Sally's words were as brittle as the brown needles scattered under the Christmas tree.

My heart beat wildly.

She stood hunched over, wearing a skimpy nightgown that hung unevenly on her body. I was shocked, not so much because she had stayed the night but because she hadn't removed her make-up. This seemed slovenly. She was like an apparition, faded and gloomy except for black-rimmed eyes and red lips blurred at the edges. But I didn't want to hurt her feelings. "I'm sorry, Sally, I didn't mean it. I was missing my mama. You made a special Christmas Eve for us. It's just that Mama died only four months ago."

"Mama." She wrested the word out like a piece of meat stuck in her teeth. "Four months is time enough to grieve. You'll have a new mama."

Never.

She was scowling at me, I knew, though my eyes were fixated on a lace angel crocheted by Mama. I had hung it on a prominent part of the tree.

"Call me *Mama*," Sally said. "For practice, say, 'Merry Christmas, Mama.'"

Growing up with Ingrid had taught me how to avoid angry outbursts. "Merry Christmas, Mama," I said, as if Senta Varsten stood before me. Now that I knew Sally lurked in the shadows, I would not speak aloud to Mama again.

"There, that wasn't so hard, was it?" Sally said, satisfied. "I see you have breakfast started. I'll get your Papa and sister to join us."

I shuffled into the kitchen, not the slightest bit hungry. I heard Sally talking to Papa in a singsong voice that quickly lost its bounciness. "It's our first Christmas together. Get up."

Papa stumbled in, unshaven and rumpled, wearing pajamas with no robe. Back in our normal life, he would not let me see him like this. "Katja." He spoke in a whine. "Sweet Katja. Merry Christmas."

I ran to him, trying not to gag at the stale unwashed smell. He patted me on the back. "I wish I could give you your mama for Christmas," he said, "and then we would both have the best gift ever." To my horror, he began weeping.

"Don't, Papa. It will make Sally angry."

He sniffled loudly. "Yes, many things make Sally angry, but Senta most of all."

"Papa?"

He looked at me.

"Please shave and dress for Christmas." His face contorted but then sagged into resignation. "Yes, I'll do that. For you, I'll do that." He grabbed me so tight I couldn't breathe. Then he let go and hobbled into his bedroom.

Shouting started in another part of the house.

"I'll get up when I feel like it!"

"You'll get up when I tell you!"

There was a loud thud, then groaning. I rushed into our bedroom and found Ingrid on the floor, rubbing her knee. Sally was yanking off the bedding. She threw it down and said, "Make your bed before you come to the table." She stomped out of the room.

I began making Ingrid's bed.

CHAPTER 11
INTO THE ABYSS

I first lost my footing and began to tumble in August of 1932. When April of the next year came around, I landed hard, sure I'd hit bottom. I was wrong. It was only a rock jutting out from the edge of the abyss. I would slide off and smack into more horrible days on my way down.

Beef stew was simmering on the stove on that April afternoon. I was curled up on the side chair in the living room, reading the novel *Lucia in London,* and chuckling at the carping between the snobby British characters. Henry was on the couch reading *The Milwaukee Journal,* and Ingrid was next to him working a crossword puzzle. The house was alive with the cozy warmth of food and people.

"What's a five-letter word for *harmony, accord,* ending with *e?*" Ingrid asked, and I was struck by how this word, whatever it was, would be a perfect fit for the day.

"Peace." Henry snorted. "Judging by world events, it will be a long time coming."

I glanced his way and was assaulted by the headline in red: *PROHIBITION REPEALLED!!!* Mama would not have been pleased.

As I headed for the kitchen to attend to the stew, I heard a raspy cackling outside. It was Sally's laughter, and it was followed by her singing, *Who's Afraid of the Big, Bad Wolf*, shrill and off-key. After several bumps and thuds, the front door swung open.

I dropped my spoon in the pot I had been stirring.

Papa's white shirt was buttoned wrong and only partly tucked in. His tie was flung back on either side of his neck and his pants were wet where something had spilled. His hair stuck up in tufts. He had an arm draped around Sally, which pulled her clingy purple chemise down over one shoulder and exposed the strap of her brassiere. Their overcoats hung loosely over Papa's other arm and dragged on the ground.

"Let's toast our girls." Sally came to the kitchen and raised her bottle of beer. Papa reciprocated and they hit the bottles so hard that beer sloshed on their clothing and the floor.

Papa laughed. "That's what we get for not drinking fast enough."

Sally brought her face close to mine and took my chin in her hand. "What's a matter, Kat-*ja*, why so hang-dog? We got good news."

I recoiled at her breath.

Ingrid snickered. "You're both drunk."

Sally straightened up, then swayed. She grabbed onto Papa to steady herself, but he started to tilt, too. "We only had two or four beers, I'll have you know," she said.

"Yeah," Papa said, "two or four hundred." They both laughed uproariously at such a witty remark.

Sally stumbled to the stove. "What's cookin'? Hey, Andy, your little girl's boilin' us a tasty ol' spoon."

"I dropped it." I reached in without thinking, then jerked my finger out and sucked on it to ease the pain.

Sally stuck her finger in her mouth. "Is this what we're having for supper? Finger food?"

She and Papa couldn't seem to stop laughing.

All at once Ingrid was at my side. "Leave her alone."

Sally's lips formed a wavery red line of smeared lipstick. With exaggerated resolve, she faced Ingrid. "You'll not be giving orders, Jew-girl." She shoved her.

Ingrid was too stunned to react.

"Shut up, Sally," Papa said in a feeble voice.

Ingrid seemed to gain power from his weakness. She slapped Sally hard across the face. A common brawl would have ensued, except that Papa grabbed Sally, who was swinging haphazardly, and Henry wrapped both arms around Ingrid. I was thankful Mama didn't have to witness this disgraceful scene but then of course it wouldn't be occurring if she were alive. *Mama, this is all your fault. Why did you have to die?*

The physical exertion overwhelmed Sally in her drunken state and she sagged into Papa's arms. As he helped her to the bedroom she murmured obscenities meant for Ingrid.

We sat dumbly on the sofa until Papa returned.

"She can't stay here," I said. "People will gossip if an unmarried woman sleeps overnight."

He fell into the side chair. "She's not an unmarried woman. She's my wife."

This was when I understood that I would continue to fall and crash into one ledge after another.

"When?" Ingrid asked, through lips barely parted.

Both of us had pushed the dreaded event so far into the future we had stopped thinking about it.

"Today." Papa lurched toward Henry and tapped a finger on the newspaper headline. "We were celebrating *this* with Sally's friends. One couple had just tied the knot and Sally called out that we should, too. Everyone was smiling and thumping me on the back and she had love in her eyes and it seemed like the right thing to do." He smiled in that helpless way Mama couldn't bear.

"I can't live in the same house with that woman," Ingrid said.

"Give it a chance. Don't judge Sally by what she does when she's had too much to drink."

"I'm not. I'm judging her by what she does when she's sober."

Henry spoke with an intensity that was out of character. "Why did she call you *Jew-Girl*?"

Ingrid's eyes narrowed. "Because that's what I am."

While Papa explained, I watched Henry. Germans came to America for many reasons—some deemed it the land of opportunity; others fled from Hitler's tyranny. Since my mind wandered during discussions of politics, I didn't know where Henry stood. What I did know was that he was looking at Ingrid differently.

"I'm sorry," Papa said to Ingrid. "Sally was going on and on about how you didn't look like Senta and she badgered me until I told her your secrets. I was weak."

"You *are* weak," Ingrid corrected, "but at least you aren't anti-Semitic." She directed her attention to Henry. "Can the same be said of you?"

Her frankness—or this new information—so addled Henry that his lower lip quivered.

Ingrid had no patience with him. "Well?"

"It's difficult to put my emotions into words," he said.

"What's difficult about saying, 'I'm not a Nazi'?"

"You didn't ask if I'm a Nazi, and the answer is *no*. Hitler is an abomination. But being anti-Nazi doesn't mean I understand how I feel about Jews. I grew up in Germany with a father who despised them and a mother who feared them, though I never understood why."

Ingrid crossed her legs and bobbed one foot, looking away.

"I'm being honest, a quality you claim to admire. It's a shock to find out your mother is Jewish. Give me time to get used to this new state of affairs."

"Get used to it in your own apartment." Her body formed a hard shell, her eyes a soft center of hurt.

"This hasn't been a good day for any of us," Papa told Henry. "It might be best if you left."

"It would be best if you both left," Ingrid said, "and take the pie-eyed bride along. If you each grab an arm, maybe you can keep her from falling on her face."

Papa said, "Here's one distinction between us, Ingrid. I never mean to hurt you and when I do, I regret it. Deep in my heart. But you...you try to cause pain, and when you succeed, you feel victorious. Weak as I am, I like me better than you right now. Good night." He shambled to his bedroom, head bowed, and the pieces of my already-broken heart fractured.

"I'll see you tomorrow after work." Henry looked hopefully at Ingrid.

Her eyes may as well have been closed, for as much as they revealed. "No, you will not."

After handing Henry his coat, I returned to sit next to Ingrid. He should have swept her into his arms and said, *I love you, no matter your religion.* Why hadn't he done that?

In the deadly quiet of our apartment, I tried to put my arm around my sister but she pushed me away. Yet when I moved to stand up, she pulled me back.

"What are we to do?" she said. "What are we to do with this hideous witch in charge of our family?"

"I feel nothing for Sally, but she'll take on more chores, which will help us both. Papa will be happier having a wife, and he'll be the head of the household, as always."

Ingrid's face was like a sack once filled with water that had drained out. She said, almost to herself, "What will it take for Katja to lose her innocence?"

"Why should I?"

"Sally won't get better now that she's hooked Papa like a carp. She's not a nice person. Maybe it takes meanness to see it in others, but trust me, there's darkness in that woman's soul."

I shivered. Ingrid was mistaken, she had to be. In my mind's eye I saw Sally's clown lips, heard her raucous voice, and smelled her stale beer breath. But that was it, the beer. It changed people. Without alcohol, she would be herself again, and while her personality wasn't sunny and warm, neither was it the dark cellar of Ingrid's imagination.

Still, I couldn't stop shivering.

CHAPTER 12
UPS AND DOWNS

The pattern of our life with Sally unfolded that April of 1933. She was either sunshine so bright it hurt your eyes or pounding rain that turned to hail. There was little in-between and we learned to be cautious when she was in high spirits for she could plummet without warning. Her "good mood" wasn't necessarily good for us anyway, since it often entailed a frenzied, overactive state, but we definitely tried to avoid her "bad mood," for then she badgered us without mercy. When I arrived home from school each day, I asked Papa, "What mood is she in?" to prepare myself.

When Sally was in a good mood, I got some relief from the duties of the apartment building, though she still dodged hard work. She was able to go dancing with Papa and not complain of her back afterward, but she steered clear of housework that required bending or lifting. *Lazy,* I thought, adding it to *slovenly.* Mama would have disliked Sally more than a little.

Thankfully, we didn't have to call our stepmother *Mama.* Ingrid saw to that.

"Each time we say the word," she told Sally, "Senta Varsten comes to mind. Can't we call you by a name unique to you?"

Sally considered this, unwilling to concede this battle to Senta, I suppose, but not wanting us to think about our mama, either. Finally she said, "I will be *mom* to you, in the American way." This suited us fine, for we didn't associate such a silly word with *mother,* which could mean that even I was still more German than American.

Because I was accustomed to living with a moody sister, I could adjust to Sally, at least at first. Ingrid, on the other hand, expected people to adjust to *her.* Sally rarely did that and then only when she was in her good mood. Otherwise she seemed to go out of her way to aggravate Ingrid, inciting angry tirades that made our lives miserable. I tried to convince Ingrid to ignore Sally, but she wouldn't listen. Or didn't care.

And so our house was filled with jarring noise—either overblown joy that didn't connect with anything of importance, or vicious arguments. The person this was hardest on was Papa. He became despondent and thus less willing to leave the house, which subjected him to the full brunt of clashes between Sally and Ingrid. And the more tumult he endured, the greater his despondency.

He pulled himself out of his lethargy when Sally was in her cheery phase, but then she would insist they go dancing, which meant drinking and then sleeping off the effects, with the result that he emerged grim and brooding. The worst example of this occurred soon after their wedding, on April seventeenth. Although many people celebrated the repeal of prohibition on its eve (Papa and Sally, on the very day), the clergy in Milwaukee managed to get the official celebration postponed until the season of Lent had ended. So on the day after Easter, Sally and Papa joined throngs of people (the newspaper estimated 15,000) at the Milwaukee Auditorium for *Volksfest*. It was all Sally talked about, how they drank beer and gorged themselves on bratwurst and sauerkraut. No singing about your Easter bonnet, as we would have done with Mama.

In her mean phase, Sally loaded me with work and then nitpicked my efforts. I got a reprieve when Ingrid came home, since Sally preferred to harass my sister. I would complete my chores swiftly so I could escape to the library, for it was impossible to study amid their squabbling. No matter what, I had to listen to Ingrid's rantings when she retired for the night.

Ingrid gradually began to spend more time with Henry. As she prepared for a date one evening, I asked the question that had nagged at me for weeks. "Does this mean Henry has accepted your Jewish background?"

She giggled. "How can I answer without making Katja's face burn ruby red? Henry mulled it over and said he realized that being Jewish made me more exotic to him." She giggled again. "So strong is his passion, I have to fight him off. He calls me his sexy Jewess. I love necking in his big car and let me tell you, we steam up the windows."

I flushed, as Ingrid had predicted, though not just from discomfort or because my sister sounded like the wrong kind of girl. She was no doubt exaggerating Henry's passion to scandalize me. What I didn't understand was why Henry would become more amorous because Ingrid was Jewish. It seemed peculiar, and in ways I couldn't explain, anti-Semitic. But I didn't say anything. I never purposefully riled Ingrid.

• • •

One evening after Ingrid stormed out and Sally withdrew to her bedroom to place a cold compress over her eyes, I said to Papa. "I can't go on like this."

He lowered the newspaper to reveal empty eyes. A cigarette burned among overflowing butts in the ashtray. "You must go on, Katja. You're the only one who will have a better life."

"How can you say that?" I felt desperate and alone. "I'm not strong."

His smile had a remnant of my old Papa, the one who would lift me in his arms and swing me around. "But you *are* strong. Let me ask you this. Do you believe your Mama loved you?"

"Of course. What a crazy question."

His eyes crinkled along with his widening smile. "And do you believe your Papa loves you?"

"Is this a game? I know you love me."

"And Grandma Rosa?"

"Yes…"

"Don't confuse anger with strength. What makes you strong is the certainty that you are loved. The rest of us don't have that."

"How can you say such a thing? Mama loved you and I love you. Ingrid and Sally do, too."

He shook his head. "I hope you're old enough to understand, but much as I loved your mama, I wasn't good enough for her. I understood this when I proposed marriage but told myself I would make her happy. I failed miserably, and after we moved to America, she didn't hide her disapproval of me. As for Sally, I'll wager she married me to avoid ending up a spinster. And Ingrid? I'm not sure she knows how to love."

No Papa should talk like this. "What about Grandma Rosa?"

He focused on something I couldn't see. "I'm a disappointment to my own mother. In reality, to everyone."

"Not to me."

His sigh was heavy, his expression tender. "I've seen the despair in your eyes when you look at me. You still love me because you were born full of love. You would love any mama and papa, no matter how despicable, because they were your parents."

His words made me feel smaller, as if my love had less value than other love.

• • •

Sally behaved like a normal person when Henry was around, evidence that she could control her moods and also that she wanted him to like our family. To be charitable, this may have been a show of support for Ingrid, but more likely she was eager for my sister to marry and leave home—this was Ingrid's theory, anyway. Naturally, when someone nudged Ingrid one way, she moved in the opposite direction, so she declared that she wanted to live on her own. She tacked a note on the bulletin board at Gimbels seeking girls to share a flat. I couldn't imagine that anyone who knew Ingrid would want to live with her. I had puzzled over how she was able to wait on people without displays of bad humor and I decided she must playact in the way she did with Henry.

The issue of getting her own apartment was irrelevant anyway, because after Ingrid's eighteen birthday, life changed. Again.

• • •

"My girls have birthdays coming up," Sally said after supper, while Ingrid and I were doing the dishes. "The three of us are going on a shopping spree to buy new dresses and foundation garments."

What Ingrid didn't know was that we had a surprise in store for her birthday in the middle of May—a trip to the dance hall. Though Papa objected that it was no place for a girl my age, Sally countered that I would turn fourteen only a month and a half later and that was old enough.

Sally could barely contain her excitement about our shopping trip (keeping the dance a secret showed amazing restraint). When the three of us stepped off the bus in front of Gimbels in downtown Milwaukee, she handed Ingrid a wad of bills. "I'm sure you'd rather choose your party dress without us butting in, so off you go. Little sis is stuck with me." Glowing with her good mood, she ruffled my hair and smiled at Ingrid. "We'll meet you back here at the women's department in three hours."

After Ingrid murmured a thank you and dashed off—afraid Sally would change her mind, no doubt—Sally and I headed down Wisconsin Avenue, window-shopping the blocks of specialty shops on the way to Boston Store. "Today you'll be fitted for a brassiere," she said. "You're long overdue."

I pulled my jacket closed. "I've been wearing layers of undershirts."

Did she expect me to try on undergarments in front of her? Mama taught me to be modest and I took great pains to conceal my body when dressing. These precautions amused Ingrid, who had no qualms about walking around unclothed.

Sally was equally uninhibited. As she waited for the saleslady to bring lingerie for her to try on, she stood before the mirror in the Boston Store dressing room appraising her naked body. "My god, what bubs," she said, cupping her hands beneath her breasts and lifting them. "Not bad for an old broad." She put her hands on her hips and twisted back and forth to gain different perspectives.

What could I reply to this?

"Oh, stop your blushing. Bodies are to be admired, not hidden."

Sally's boasting was remarkable given that her stomach bulged and her breasts hung like the feed bags of carriage horses. Her legs were her best feature, the only part of her body with any firmness, probably because of regular visits to the dance hall.

She ran the poor saleslady ragged, asking her to bring all sorts of lingerie in different sizes and styles. I didn't let myself dwell on how the silk pajamas and negligees were meant to please Papa. After selecting a corset, followed by a bra and panty set, Sally said, "See how underclothing can enhance the female form?" She didn't wait for my answer. "It's your turn. Let's have a look at you."

I took a step backward. "Oh, no."

"Listen, someday you'll marry and your husband will admire your body—"

"I won't marry then."

She laughed, not unkindly. "This can be your rehearsal." With that, she unzipped my dress and gestured for me to step out of it. "Off with the underwear, too."

I wanted to run from the dressing room, but my feet were rooted to the floor.

"We have to make sure the lingerie fits."

After removing my bulky, yellowed, cotton underwear, I stood in front of the mirror and stared at my toenails. Sally tilted my chin up. I blinked and shivered and saw my nipples harden. I thought I might die of embarrassment.

"Katja," she said softly, "your nipples will do that when you're cold. It's natural. Later, if you become excited in bed with your husband, they will do the same thing. Has anyone explained sex to you?"

"Ingrid, when we were younger." I crossed my arms to cover my chest. "She maybe didn't get all the particulars right."

"When we get home, I'll tell you whatever you want to know. Now put your arms down and look at yourself."

I took a deep breath and did as she asked.

"Check out that gorgeous figure, will you? Everything in the right proportion. Be proud of your body. Ignore the flaws—though damned if I see any—and then when the day comes, you'll feel at ease with your husband. Okay, let's find out if any of the unmentionables we picked out are worthy of such perfection."

I will always be grateful to Sally for this day.

She loved nice clothing and had me try on lingerie that was feminine and grown-up. Even the word *lingerie* was nicer than *undergarments*. I ended up with brassieres, panties, a chemise, and a slip, all accented with lace and in the newer tea rose shade.

Once the foundation garments had been selected, we began our search for dresses. I was able to temper Sally's garish taste by pointing out what Papa would like, and she steered me away from childish frocks with rounded collars and buttons down the front, saying I had enough of those in my closet.

"You've been the baby of the family long enough. It's time to see yourself as a young woman," Sally said. "Your papa is no help at all; you'll always be his little girl."

And so I got my first store-bought fancy dress. I would treasure it, even though Mama would judge its peach taffeta too sheer, its double layer of ruffles across the shoulders too showy. From the moment I put it on, the dress made me want to twirl like a ballroom dancer. For Sally we chose a cream satin gown that tapered over her hips and flared out mid-calf. With the corset, her body hinted at the hourglass figure she had as a young girl. After the saleslady boxed our purchases in tissue, we hurried to meet up with Ingrid.

My sister had narrowed her choice down to three dresses and flattered us by asking our opinion. The gleaming emerald gown with its cowl neckline and flowing skirt won our vote because it made her look feminine. With our final purchase complete, we boarded the bus. Our shopping excursion had been a success and we shared a rare girlish closeness on the ride home. In private I'm sure each of us pictured herself as belle of the ball.

Within hours of walking in the door of our apartment, I panicked. I didn't know how to dance. Sally said that she had no patience for teaching, and so each evening that week after my housework was done, Papa instructed me in the waltz. When I asked to learn the faster steps, he shook his head. "That's for when you are older," he said. "You'll bounce and jiggle too much." I complained that he was babying me and he said, "Yes, and I don't intend to stop."

Ingrid went off to work on Saturday morning thinking that her birthday present from the family was a new dress and a promise of cake when she got home. But the minute the door closed, Sally bustled about organizing the celebration. We each had duties: she made the cake and put together the supper menu; I cleaned house and helped with the cooking; Papa tacked up paper streamers and a homemade sign that read *Happy 18th Birthday, Ingrid!* Throughout our preparations I tried to squelch my growing apprehension that Sally would switch in an instant from giddy to sullen. We never knew how long the good mood would last.

By late afternoon, we were ready. Papa got dressed, then had a smoke. "Go get yourselves dolled up," he told us. "I'll be on the lookout for Ingrid, though we can count on Henry to be on time in picking her up from work."

Sally and I primped in her room. We began by removing pin curls and styling each other's hair. She made up her face and then had me sit at her vanity table while she applied a light shade of lipstick and a touch of blush. "I'd do more," she said, "but I don't want to upset your papa." It was just as well, since she had a heavy hand with make-up. We put on our chic lingerie and sophisticated gowns and admired ourselves in the mirror. Then we locked arms and strolled into the living room like models.

Papa gave a wolf whistle. "You two look ritzy—" He cocked his head. "I hear Henry's car."

We crouched behind the sofa and then, when the door creaked open, jumped out, yelling, "Surprise!"

Ingrid was genuinely surprised, but her eyes didn't light up as I had anticipated. "Just the three of you then?" she asked.

I couldn't think what to say; our invitations to the salesgirls at Gimbels had been met with polite excuses.

"Oh, *no*," Sally said, hands on either side of her face. She looked at Papa. "I knew we should have invited people outside the family. I'm sorry, Ingrid. We thought you would like a cozy get-together."

Unpredictable, that was Sally. Kindness blossoming like a flower from a prickly cactus.

Ingrid was nodding. "Yes, yes, you were right. Just the family."

"And Henry." Sally smiled at him in a way that suggested he *was* family.

"And Henry," Ingrid agreed, without looking at him.

Sally donned a cook's hat and sashayed to the kitchen, pointing to a sign overhead that read, *Sally's Diner*. While Papa escorted Ingrid and Henry to the table, I put on my apron and *Kat* nametag.

"I'll be your waitress tonight." I said, setting a plate of hamburgers on the table. I went back and forth to the kitchen bringing out condiments, fried onions, hot German potato salad and coleslaw. Once everything was arranged, I took my place at the table.

When Sally brought out a tray with five beer steins, Papa raised an eyebrow. "The girls are underage."

"This is a special occasion." She winked at Ingrid. "Is the birthday gal interested?"

"Oh, yes." Ingrid beamed and held up a stein.

So that was what it took to make her smile, I thought uncharitably.

"I'm so wicked." Sally laughed, with a sidelong glance at Papa. "Katja?"

"No, thank you." The smell of beer made me queasy.

"Try it, little sister," Ingrid said. "You could do with some adventure in your life."

"She said *no*," Papa snapped. He turned to me. "Lemonade?"

I nodded.

Ingrid's grin slid into a sneer. "Bunny Boo will never grow up."

"A toast then," Sally said, "to our grown-up Ingrid Varsten."

The tension dissolved with the clink of our glasses.

"Don't let the food get cold." Sally shoveled a huge mound of potato salad on her plate, then passed the dish on. When she hit the peak of her good mood, she gobbled up food and washed it down with too much drink. I prayed that her joviality would outlast the evening.

Sally inquired about Henry's day at work and stifled yawns during a lengthy explanation of his duties as an accountant. Ingrid feigned interest (obvious to me, though not to Henry), but I listened closely. While English was my favorite subject, mathematics appealed to me because there was a right answer, so unlike real life. Junior high counselors steered girls into secretarial classes and boys into math and science, but because Sally welcomed a fight on behalf of the female sex, I was enrolled in a mix of subjects. When Henry described balancing budgets and calculating paychecks, I blurted out that this was a job I could do.

His expression was scorching. "Accounting is complex, detailed work." He set his fork down as if this point was too important to make while masticating. "It's hardly something a schoolgirl can handle."

Ingrid took a long draft of beer, then said, "When Katja begins job hunting, she won't be a schoolgirl. She'll be a high school graduate with plenty of smarts, equal to any schoolboy graduate."

Ingrid was defending me, a shock all by itself, but she was defending me to Henry, the one person she deferred to.

Henry's features constricted in anger. "No girl can equal a boy in the business realm," he said. "The female intellect isn't designed for computing."

Sally tapped a fork against her glass. "Time out. This conversation is far too serious for a party. Katja, I need your help in the kitchen."

I rose slowly. Ingrid was glowering at Henry; the alcohol seemed to dissolve her ability to behave herself. At the kitchen counter, Sally was lighting candles on the cake. I smiled, remembering how we had laughed decorating it. The *Happy 18th Birthday* had come out crooked and we'd had to cram the letters of *Ingrid!* to make them fit.

"Turn out the lights," Sally said. "The lovebirds will simmer down if they can't see the daggers zinging from each other's eyes."

I flipped the switch and we walked to the table singing "Happy Birthday." Papa joined in, though I didn't hear Henry.

"Make a wish," Sally said.

"Foolish custom," Ingrid said, though she paused before blowing out the candles.

While we ate, Sally brought up less controversial subjects like my softball team, though it occurred to me that a girl playing softball supported Ingrid's point. When Papa bragged about me and my team, I glanced at Henry to gauge his reaction. His eyes kept darting to the side table, where Ingrid's gifts had been placed. Sweat glistened on his forehead and he bit his lip nervously.

I caught Sally's eye.

She gave me a quick nod. "Ingrid should open presents. Give her yours first, Katja."

I slid Ingrid's plate over to make room. She picked up the narrow package and shook it.

"Too bad you did that. It's breakable." I giggled. "No it isn't. Open it, open it."

She tore off the wrapping paper—newspaper comics—and brightened when she saw what was in the box. I had saved my allowance of ten cents a week to buy the simulated-emerald necklace. "It'll be perfect with my dress," Ingrid said, and she came round to kiss me on the cheek. Did she mean to show affection or merely shock me again? I wondered.

"Open the one from your papa and me." Sally was like a child who couldn't sit still. She plunked down a large and stylish round box, white with silver stripes and an elaborate green bow.

Inside Ingrid discovered a beautiful feathered hat that matched her dress. "Oh, Sal...I mean, Mom, I love it." She kissed Sally on the cheek, too.

"What about me?" Papa said, with mock indignation.

"Thank you, Papa. I know how nerve-racking it is to select the proper lady's hat. You must have spent hours at the millinery store." She kissed him with a loud smack.

We all laughed except Henry, who was paler than usual.

"Are you all right?" I touched his forearm and he flinched.

"Yes, yes." He thrust a small box at Ingrid. "For you."

Ingrid took her time—could she be teasing him?—but finally, there it was, the glint of a small diamond. An engagement ring. Her mouth formed a crooked line. "How sweet of you, Henry. How very sweet." Her eyes held more compassion than I thought she possessed.

"We'll get married." He may as well have been declaring his intention to buy new tires for his automobile, his tone was that uninspiring.

I ran a finger along my plate to collect vestiges of frosting. Hadn't he rehearsed this important scene? He should have been down on one knee, asking instead of telling Ingrid, and he should have chosen a romantic setting, not the kitchen table with an audience of relatives. I licked the sugary concoction from my fingertip.

"I can't get engaged," Ingrid said. "It's too soon. I haven't been out in the world yet."

The tic-tock of the cuckoo clock seemed louder than usual. We had purchased the clock from a family who moved out of our building for an exultant return to the Black Forest region of Germany. Their plan was to buy another clock when they got there. I hoped the bird wouldn't pop out now with its mocking, "Cuckoo, Cuckoo." It would be hard to know who it was taunting.

I felt an unreasonable urge to laugh. The room was so quiet. Just that clock.

I looked around the table. Sally's demeanor had darkened. She was trying to keep the bad mood inside but it was seeping out through her eyes. Papa was saying, "You're both young. There's no rush to decide your future." Henry's face held no softness, just crevices and jutting angles.

"Why don't we all go to the dance hall?" Sally said. "The two of you can talk about this later, when you're alone."

I waited, the large piece of birthday cake I had eaten lodged like a brick in my stomach. I could see that Ingrid was calculating what to say and I was grateful, for her most biting words were uttered without forethought. "Yes, you're right," she said at last. "We'll go dancing."

Henry stared straight ahead.

Sally stood up. "Give her time," she told him. "A sensible girl takes a marriage proposal seriously and doesn't answer quickly."

He nodded.

Although what Sally said was true, I couldn't help thinking that Ingrid was hardly a sensible girl.

"Change your clothes, Ingrid," Sally said dully, "and we'll be on our way."

Ingrid snapped the ring box shut and gathered it with the other gifts.

• • •

My sister took her time getting dressed, making our nerves even more frayed. When she emerged looking strangely radiant—but then Ingrid seemed to thrive on discord—she was wearing all but one gift with her lovely dress. The hat was at a jaunty angle on her head and the green stone gleamed from her neck, but there was no ring gracing her finger.

Henry had regained his composure. "Shall we go, Ingrid?" He held out her wrap.

She smiled. "Let the dancing begin."

It was the end of the dance that worried me.

CHAPTER 13
THE DANCE

The dance hall pulsed with whirling people and big band music, almost too much to take in. I wished for Mama's company but this was a ridiculous notion because she would not have allowed me to enter a dance hall. Sally led Papa into the reeling throng and they disappeared like swirls of color into a lollipop. My stomach fluttered and I stood with my hands tightly clasped. Where would I go when Ingrid and Henry started dancing? I scanned the hall to locate the ladies' room.

Ingrid nudged me. "You have your first suitor."

Watching a boy make a beeline for me was scarier than the prospect of standing alone. His hair was plastered down and his suit looked brand new. He was a nervous Nellie, too. Nervous Neil. I chuckled to myself.

"Would, would, you like to dance?" He swallowed, drawing attention to a prominent Adam's apple.

"Oh, I don't think—"

Ingrid gave me a push. "She'd love to."

As I followed him, I looked back at my sister, who pantomimed dance moves by way of encouragement. The music had switched to a waltz, which was some consolation, as my brain knew how to instruct my feet in this step. At first we were clumsy. Then I relaxed my hand so he would do the same, and this helped. He told me his name was Joseph, that he was a senior at my school. I didn't remember him but pretended I did. Though I felt no stirrings of a Prince Charming, Joseph was a good partner for my first dance because I became more confident by practicing with him. When he delivered me back to the dour couple of Ingrid and Henry, he hung around a bit before asking me to dance again.

"Maybe a little later?" I said. "I'd like to talk with my sister."

Joseph stumbled as he turned to leave but then collected himself to approach another girl. I had helped build his confidence, too.

"What did you want to talk about?" Ingrid asked. "I hope it's more entertaining than my conversation with Henry."

Henry struck back. "Why would you expect to be entertained? You disgraced me in front of your family."

"You should not have asked me in front of them, I mean *told* me."

I shifted to a few feet away, but Ingrid jerked me back by the elbow. "Stay. Henry likes an audience."

Henry pulled himself to his full height. "Ingrid has that wrong. She's the performer."

I secretly sided with him on this point.

"In that case, enjoy the show." Ingrid swooshed off, headed for a handsome man with sleek black hair. She asked him to dance and they engaged in what I thought was an improper version of the foxtrot.

"She's only trying to get even with you," I told Henry.

His eyes gleamed as if a new person had taken charge of them. "Ingrid is like a high-spirited racehorse who needs the right jockey."

I winced. "She's not Man O'War, make that Woman O'War."

He looked down his nose at me. "Flippancy doesn't suit you, Katja. I thought you were the Varsten girl who knew her place."

My feelings bubbled inside like soup with the heat turned on high. I wanted to be a good German girl, yet he made that seem demeaning, so I took pride in defying him.

Papa approached with Sally, who was finger-snapping happy until she sized up the situation. "What's going on?" She gestured in Ingrid's direction.

Henry adjusted his tie. "Ingrid did not wish to discuss our engagement."

"Not in public, anyway," I said.

He frowned. "This is not your business."

Papa bowed to me. "Would the lovely young maiden consent to dance with an old codger?"

I looked around, then met his eyes. "I don't see any old codgers, but I'd be honored to dance with a distinguished gentleman."

Papa swept me onto the dance floor and away from escalating emotions. But I hadn't really escaped. I worried there would be fireworks when Ingrid returned to Henry—if she returned, for I spotted her across the room dancing with another man. Maybe this meant she and Henry would no longer keep company, which could be for the best.

The evening wore on. Each swell in Ingrid's gaiety deepened Sally's brooding. Sally danced often with

Henry, to make up for Ingrid's neglect, I assumed. He did ask another girl to dance, but it was a transparent attempt to rouse Ingrid's jealousy, as his eyes constantly sought her out. She seemed oblivious. Papa and I danced one song after another in his efforts to discourage possible suitors. I thought he was being overly protective until he stopped to have a smoke and a man with gray at the temples invited me to dance. This man held me too tight and stroked my hair in a way that made a scream bottle up in my throat. When the dance was over I ran to Papa.

"What's the matter with you?" Sally said. "You're too old to cling to your papa. Andy, you treat Katja likes she's four instead of nearly fourteen."

Papa gripped my arms. "Did that man do something bad to you? Tell me."

I could still feel the stranger's moist palm touching my head. "No, but I was afraid he would."

Sally rolled her eyes. "Such an imagination. He was being friendly, that's all."

"An older man who is too friendly with a young girl bears watching," Papa said.

"What about a young girl who's too friendly with older men?" Sally pointed a rigid finger at Ingrid, who was dancing with a well-dressed fellow, her head thrown back in laughter. I glanced at Henry and was taken aback by the smile flickering on his face.

"You aren't angry?" I asked him, the question slipping out before I thought better of it.

"I like the fact that Ingrid is attractive to other men."

"It's what she's offering that attracts them," Sally said.

A tremor ran through Papa. "Don't speak that way about my daughter."

"She's our daughter now and she'll behave like a lady or we grab her by the hair and drag her home."

Henry blinked as if he'd been shaken from a dream. "Please, don't make a scene." He surveyed our surroundings. We were off to the side, separate from potential eavesdroppers. The noise and festivity in the dance hall, which had increased along with the consumption of beer, drowned out most conversations anyway. "I'll fetch Ingrid," Henry said, and with that, he strode through the dancing couples and tapped Ingrid's partner on the back.

"About time he did something," Sally said with a harsh laugh. "He must have a small pecker."

Papa's hand came up as if he might slap her. "You talk like a woman of the street. It disgusts me and I won't have Katja exposed to such vulgarity."

"Innocent little *Katja*." My name was hurled like a rotten tomato. When Sally was like this I told myself it was her bad mood and the beer talking, but it always hurt. And kept hurting. She said, "Your darling baby will have a man's pecker in her someday. You can't shelter her forever like your precious Senta tried to do."

He did slap her then, though not hard, for I could see him fight to restrain himself. Sally stepped back, stunned, one cheek a faint pink. "Strike me again, Andy, and I'll leave you."

He jammed his hands in his pockets. "Don't tempt me. Katja, get your sister and Henry. Tell them we'll be in the car."

I did as I was told, but couldn't stop trembling. Never had I seen Papa hit anyone. And the thought of being in the closed space of Henry's automobile, squished against everyone's anger, filled me with dread.

• • •

At some point during the ride home it was as if the car made a sharp turn and the power rolled from Papa to Sally. Or maybe it was that he'd used up his limited capacity, while Sally had a supply in reserve. When we pulled up to the building, she told Henry to go home, that we had family matters to discuss. He kissed Ingrid on the lips and said he would pick her up after work the next day. She made no reply.

My heart pounded and my palms sweat. I shuffled into the apartment after my family, fighting the temptation to bolt back outside where I could breathe. Sally flung open the door and yanked down the *Happy 18th Birthday, Ingrid!* banner. She ripped it to pieces in a kind of rhythm while she spoke. "You ungrateful bitch. We try to give you a nice birthday and you throw it back in our face." She hurled the shredded paper at Ingrid.

In a blur of ferocity, Ingrid seized Sally by the wrists. "I don't have to take this anymore—your insults, your slaps. I'm done with it."

Sally struggled to free herself and when she couldn't, she began kicking. "You goddamn whore. I hope Henry doesn't expect a virgin."

Ingrid snorted. "Oh, the irony, Sally Rand calling me a whore. What's your count, Madame Rand?"

The kicking intensified, but Ingrid stopped it with a blow to Sally's face, causing her to careen backward and fall over a chair. She thrust the chair aside, scrambled to her feet and came at Ingrid. They wrestled and scratched and tore rips in their lovely dresses, like common women with no sense of propriety.

I leaped out of the way. "Papa, stop them!"

He was slumped on the sofa as if his bones had turned spongy. "I'm worn out trying to keep them apart. Let them fight it out."

"I'll get the police."

The sudden quiet was loud, like the aftermath of a gunshot.

"No cops," Sally said. "I won't lay a hand on her except in self-defense."

I waited. "Ingrid?"

My sister was panting like a wild animal. She wanted nothing more than to beat Sally senseless, that much I could tell, and so could Sally. She was afraid and Ingrid knew it. I flashed back on the boy dragged from the tree screaming. So this was where that fury could lead.

Ingrid's eyes darted from me to Papa. She put a hand on her heaving chest as if to steady herself. "You two are no help. You can't even defend yourselves against her." She appraised Sally coldly. "If I'm to control my fists, then you'll control your mouth."

Two bullies at a standstill and only because one was physically stronger than the other.

"Go to each end of the table." As soon as I said this, the boxing ring came to mind. I wanted to laugh at this absurd image, but it seemed as if I would never laugh again. "You have brought dishonor to the Varsten house," I said, "both of you have done this." I struggled not to break down.

Sally picked up the fallen chair and plopped down on it. Ingrid turned hers around and straddled it, the shimmery fabric of her dress hiked up around her knees. I took Papa's hands and guided him to the chair across from me. He moved like a wisp of a person and sat down to examine his fingernails. I may as well have left him on the sofa.

No one spoke. Ingrid grabbed the newspaper and made a show of turning the pages. Sally slouched in her chair, eyes closed. Papa put his head in his hands. I let my thoughts pursue every nook and cranny of worry.

When the wooden cuckoo mocked us with his performance, I saw that an hour had passed.

"I want you out of this apartment," Sally told Ingrid, as if the silly bird had given her permission to speak. "If you won't go with Henry, then find another way. You can't live here."

Ingrid laughed in caws, like a crow. "So that was the reason for this party, to get rid of me?" She cawed again. "I should have known. Why didn't you just put me in a box with a ribbon on it for Henry? No wonder you didn't invite my friends. He was the only one who needed to attend."

Sally's laughter took a different pitch—higher than Ingrid's, but just as ugly. Screeching owl, talons out. "Friends? We couldn't *pay* anyone to come."

That had to hurt as much as a punch in the face; Ingrid appeared shaken but quickly recovered. "You probably asked at work, that's why. You haven't met my friends. I surely wouldn't bring them here."

Sally rapped her fingers on the table. "No, I wouldn't be acquainted with men who pay for sexual favors."

Ingrid shot up, brandishing a fist. "I told you to watch your mouth. Do you want me to mess up the other side of your face?"

Sally touched the cheek that had turned scarlet and would be purple in the morning. "All right, all right, I take it back. I don't know your friends." I heard her legs jiggling under the table, betraying her fear.

"You've got money stashed away," Ingrid said. "Give me boat fare to Germany so I can reunite with my real mother. I'll be gone before you can invent another insult."

Sally's eyes lit up from within, a curious reaction. She couldn't possibly have the means to honor such a bargain, could she? I was baffled. She leaned back in her chair and looked at Papa with a smile playing at her lips.

He lifted his head and placed his hands in front of him. "Hush, Sally."

"What?" Ingrid leaned forward, searching their faces. "Do you have the money?"

Still smiling, Sally said, "For you to see the mother who tried to abort you? I'd rob a bank to give you that experience."

Something inside of me twisted like a wet towel wrung out. I should have let Ingrid beat her up, for then Sally wouldn't have been able to inflict this pain. And Papa? I shot him a fierce look.

I expected Ingrid to attack Sally and I wouldn't have stopped her, but she was composed. "Is this true?" she asked Papa.

Say it's a lie, I begged him silently. *Say it's a lie.*

His hands twitched. "Yes, it's true."

Ingrid didn't throw back her shoulders in proud defiance as was her way. I believe her posture changed that day, that forever after her shoulders drooped forward, the way they did when she left the table.

"Ingrid..." Papa said.

She walked unhurried.

"Let the kike go," Sally said.

Ingrid froze. She swerved toward Papa in slow motion. "This monster is what you gave us to replace Mama? You should be ashamed." She went to our bedroom and closed the door.

I stood up and said, "I hate you both," and absorbed the shock of meaning it. Then I went to tend to my sister.

She was packing.

"Where are you going?" I asked.

She didn't look up. "To Henry."

"A place to stay until you find your own apartment?"

"I'll marry him."

"Ingrid, no."

She looked at me. "Sit down."

I sat on her bed because her suitcase dominated mine. She shoved the case over and sat across from me. "I can't live here, don't you see that?"

"Yes, but be patient. You know Sally's explosions lead to a period of calm. Stay until you have your own apartment. Surely one of your friends will put you up for a while."

She sighed. "You fell for that, did you?"

I nodded, even though I hadn't, really.

"I have no friends. People don't like me. Not one person answered my note on the bulletin board. I take that back, someone scribbled *Ingrid Varsten, Roommate from Hell* on it." She grabbed a torn piece of fabric that dangled from her dress and ripped it off completely. "People don't take to Henry, either, so unless we are to live alone, it's appropriate for the two misfits to be yoked together."

"But you said you didn't mind being alone."

"I can't support myself. They cut my hours at Gimbels. Haven't they taught you in school that our country is in a depression?"

"Please don't leave. I'll get between you and Sally, like a referee."

"A kitten trying to tame snarling curs," she said, more teasing than mean. She stared at the picture tacked on the wall above her bed, a forbidding German castle. "Sally is ignorant and spiteful, but I can manage her. She's not the one I have to get away from."

My breath caught in my throat. "Me?"

Now she laughed. "Katja sees herself in every photograph. No, I mean Papa. I can't stomach him anymore." She stood up. "Unzip me." After I did, she pulled the dress over her head and tossed it on the floor. "He's a spineless liar who can't be trusted." She kicked the tattered dress into a corner.

"Don't talk like that about our Papa. He would never hurt you on purpose."

"But he keeps doing it *not* on purpose, doesn't he? Proof of how little he cares about me. He doesn't keep hurting you."

I almost agreed, then thought about it. "But he does. It hurts that his pride was more important to him than my schooling. After Mama died, he refused to help with the chores of the apartment building. He wanted me to quit school and devote my life to cleaning."

Ingrid removed her underwear and pulled a flannel nightgown over her head. "He doesn't give away your secrets. Then again, you don't have any. Your mother wanted you."

"When he tells your secrets, he tells mine. We're family."

She went to our dresser and began tossing clothes in the suitcase. "Not anymore. I'm divorcing myself from this family to make one of my own."

Ingrid has always been able to do that—dissolve my existence like powdered milk in water. *Poof,* and I'm gone. Nothing.

I put on my pajamas, moved the suitcase to Ingrid's bed, and crawled under the covers.

CHAPTER 14
NO BELLS ARE RINGING

Ingrid asked me to be a witness for her marriage ceremony at the courthouse, which took place in June of 1933, only a couple of weeks after her birthday. She made me promise not to say anything to Papa or Sally. "Don't go back on your word," she warned, "or I'll break my ties with you, too."

The other witness was Henry's younger brother, Hans, who had recently graduated from high school and would live with the newlyweds until he found a job. Ingrid confided her hope that he would stay on when he was working, as he could help pay the rent. Hans had thin hair and pale skin like Henry, but I vowed not to judge him to be similar in personality, since I would not want to be judged on the basis of Ingrid.

Instead of a wedding dress, Ingrid chose a tailored suit, which meant I had to trade my dream of a pastel bridesmaid's gown for a shirtwaist with dressy shoes and gloves. The couple that came out while the four of us waited seemed tense and unhappy, maybe because the bride looked to be with child. Though Ingrid was too smart to get in trouble, her marriage was also forced and I expected her to emerge with the same expression, a thought that turned my own mood glum.

It took only minutes for my sister to change her identity to Ingrid Spengler, but that's to be expected when a justice of the peace does the marrying. When he said, "I now pronounce you man and wife," I bit the inside of my cheek, and when he added, "You may kiss the bride," I cringed, for Henry gave Ingrid a quick peck, as if to get it over with (public shows of affection were *verboten*). In the wedding fantasy for myself, my new husband and I gazed at each other with lovesome eyes, then embraced in a way I couldn't quite visualize but was nothing like what I saw between Ingrid and Henry. Perhaps Mama had been right, I needed to marry an American man.

On our way out, Hans held the door for me and whispered, "My brother has not a shred of romance in him."

"Neither has my sister," I whispered back. "I've been wishing on stars for these two."

He smiled, and any resemblance to his brother vanished. "I can't help but like someone who wishes on stars." With that we were friends.

And I would need a friend in the months to come.

• • •

I thought life would settle down with Ingrid gone, but instead Sally and Papa argued more often and in louder voices. It could be that Sally needed someone to fight with and goaded Papa as a substitute for Ingrid, or maybe their bickering arose from Ingrid's departure and the dreadful words that had been exchanged. Regardless, peace and quiet were rare in the Varsten apartment.

I never apologized to Sally for saying I hated her, though I did try to make up with Papa. "I understand why you said it," he replied. "Most days I hate me, too." I said over and over that I loved him, that I had spoken in the heat of anger, but he refused to believe me.

My feelings for Sally were different; there was a part of me that did hate her. And this part grew in the ensuing weeks. The minute I set my books down after school, she sent me out to clean apartments. When I complained that I had to study, she told me to stop shoving my education in her face. I asked Papa why she would make such an accusation and he explained that Sally dropped out of school at age twelve and was sensitive about her lack of education.

"She had no choice," he continued. "Her mother had an affair with a married man and they both divorced to marry each other. Sally was sent to live with her father in America. He needed help with his business, so school was out of the question."

I felt a twinge of pity. "Why did her mother send Sally away?"

"The man she married had four children. He said five was too many. Sally never saw her mother again."

Though my hatred shrunk a bit, Sally always did something to expand it again. If Papa displayed any affection, she accused him of coddling me. At first he objected, saying, "How can it be coddling to give Katja a hug when I haven't seen her all day?" or "A father should thank his daughter when she has done the ironing for three people," but her badgering persisted and he began to seek me out only when she wasn't around. And then he seemed to lose interest altogether. My loneliness was profound.

Henry was unwilling to hide his marriage indefinitely and asked Hans and me to help broach the subject with Ingrid. "It's not as if she ever listens to me," I protested, but he said he needed someone on his side. It did pay to outnumber my sister and I *was* on his side, but it was for Papa's sake that I agreed to help. Since Ingrid had left, Papa's sense of failure had darkened his features until it seemed he would dissolve into the shadows. Sometimes when I came home from school, he didn't bother to look up. When I talked to Sally about this, she said, "Your father pouts. Ignore him, he'll come out of it sooner or later."

One evening, when Hans and I were playing cards at the Spengler apartment, Henry declared, "Ingrid, it's time you opened communication with your family."

Hans tilted his head at me. "I see he took our advice to ease into the topic."

Ingrid was sitting on their sofa, a utilitarian design the color of concrete, listening to the radio and smoking a cigarette. "I don't ever want to see Papa or Sally again, if that's the family you're referring to."

"Papa loves you," I said.

"If he loved me, he wouldn't permit Sally to speak to me the way she did."

I set my cards down. "He was put in the middle and didn't know what to do. We should heal this wound and become a family again."

"*Family*." She grimaced.

"Katja speaks for me, too," Hans said. "My brother and I have no relatives in this country except the Varstens. Sally spoke from ignorance of Jews. We can teach her about other cultures and religions. Don't cut all ties to your father, for then you cut ties to your mothers, Senta Varsten and Nadine Oberlin both."

Ingrid reddened. "What do you know of this?"

"Enough." The word floated on the air like a wisp of smoke. "Henry and I have personal experience of what it means to lose a mother."

Ingrid budged a few inches, giving us permission to inform Papa and Sally of her marriage, though she would have preferred them to assume she was living in sin. "Visit them all you want, without me," she said, "and that woman is not to set foot in my home. Ever."

Hans and I looked at each other. Nothing with Ingrid ever came easy.

"What if Sally apologized?" I asked, though I wasn't sure I could bring this about.

Neither was Ingrid. "You won't get that bitch to make the first move."

Henry stood up, clenching his fists. "I won't tolerate my wife speaking like a common woman."

She stubbed out her cigarette and gripped the ashtray as if to hurl it. "Maybe your wife *is* a common woman."

Hans cleared his throat. "Leave such matters for now, Henry."

"A wife should respect her husband's wishes regardless of the circumstances."

"You knew what I was when you married me," Ingrid said.

"No, I did not. You hid your smoking, and it proved to be the least of your foul habits"

"Ingrid," I interrupted, "answer my question. Would you accept an apology from Sally?"

Ingrid's eyes were still on Henry. "That would depend on whether the bitch was sincere or not."

Henry fetched his overcoat from the closet and slipped it on. He took his hat from the shelf and adjusted it while looking in the mirror. Then he walked out the door.

I was saddened that in his absence nothing seemed missing, as if he had taken up no space.

"Why do you provoke him?" I asked. What possible satisfaction could it bring?

Ingrid smiled. "I don't have to be an actress anymore. He's hooked, as the Americans say. I can be myself and he'll have to adapt."

"The adapting should go both ways," Hans said.

Ingrid considered this. She liked Hans, so she never directed her wrath at him, though the rent money might have had something to do with her restraint. "What is it I should adapt to?"

"Unless you want always to fight, you must try to understand my brother."

"Go on." Her face was set.

"Henry despises cussing. Our father swore at us before hitting us and while he hit us. Ask Henry how this affected him."

She laughed. "You're assuming I care enough to bother."

What a contrast there was between the faces of Hans and Ingrid: elegant lines versus granite fissures; soft butting against hard.

"Yes," he said. "I'm assuming you have the integrity to honor your marriage vows. Henry gave himself to you with love, no matter how flawed. Cruelty in the face of such love is dishonorable."

Honor was something Ingrid valued. "What else should I understand about your brother?"

"He detests surprises. You can get what you want by preparing him in advance. And don't lose the co-quettishness that 'hooked' him. It'll get you far. Henry thrives on flattery."

Ingrid slammed the ashtray on the coffee table. "And what about me? Is Henry expected to understand anything about me?"

Hans cocked his head, pondering her question. "Nobody said the world was fair. You'll have to coach him on what's important to you."

"I intend to help make the world fair to all women. Men will be compelled to understand, whether they want to or not, and that includes Henry."

"Do you teach a child to like spinach by cramming it down his throat or by adding flavor to tempt him?"

"Some kids will never learn to like it. What would you suggest we do with them?"

"Don't marry one," I said.

They both looked at me.

"Too late," Ingrid said.

I shrugged. "Then season the spinach well."

CHAPTER 15
FRIENDSHIP

Hans and I were destined to be close. The fact that we grew up with difficult, strong-minded siblings contributed to this bond, but we also shared interests in music and books. Beyond that, we were good for each other. Hans was knowledgeable about current events as well as history; his political summaries taught me more about power and corruption than Ingrid's rants ever could. Yet he was the shy one who became more outgoing in the security of my company. It was easy to include him in activities with my classmates, who eagerly welcomed a handsome older boy. There was never a hint of romance between Hans and me, it wasn't that way, and I hoped he would meet a nice girl to go out with.

I was playing matchmaker when I threw Doree and Hans together. Doree had confessed that she was "keen on Hans," so I hatched a plan where the three of us would go to a Saturday night dance and I would drift off to allow them time alone. Since Papa deferred to Sally, I needed her permission to attend the dance and stay overnight at Doree's flat afterward; this I obtained by offering to work in the apartment building all day Saturday.

The evening was a success. My best friends danced together with grace and beauty and the three of us left the building with arms linked. While Hans was driving us home in his brother's car, I pictured myself as maid-of-honor at their wedding, godmother to their children. I had already calculated my next move aimed at ensuring their future together. When we pulled up to the flat, I jumped out of the car, saying, "I'll run in ahead and let you two talk."

Doree came in only minutes later and flung her coat on the bed.

"What's wrong? Did Hans get fresh?" This didn't fit the Hans I knew, but he was a boy, after all.

She shook her head, then checked her hair in the mirror and patted it approvingly. "I wish he *had* made a pass at me. At least then I wouldn't feel insulted. He shook my hand." Judging by her tone, Hans had committed a heinous crime.

Doree was one of the most popular girls in school. Boys mooned over her in study hall, and when we walked past construction workers on our way home, they whistled. She insisted they were whistling at me, too, but I wasn't the type to draw that kind of attention. I didn't have her easy, swaying gait. It's not that she was brassy—the opposite, really—more what I would call smooth. While I stiffened under their ogling, Doree preened like a tropical bird. She had come to expect boys to be attracted to her and so she was dumfounded by Hans' lack of interest. I promised to play detective.

I kept my promise, but I never shared what I discovered with Doree.

• • •

Hans and I sat at the counter of Moser's Drugstore on Sunday afternoon, joking about a boy from school who had made a spectacle of himself at the dance.

"He thinks people watch him because he's a great dancer," I said, "when it's really because he flails about like a silly ostrich. He steps on the feet of his partners and doesn't even notice. Every girl he escorted from the dance floor was limping."

Hans chuckled. "On Monday you'll be able to spot Tom's partners. They'll be the ones with flat feet."

"Big flapping clown feet." I was laughing so hard I had tears in my eyes.

We sipped our milkshakes, comfortable with each other. After a while I said, "You and Doree made quite a couple last night."

It was as if I had informed him of someone's death, the way his demeanor changed. "Yes," he said, "she knows all the latest steps and performs them with ease."

Usually we talked over each other in our eagerness to share our thoughts, but not today. I became impatient with his silence. "Do you like her?"

"I've always liked Doree."

"Do you *like* her?"

He twisted his stool toward the booths and stared at a couple sharing a milkshake with two straws.

Maybe Doree had done something to offend him and he was afraid to tell me.

"I don't *like* any girl."

Here was more information at least. "You're waiting for the right girl to come along?"

He swirled his chair back and propped his elbows on the counter. His eyes flickered with emotions, none of them happy. "You don't get it. I like boys, not girls. I'm what your friends would call a *sissy*, a *fag*."

He had to grab me around the waist to keep me from falling off the stool. And with that, one emotion took charge of his face. Fear. "I haven't admitted this to anyone else," he said. "I thought I could trust you."

I covered up my distress with indignation. "What, and now you think you can't?"

His expression settled, became less agitated. "I wasn't sure how you'd feel."

How *did* I feel? It was hard to sort it out with Hans right beside me. Or maybe that made it easier, because here was a real person I cared about telling me he had cravings the Bible called sinful. The idea of homosexuals in couples made me cringe; on the other hand, so did intercourse between men and women, though I had only shared this reaction with Doree. Our church condemned homosexuality, yet one thing Ingrid had hammered into my head was that I didn't have to accept everything I was told. There was no way to reconcile "sinful" with Hans any more than I could associate "kike" with my old skating partner. Did the fact that Hans was homosexual make me like him less? Nothing could do that.

I smiled at him. "We're friends, no matter what. Your secret is safe with me."

His relief was palpable, which made me feel sad for him. What would it be like to know that revealing something about yourself could turn friend into enemy? To think those who love you could hate you in the blink of an eye? And what did a friendship mean if you could only keep it by hiding your true self?

"In here"—Hans put his hand to his heart—"I knew you would accept me, but doubt creeps in. It feels good to finally tell somebody."

"There's no one in your family you can trust?"

He rolled his eyes. "Has Ingrid told you anything about the Spenglers?"

"Only that your parents still live in Germany and your father was severe in his punishment, but that's true of many German fathers."

"Henry and I ran away from Father. The truth is, we ran for our lives and we didn't stop until there was an ocean between Herr Spengler and his boys. His method of discipline was to beat us. If he knew his son was a faggot he would kill him."

"Don't call yourself that." By using the word, I believed Hans accepted the loathing that went with it.

"I'm speaking as he would. And my mother? Everything had to be just so. Line the forks and knives precisely or have your fingers whopped with a serving spoon. Sit straight in your chair or have your toes stomped on. Any messiness? Scrub your hands raw. Henry has inherited some of this need for perfection—God help his bride."

"Don't worry, Henry has met his match in Ingrid. But what did *you* inherit from your mother?"

"Hmm, let me think..." His words drifted out. "Good qualities, mostly. Her appreciation of beauty, for one. She used to embroider intricate flowers on linens. Of course the design had to be exactly symmetrical, but she created her own patterns, which were quite artistic. I took some linens from her bureau before I left; I'll show them to you someday." He formed a tent with his fingers, deep in thought, then said, "Mother was harsh, but I hold my father responsible for that. She knew if we strayed from his expectations a beating would follow."

"Were your parents upset when you moved out?"

"They didn't know we were leaving until they opened the door to an empty bedroom. Father must have been fuming, cursing the loss of free labor. There was nothing he enjoyed more than sitting in front of his cobbler's shop, gabbing about politics with other idle fathers who forced their sons to do their work. As for Mother, she lost her mind months before our departure. Her speech had become incoherent and she didn't seem to recognize us. She also developed a tendency to wander off. We aren't sure if her madness came from a blow to the head or the stress of living with Father. Henry speculated that Father might have drugged her."

"He makes my grandfather seem kind, and Frank Varsten was as hardhearted as they come."

"Something else I inherited from my mother," Hans said, "is the expectation that I'll be hurt."

"Not by me." I kissed his cheek. "But it's my turn to confess. As a little girl, I secretly wished for a different sister than Ingrid, or a brother. I think my wish has come true."

Hans was laughing. "It's funny you say that, because I always wished for a different brother than Henry. A sister will do just fine."

We sat until we had drained the sweetness from our glasses, until we made rude noises with our straws and couldn't stop laughing about it.

• • •

I would be painting my self-portrait as too flattering if I gave the impression that I accepted Hans' homosexuality without qualm. The society I lived in viewed his way of life as a perversion and if I let myself dwell on it, I was like foil crunched in a fist of morality, with sharp peaks of guilt and misgiving. Mama would have denounced Hans on religious grounds, yet I couldn't conceive of her disliking him. In the end my strategy was to simply not think about it. Mostly this worked and let me love him as my friend.

When I went to Doree's flat for lunch a few days later, I told her Hans was recovering from a broken heart and had decided to focus on his studies for the time being. I didn't even ask Hans if I should tell her the truth, for I knew secrets were like air to Doree—she took them in and let them out again. She accepted my explanation, probably because she couldn't imagine a boy rejecting her. Hans wasn't her type anyway, she said. I heartily agreed with her.

Doree was drawn to the outgoing, fast-talking charmers Mama had taught me to distrust, though I couldn't help turning wobbly around them. One in particular kept trying to catch my eye and I did my best to ignore him.

"Roberto likes you," Doree said. "Why won't you smile at him?"

"That would displease Mama."

"Your mama would want you to make decisions for yourself now that she's gone, or get guidance from your stepmother."

We were sprawled on the plaid sofa in Doree's cozy living room, the smell of potato soup wafting our way. How I wished I could change places with her and live in this flat with its warm stuffiness and friendly clutter. "Mama would not want Sally to guide me," I said. "Sally's goal is to push me out of the house, like Ingrid, so she can have Papa to herself. She'll encourage me to pursue any boy whether he's good for me or not."

"She seems nice enough. I can't believe she's that heartless."

The blood rushed to my head as if I'd been turned upside down. "You have a normal mother!" I heard myself shouting. "You don't know what it's like to live with a selfish woman who never wanted children and then got stuck with somebody else's kids."

Doree's mother appeared drying her hands on a dish towel. She wore a flowered housedress and an apron with ruffles. Her eyes were filled with concern. "What's the matter, honey?" she asked me.

"I miss Mama." My voice came out squeaky as a mouse.

She opened her arms and I ran into them, wishing with all of my might that I would turn into Doree and have this mother.

"There, there," she said, until my breathing slowed to normal. She stood back to look at me. "Feel any better?" Her expression was so tender I wanted to beg her to adopt me. But I only nodded, embarrassed at my loss of control.

Same old weepy Katja.

• • •

Roberto was a handsome Italian with curly black hair and a smile that held more than friendliness. The less I took notice of him, the more he sought me out.

Doree said it was a terrific technique for keeping a boy interested, but I was never one to use techniques.

A week before my birthday in July, Sally asked what kind of celebration I would like. I had no answer. The anniversary of Mama's death loomed a month away, so it was like trying to bask in the sun while storm clouds darkened the sky. Roberto had invited me to the movies and to ensure my acceptance, Doree agreed to go out with his friend, a sacrifice on her part, she pointed out, since the boy was not up to her usual standards. Doree's manipulation gave me the reason I needed to say *yes*.

Sally thought the double date was a *marvelous* idea and declared that we must bring the boys to the apartment afterward for cake and ice cream. I expected Papa to put his foot down, since Mama's rule was no dating until age eighteen. Yet when I requested his permission, he barely glanced up from the newspaper. "Whatever you want to do."

I found myself arguing with him. "You don't care if I go out with a boy?"

"I trust you. You wouldn't do anything to make me or your mama ashamed." He said this in Sally's presence and we all knew "Mama" did not mean her. Sally left the room. Papa turned the page of his newspaper and gave no indication that he had been aware of her.

Hans made up for Papa's disinterest the next day when we went shopping together.

"You're going on a date with that snake Roberto?" He held open the door of Goldman's Department Store. "He's too smooth for you."

I halted before going through. "What do you mean? I can take care of myself."

"Not with that ladies' man. You won't stand a chance against his clever tricks."

An older lady with a flamboyant feathered hat was crowding me, so I went inside the store and stood off to the side to let her pass. When Hans joined me, I said, "You treat me like a child."

"In some ways you are like a child, and by that I mean naive." He fell behind me so we could walk between the open bins of women's clothing, though he leaned forward to continue talking. "Here's how Roberto will operate. After the lights go down and the movie starts, he'll rest his hand across the back of your seat, careful not to touch you, pretending to be a gentleman. Then at a romantic part—you're going to see *It Happened One Night,* aren't you?—he'll bring his arm around your shoulders and when the time is right, he'll pull you close to him. After that—"

I swung round to face Hans, almost causing him to smack into me. "And how would *you* know about such things?"

We both backed off as if my words had exploded between us.

He said, "You don't have to be interested in girls to know how boys operate."

"I'm sorry. I'm nervous and you're making it worse." I twisted a paisley scarf in my hands. "You want to protect me, but what's so terrible about a boy putting his arm around a girl?"

Of course I was old enough to know the answer to that, but Hans made sure to tell me anyway.

• • •

My birthday was on a Thursday, and my date was the following Saturday. When Sally announced that she would bake a cake for both occasions, I didn't let on that Ingrid had promised to make one, too. Better to stuff myself with cake than set off Sally's temper.

One of Sally's birthday presents was to free me from chores all day, so on Thursday I meandered to the Spengler apartment with the luxury of time to waste. I stopped to admire a window box of geraniums and smile at a baby in a stroller, but mostly I replayed my conversation with Roberto a couple of days ago.

I had been going down the steps at school when he appeared at my side, so close I could smell his lime aftershave lotion. Brushing aside a strand of my hair, he whispered, "I have a gift for lovely Katja's fourteenth birthday"—his breath in my ear set off a tingling sensation—"but she'll have to wait until Saturday." He ran his finger along my cheek and when I gazed into his eyes, I understood what it meant to swoon. Roberto could have been the leading man in a romance magazine.

These thoughts tumbled to the back of my mind when I arrived at the Spengler apartment, where I was showered with confetti and *Happy Birthday* sung in three distinct voices. Ingrid was off-key and Henry had a flat monotone, but Hans...oh, how to describe it...if the neck of a swan, the leap of a deer could be translated into sound, each might convey the grace of his voice. I vowed to have him sing for me later; at the moment I wanted to savor my birthday celebration.

As a little girl, I was treated like a princess on my birthday. I never dreamed Ingrid would re-create the joy of that experience for me, since jealousy had caused her to ruin many of my birthdays. One year she spilled raspberry sauce all over my party dress; on another she bumped the table so my new ceramic whistle rolled onto the floor and broke. Yet today she proudly presented a lopsided cake with precise lettering. Hans and I would chuckle in private over how obvious it was who did what, how irked Henry must have been to place his perfect letters on an imperfect surface. I hoped he hadn't criticized Ingrid but guessed he had, and for that reason I went overboard in praising the cake. She didn't leave out any ingredients, so it tasted fine.

Ingrid beamed and Henry was content because his wife was smiling. We were able to play charades without Ingrid accusing me of cheating or Henry getting mad at the phrase he was expected to pantomime. Ingrid didn't move Henry's hand away when he idly picked lint from her green sweater and he tolerated her talk of women's rights. All in all, it was an afternoon of goodwill. I didn't want to leave, but delay would invite Sally's annoyance.

She greeted me at the door with a German chocolate cake that lacked the distraction of lettering. The atmosphere was dreary and my efforts to be cheerful went flat as a run-over tin can and I got tired of trying. I was filled with resentment—Sally and Papa should have been the ones making the effort—until I realized with a sinking heart that this *was* an effort. Normally they would be trading hostilities.

My gifts were secondhand books: from Sally, *Brave New World*, which Papa said was too grown up, and from Papa, *The Wind in the Willows*, which Sally said was too juvenile. I ended the argument by declaring that I was eager to read them both. We spent the rest of the evening in the living room, Papa with the ever-present newspaper, Sally listening to Charlie Chan on the radio, and me with *Brave New World*. After an hour or so, I switched to *The Wind in the Willows*.

• • •

Hans was right and wrong about my first date. Roberto put his arm around me, but he did so from the start and without apology. I liked the feel of it there. When we returned to the apartment after the movie, he made a good impression by complimenting Sally on her first try at lasagna and by showing the proper respect to Papa. Best of all, by bringing up the subject of boxing, he encouraged Papa to be more animated than I had seen him in months. Papa even went so far as to imitate the moves of someone named Max Baer. This day marked not only my first date—a good one—but my first box of candy from a boy. As we said our goodbyes at the door, Roberto tried to steal a kiss. I let him know I wasn't that kind of a girl, candy or not.

Roberto became harder to resist as we saw more of each other. One weekend, Sally and Papa took us to the Mitchell Park Horticultural Conservatory and arranged to meet us in an hour. It was like being inside a huge aquarium filled with flowers instead of water. When Roberto had had his fill of flowers, we strolled along the pond out front. Under the warmth of the sun, he kissed me. ("In broad daylight," Doree would exclaim later, with unmistakable envy.) In a flash of electricity I knew he was *The One*.

We joined up with Sally and Papa at the park diamond, but I couldn't keep my mind on sandlot baseball. Roberto must have had the same problem, for he whispered, "I wish we could go back to the conservatory, and not to smell the flowers, if you know what I mean." I giggled and said, "Watch the game, Roberto."

I still think of him with fondness and wonder what might have been. Roberto created such turmoil, anxiety and desire wrestling within me. I was fascinated by his maleness. I didn't admit this even to Doree (though she had no problem sharing such thoughts), but I wished for an Indian summer so we could visit the bathhouse and I could see Roberto in his bathing suit. That never happened, though.

It would be a long time before I wished for anything so frivolous. Nearly a lifetime, in fact.

CHAPTER 16
ANNIVERSARY

The trouble with Roberto was that *happy* was the only emotion he did well. As the anniversary of Mama's death approached, he maneuvered me away from expressions of grief. I tried to be jovial for his sake, but I have no talent as an actress. One evening when we were in the lobby of the movie theatre, he cocked his head, a charming curl of hair falling across his forehead, and asked why I was acting so peculiar.

His question unlatched a floodgate. I flung my arms around him and cried, "I'm trying not to think of Mama, but it isn't working."

He didn't hug me back but instead freed himself. "Not here," he said.

My eyes pleaded with him, as they used to do with Ingrid, to *understand*. But he was as immune to this message as she had been, although instead of belittling me, he let his gaze fall on a faraway spot as if that was where he wanted to be. To hold onto him, I reeled in my despair. "I'm sorry," I said, "I don't know what's gotten into me. How about if we ask Doree and Mike to go to Moser's after the movie?"

"Yes, let's do that." He fiddled with the cuff of his shirt, making sure the button fit in its proper hole. "About next Saturday—"

The very date, one year ago, that Mama left the world. I was grateful he brought it up. Being with him would get me through the day, even if we didn't talk about her.

"—my parents are counting on me to visit my aunt and uncle."

"The whole day?" I squeezed the words through my lips.

"Actually all weekend."

"But surely not Friday night? That's our usual time together."

"We'll have to skip this Friday."

"All right," I said brightly. "The next weekend, then."

At the soda fountain, I concentrated on hiding my feelings. This proved to be a strain and finally I told everyone I was tired and asked Roberto to walk me home. Outside the apartment building, I let him kiss me. I let him do this more than once and I also allowed our tongues to mingle. I wanted a magnet that would draw him back to me.

He was the one to end our embrace. "You're making me wild. If I don't stop now, I won't be able to stop, and your father will come at me with a shotgun. I'll find us a place to be alone next week."

Don't worry about Papa, I wanted to say. He doesn't care what I do and even if he did, he wouldn't have the energy to lift himself from the sofa to object.

I watched Roberto swagger down the sidewalk and knew I must get hold of myself.

• • •

On Saturday morning, I spoke to Papa through a closed door. I tried to be grown-up when I asked him to accompany me to Mama's grave, but when he said he wasn't up to going out, I turned into little girl Katja. "Papa, please, I need you."

His "I can't do it" was muffled.

I sunk to the ground with my back to the door, arms wrapped around my legs.

After a few minutes, the door gave a bit and I twisted around to see Papa's face in the crack. There was a dinginess to him. He hadn't shaved and the one eye I could see was glassy.

I stood up. "You'll come?"

He squinted at me. "You go ahead and I'll catch up."

"I can wait."

"Go. Ingrid will be expecting you. I need to bathe and dress nicely for Senta."

• • •

The cemetery was deserted, as it often was, not the meeting place of Brühl. Milwaukeeans tended gravesites lovingly, but they seemed to do it alone and without fanfare.

I was glad Ingrid hadn't arrived yet, so Mama and I could be alone. I set pots of pansies by the headstone, then walked the length of her body and stood taking in the permanency of her name in granite: *Senta Varsten, Beloved Wife of Andreas, Adored Mother of Katia and Ingrid.*

"I hope you like the pansies," I told Mama. "Grandma Rosa wrote that they should be a mix of purples, with yellow added for contrast." A tear wandered down my face and splotched onto my white blouse. "Papa said he would visit, but you know how he is. You'll have to make do with me for now." I glanced over my shoulder and saw Ingrid and Henry approaching. "I have to talk fast, Mama. I miss you with my heart and soul. I have so much to ask you. How do I say *no* to Roberto without losing him?" I saw him in my mind's eye and felt a fluttering inside. Then I apologized to Mama if it was disrespectful to bring him up at her gravesite.

The crimson of the zinnias Ingrid carried was vivid against her black dress. I hadn't thought to wear black, though I did put on my nicest white blouse and navy skirt to please Mama. Henry in his three-piece suit might have been comical toting a little pail but he managed to look distinguished, even when he pulled out a small spade and began digging.

"The zinnias will come up year after year," Ingrid said, setting the plant in the damp earth just excavated, "and Mama will like tulips every spring, won't she?" She drew a bulb from a basket hanging at the crook of her arm.

"That was smart," I said. "My pansies won't last more than a month."

"But they'll look pretty for thirty long days," Henry said. Now and then he surprised me with a comment like this.

Only Henry Spengler could work in the soil wearing a suit and not get dirty. Of course he brought a damp washcloth for tidying up. After Ingrid watered Mama's new plants, we stood admiring them. And waiting.

"I'll come back tomorrow to water again," Ingrid said.

I nodded, then met her eyes. "I'm not sure Papa will show up."

Her face hardened. "In that case we may as well leave."

They offered me a ride, but I turned it down, preferring to walk. If I had taken the ride, I might have reached the apartment in time.

• • •

I was outside the building when I heard the gunshot, though I didn't know what it was at the time. As I reached for the door to our apartment, Sally rushed out sputtering words I couldn't understand. She had the face of someone in a horror movie without the phoniness of overacting.

The bedroom door was open and I approached with halting steps. Papa hadn't changed clothes as he said he would. His sprawled legs wore the same grubby brown trousers. His far-flung arms emerged from the same yellowed short-sleeved shirt. He lay on the bed with viscous splotches of blood around him. This is all I remember now. I've racked my brain to recall more, but a hazy blackness comes, like fog without even a dull light shining through. *Thank God,* Ingrid would say later; thank God for that impenetrable fog. I had left the outside door open and neighbors jammed the doorway and spilled into the apartment. Screams, I remember screams, but I don't think they came from me. Maybe they did. Someone guided me to another apartment; there was the warm pressure of a hand on my arm. The police appeared amid high-pitched sirens and tried to talk to me but I was a deserted house with boarded-up windows and doors. Dr. Perry appeared and gave me a shot. I was in a bed I didn't recognize. A day bed. I slept, falling down the chasm that has no end.

I saw Papa's body in a painting of spattered scarlet, without Papa's face.

CHAPTER 17
SUSPENDED ANIMATION

I awakened to Hans' troubled eyes. He told me he had carried me to the car and then up to his room on that terrible day, The Day of the Orphan. Henry remained at the apartment building for more than a week, cleaning and painting the room where Papa had been found. I would always think of Papa under that paint.

Henry made Ingrid stay away from the apartment. He was afraid of what she would do to Sally, since Ingrid believed she killed Papa. Sally as murderess never entered my mind, even when I saw her fleeing the building. The police had to investigate and for three days Sally's whereabouts were unknown.

She turned up at a tavern. After questioning her and examining the scene of the crime, the police determined that Papa's wounds were self-inflicted, that was how they put it. Henry told me that Sally was drunk when they located her, that she had been "trying to drown her sorrows" since she discovered Papa. She blamed herself for his death and at first, I did, too. I had warned her of the signs but she brushed my concerns aside and so she deserved blame.

After Papa's death, I would not speak to anyone. I only wanted to lie in bed without moving. For a few weeks this was tolerated by Mr. and Mrs. Henry Spengler, but on Sunday afternoon of the third week, Ingrid burst in and yanked back the covers. My lips formed a circle of disbelief.

"School tomorrow, Katja. I have make-up work from your teachers. They were lenient. You can get it done today."

I rolled onto my stomach and placed a pillow over my head.

Ingrid picked me up. She actually lifted me and sat me on the edge of the bed. I fell onto the blanket and curled up against the plaster wall. In my life I had never defied Ingrid, but that was because I was afraid. Now I didn't care. She could slap me, beat me up. I did not care. Part of me thought I deserved to be punished, anyway. I should have kept Papa from leaving us. We all assume we have more control over others than we do.

Ingrid sat down and began talking. "I won't say my feelings for Papa compare to yours. I was born mad at him and never stopped being mad. There were times I loathed him, but these times were better than when I pitied him. All of my feelings, though not loving like yours, well up inside of me now that he's dead. What I'm trying to say is that I feel it, too, the enormity of Papa killing himself on the day Mama died. You want to curl into sadness—I want to curl my fingers in rage. But who should I hit? The main thing is we both *feel* and we can't let these feelings destroy us. You must go on. You must finish school."

"I can't go to school. The kids will point and stare. I only want to be left alone."

She waved a hand as if I were fussing about one ant in the pantry. "So, you'll be an object of curiosity for the first few days and then they'll lose interest."

"I can't go on without Papa."

A burst of air escaped her lips "You've been going on without Papa for years. The Papa you knew and loved died long before this helpless one."

"I can't."

"You have an hour to get dressed. If you don't, I'll drag you out of bed and dress you myself. Tomorrow I'll carry you to school and keep you propped up at your desk. You know I care not even a grain of sand what others think."

I said nothing.

"Don't be weak like him."

"I am weak like him."

She grabbed me by the shoulders and shook me, hard. "No, you are not. You carried on after Mama died, doing twice the work and living with a stepmother who hissed one moment and purred the next. You will graduate from high school and be a success. You are *strong*."

• • •

The Katja Varsten of this time was a sleepwalker who attended school in a trance, who took out her book as the teacher instructed and learned how to calculate the angle of a triangle, then went home to figure out the angles of more triangles. A spell had been cast on me.

The other students did gawk and whisper, but as Ingrid predicted, this did not last overly long. It helped that Doree glared back at some and enlisted the sympathy of others. With time, a few girls approached to tell me they were sorry for my loss, carefully avoiding any reference to suicide. To this day, I remember every one of them by name. I also remember those who were silent when I passed. Like Roberto.

I was invisible to him. If he did glance my way, his eyes registered nothing, as if we had never met. And I discovered that a broken heart can always splinter into smaller pieces.

• • •

Two months had passed when Henry sought me out for a conversation "between just the two of us." Ingrid would be home soon from the beauty parlor and I was setting the table for lunch. "We need to discuss your future," he said.

I was mildly surprised. "I'll live here."

He shook his head. "Haven't you noticed that you took Hans' bed? The apartment is too small for four people. I have another proposal for you, but first let me give you the background leading up to it."

I sat on the wooden rocker. He remained standing.

"I went to fetch Sally after the police had finished with her," he said, pacing before me and doing a neat pivot when he reached the rocker's edge. "I took her home, poured all her liquor down the drain, and guarded her like an Alsatian in a jewelry store. I slept on the sofa until she had gone a week without drinking. I could only do this with her consent. She has been sober ever since but she needs support getting back on her feet."

He went on to explain that the apartment where my mama and then my papa died had been put up for rent. The owner told Sally she could have another apartment, but he would not permit a woman to act as manager of the building. This jerked Sally from her despondency and she declared that she had been the one running the apartment. "No matter," the owner said, "a man must be the official manager."

"No wonder Ingrid fights for women's rights," I said without interest.

Henry mumbled something noncommittal, then said, "I negotiated with the owner and he agreed that Sally could manage the Cherry Street Apartments with Hans, in exchange for a small two bedroom apartment plus efficiency unit. They will share a meager allowance. Hans has the foolish notion of becoming a nightclub singer and claims this arrangement will give him a roof over his head while he establishes his singing career. With any luck he'll come to his senses and get a real job, but for now both he and Sally will benefit from this joint venture."

"Then Hans' room will be freed up here." I marveled that this fact had escaped him.

Henry shook his head. "Ingrid and I want to have a family. We need to be alone and become closer as a married couple."

The room will stand empty for a long time, I thought, but I did not voice my opinion. "I could be your baby-sitter."

"You have four years of high school left. Plan on moving into Sally's apartment—" He held up a hand when I started to protest—"Hans and I will make sure your duties in the building are limited and we'll put everything in writing. Sally has agreed to this. She is lonely and eager for you to move in. Hans will be right next door in the efficiency unit."

"Sally wants a live-in maid. Would we put in writing how the housework will be shared?"

"If that's what you want."

I moved in with Sally because I had no choice. I referred to her by name and never called her *Mom* again.

CHAPTER 18
FAMILY
1935

I learned to be an orphan, to identify myself as someone without parents. Strangely enough, I was able to get along with Sally much better than when Papa was alive. This might have been because she no longer had any grounds for jealousy, but what I think really is that I had no expectations of her. I accepted Sally for who she was rather than as a poor replacement for Mama. She was just a person, flawed but not horrible.

I came to comprehend the insecurities that chewed at Sally's heart and created ragged borders. One evening, after a backbreaking day in the apartment building, when many tenants had left in the night to avoid paying rent, she and I sat on the porch sipping tea. After waving to Hans, who was on his way to a singing engagement, Sally turned to me and said, "Your Papa married me because I look like your Mama."

I flinched as if I had been jabbed with something sharp.

"I thought he'd come to love me, but instead he tried to make me into Senta. First he nagged at me to wear her dresses." Sally swallowed hard. "I couldn't do that, wear a dead woman's clothing. Besides, I have my own style. What made it stupid was that her clothes would never fit. Try putting a cocker spaniel's collar on a St. Bernard and you'll know what I mean." She shook her head. "His desire to change how I looked was bad enough, but when Andy wanted to change my personality, that was humiliating." She leaned forward, dangling her hands over the railing.

"Papa loved qualities about you that Mama didn't have." I felt a twinge of guilt at my disloyalty, but Mama would want me to ease this woman's pain.

"Me?" Sally wasn't about to let herself believe this.

"Yes, you. He told me he liked your fun-loving ways. He looked forward to going dancing."

"The beer." Her eyes dulled. "It helped him forget Senta and gave him permission to dance."

"No. It wasn't the beer. It was you."

And so we developed a kind of friendship.

When Sally became lazy and put her work off on me, I had only to joke that I would tell Henry. She would buckle down the very next day. I found this odd and said as much to Ingrid.

"Not so odd," she said. "Henry is the German father figure Sally yearns for."

I cocked my head at her. "Why, Ingrid, you sound like Sigmund Freud."

"As long as I don't look like him." She offered one of her deep laughs.

Ingrid's attitude toward Sally had gradually shifted; she didn't spout off in anger or call her names, and she even made an occasional sympathetic comment. High time for these women to become reacquainted, I decided.

It was spring of 1935. I asked Ingrid to help me plant flowers on the graves of Senta and Andreas Varsten so the anniversary of their deaths in August would be marked by color and beauty. I also asked Sally. In both cases I failed to mention who else would be there, though Henry was in on the secret. I apologized beforehand to my parents, should an angry scene erupt, and went on to explain that I was ready to unite the broken-down people who used to be a family.

From five gravesites away, Sally recognized Ingrid and Henry, who were engrossed in conversation. She stopped in front of *Anna Fitzgerald, Beloved Wife of Samuel.* "You shouldn't have tricked us," she said. "Ingrid will leave when she sees me."

I shrugged. "Then she leaves. Let's put her to the test."

We had passed three gravesites when Ingrid noticed us. She assumed a rigid posture, but as Sally drew near with eyes downcast, wringing her hands, Ingrid became a soldier at ease.

Henry's welcome had a jolliness that was so out of character I couldn't wait to mimic it for Hans later. Henry held out his hands to Sally, saying, "Come join us in cultivating a garden."

Sally nodded to Ingrid. "How are you?"

"I'm doing well," Ingrid said, unsmiling. "And you?"

"Getting by. I miss your father."

"Yes." Ingrid bent down to dig in the earth. "I miss him, too."

Sally gestured at Mama's grave. "Which plant would you like here?"

Ingrid gave her a sharp look, then reached for a pot. "The climbing rose bush. Put it behind the headstone.

That way the roses will form a border around Mama's name, like a portrait with an ornate frame."

"I'll need the shovel when you're done with it."

For the next hour we worked on our memorial garden. When it was finished, we stood remembering. And from then on, Ingrid and Sally were speaking to each other again.

• • •

The plan for a trip to Germany was hatched that summer (I like to think the breeze at the cemetery was really Papa whispering the idea; it didn't come from Mama, that much I know). We were at an elegant supper club, an audience for Hans and his new pianist. I felt grown-up seated in a booth of tufted maroon velvet, the scent of perfume, cigarette smoke and candles creating the feel of an exotic land. With an overlay of muted conversation and clinking glasses, the duo performed *It Was Just One of Those Things*. When Hans finished singing, he bowed to our enthusiastic applause and joined us for his break.

Henry cleared his throat, but instead of complimenting Hans, he said, "Ingrid has it in her head that she must go to Germany. I've done my best to dissuade her but as usual she turns a deaf ear to me. Perhaps she'll listen to the rest of her family."

"Since when?" I said, and even Ingrid laughed.

Hans set his water glass on the table, empty. "I say if she needs to go, let her. Why must we dissuade her?"

Ingrid's face brightened as if she had been floundering in the sea and was suddenly saved by a kind soul in a lifeboat.

Henry grunted. "Do you pay attention to anything besides your silly birdsongs, brother? Do you have any notion of what's going on in Germany?"

"Of course he does," I said. "All the more reason to go. Grandma Rosa is worried sick. She writes that Hitler replaced the Storm Troops with the brutal Schutzstaffel, or SS, and what was that other secret police force she wrote about?" I turned to Hans, with whom I shared all of my grandmother's letters.

"The Gestapo, subject to no laws or restraint." He signaled the waiter and pointed to his water glass.

"But these Gestapo forces, they don't bother regular Germans, do they?" Sally stirred the lime in her soda pop with a swizzle stick. "Only Jews, I thought."

Ingrid was up in a flash, bumping the table so we scrambled to keep our glasses from toppling. "Jews are Germans, you idiot, and don't ever say otherwise."

Henry yanked her down. "She intended no harm."

Ingrid pried his hand from her arm and glowered at him. "Your anti-Semitism is showing, dear."

"Lower your voices." Hans glanced at the owner of the club, whose eyebrows had unified in a threatening glare. "There's no need for all the patrons to overhear your conversation."

Ingrid nodded, lips drawn tight.

"I wasn't trying to insult anyone," Sally said. "I only meant that we wouldn't have to worry because we're not..."

"Jewish?" Ingrid said. "Is that the word you stumble over?"

"You're only part Jewish, and no one will know unless you announce it."

Ingrid took a long drink of her beer. "I'm a Jew, period. I should be able to shout it from the rooftops."

"Whether you should be able to do it is beside the point," Henry said. "If we go to Germany, you cannot reveal your heritage for reasons of your own safety and the safety of your family. You must represent yourself as one hundred percent German, declaring your parents to be Andreas and Senta Varsten. Don't give me that look, Ingrid. From the furor's standpoint, Jews are not Germans, fairness be damned."

Ingrid was about to object, but then I could see her calculating. "Are you telling me I can make this trip, and that others will be going, too?"

"My wife will not travel without her husband. What's more, Hans has expressed interest in learning the fate of our parents. Travel will be feasible even in these dangerous times because Berlin is preparing to host the Olympics next year. With the world watching, Germany will strive to present itself in a favorable light and will be more accommodating to visitors. So yes, I'm yielding to your wishes." Henry raised his hands in resignation.

I could no longer contain myself. "To see Grandma Rosa and Uncle Albert again would be a dream come true. A day doesn't go by that I don't think of them. I want to go."

"And me," Sally said.

We all stared at her.

She held her chin up. "I have a mother, too, and a desire to see her."

An acceptable answer.

"All well and good," Henry said, "but where will the money come from to pay for five round-trip tickets to Germany?"

I coughed, the secret of hidden money lodged in my throat. The December after Mama's death, I discovered her nest egg in a box of Christmas decorations no one else wanted. My first impulse was to tell Ingrid and Papa, but then the strangest thing happened: I got a message from Mama, I swear I did. The money must be used to buy a house. A house, nothing else. I could not use it for a trip to Germany. If I did, I would be breaking a promise to Mama.

Henry drummed his fingers on the table. "So we have a grand plan and no cash to fund it."

Ingrid seldom got close to tears, but she seemed on the verge now. Then she was herself again. "We'll have to earn the money for our passage," she said. "If that means taking on extra jobs, so be it."

Sally's laughter was a series of snorts. "In a depression, we'll find extra jobs?"

Ingrid's eyes narrowed. "Yes. We will."

"We might have items to sell." I pictured the Hummels, cuckoo clocks, and furniture crowding the apartment Sally and I shared.

Sally frowned at me. "People are out of work. They don't have money to spare, and even supposing they did, curios and antiques wouldn't fetch what they're worth."

Ingrid snickered. "They're probably worth less than you think."

It would take two years, Sally's grudging disclosure of a hidden inheritance, and a shameful act to get back to Germany, but we swallowed our pride and did what we needed to do.

PART 3
GERMANY

Summer 1937

CHAPTER 19
VISITING THE HOMELAND

"Grandma Rosa." I hugged her and drew strength from her sturdiness.

We stood back to examine each other and I saw that her eyes had a softer hue now. She said, "A child left and an eighteen-year-old woman returned. I missed seeing you grow up." When she spoke German in her rich tones, it was like hearing a beloved song after many years.

I slipped into my mother tongue like a comfortable old jacket. "You look younger. How can that be? And you aren't in black." She wore a dress printed with roses and her cheeks had roses to match.

"Both may have to do with your grandfather's passing last year." She hurried to add, "God rest his soul."

I nodded solemnly and we paused to honor the dead. Then she asked about my trip.

Taking the train from Mannheim to Brühl had not been the ride of ten years ago. The friendly atmosphere that had reportedly characterized the Olympics was no longer evident and the anti-Jewish signs had been reposted. The SS dominated the cars and these were not policeman who made you feel protected, like those in America who smiled at children. These men with a lightning-shaped *S* on their black uniforms smiled at no one unless they jeered. Ingrid told me afterward that she had imagined her Jewish blood setting off an alarm that caused the SS to attack; when her blood spilled out it was purple and they licked it up like devil dogs. I told her she should write horror stories.

It was not just the military presence that tainted the train ride, but also the submissive demeanor of the passengers, their faces taunt and their bodies stiff in a complete absence of joy. Even a baby cradled in her mother's arms brought no coos of pleasure from those seated nearby. I couldn't wait to disembark.

To my relief, the farm was much as I remembered it. With Uncle Albert's help, Grandma Rosa had kept it from becoming run down like many of the surrounding properties, although the buildings did need painting. "We can't afford to buy the paint," she said as we stood surveying the property.

"I can get a good price from Herr Simon," Uncle Albert said, "if you would only agree to the deal."

Grandma Rosa's eyes darted nervously. "Let's go inside."

Once we were in the living room, she said, "What is our answer when the SS inquires where the paint was purchased?"

Uncle Albert sat in the rocking chair. "If Herr Simon doesn't sell the cans stockpiled in his basement, the Nazis will seize them. We need paint and he needs money."

"We aren't permitted to buy from Jews," Grandma Rosa explained to us, "even those we have known for thirty years, like Herr Simon. The government forced him to sell his business for a paltry amount. He was able to keep some supplies for personal use. He considers himself fortunate, as many Jews have been chased from the country."

Ingrid flopped onto the sofa. "Buy the paint and we'll do the house together. If the Gestapo goons raise questions, tell them you bought it long before they stole Herr Simon's business, that he was storing the paint until your relatives arrived to help you."

Grandma Rosa tapped a finger to her chin. "A clever strategy that just might work."

"A word of caution," Uncle Albert said. "Never speak disparagingly of Hitler and the Nazis. You can be arrested and taken away."

"But it's just us talking," I said.

He looked around, careful not to rest his gaze on the Spengler brothers or Sally, but lingering for a fraction of a second, nonetheless. "It's perilous to get in the habit of speaking your mind, even in confidence. You might forget and loosen your tongue in public. And the person you trust could have a change of heart where Hitler is concerned. Such converts have long memories."

I never pegged Uncle Albert as the suspicious type, and when Ingrid and I went upstairs to unpack, I got my second surprise. "Uncle is right," she said. "We must be careful. It's not inconceivable that Sally—even Henry—would betray me."

The candlelight from the dressing table flickered as if a shrouded figure had passed, or so my imagination suggested. "How can you say that? I can appreciate your misgivings about Sally, although you probably have nothing to worry about, but your own husband?" In my agitation I stuffed two blouses back into my suitcase in a wad; I had taken them out only minutes ago to hang up in the closet. The wrinkles would need to be steamed.

Ingrid brushed her hair vigorously. "Henry loves me, that much I know—why he loves me, I do *not* know—but he was raised to distrust Jews. Whether the clay of that distrust could be pummeled into a grotesque shape by Nazis, I can't predict. Good people can also be weak. I'm only admitting the possibility."

"But you're telling me you can stay with a man who could hand you over to the Nazis?"

Ingrid's mouth formed a slanted line; her eyes shone ebony. "For better or worse, sister dear."

She was being sarcastic, I knew, but how did she cope with these doubts? Surely betrayal goes beyond what the marriage vows meant by *worse*.

I knew even then that Ingrid was wrong to doubt Henry. He was a man with a strict moral code who loved her and would never betray his wife. Why didn't she realize that? I believe it was because she made no effort to understand him.

• • •

Within a few days of arriving at the farm, Henry and Hans motored off in Grandfather's old truck to revisit their childhood home in Frankfurt. After they left, we women sat at the kitchen table to make plans. Sally needed to arrange transportation to Düsseldorf, about thirty miles away, the last address she found for her mother. Ingrid had only to go into the city of Brühl. Both asked me to come along (Ingrid had turned down Henry's offer to escort her). I was puzzling over how to please two people at once when Grandma Rosa said, "I'll go with you, Ingrid, if you'll have me."

Ingrid set her cup down and held tight to the handle. "Why? How would this benefit you?"

Grandma Rosa walked behind her and placed a hand on each shoulder—Ingrid could not see her face, but I was struck by how much an expression of unhappiness will age a person—"The benefit would come from whittling away regret for a lifetime of harshness toward you."

Ingrid's cup rattled. Emotions flashed on her face like a newsreel spinning through different stories. "Join me, then," she said in a level tone.

"I will." Grandma Rosa came around the table to face her. "Nadine knows me. And before we go, I must prepare you for what you will find."

• • •

Sally and I took a bus to Düsseldorf. She had made no contact in advance. If her mother and stepfather knew she was coming, she joked, they would hide behind the drapes and pretend no one was home.

We stood on the porch of a fashionable two-story house, daunted by an elaborate brass knocker on a heavy wooden door, until finally Sally grabbed the metal loop like a chicken's neck to be wrung. At the resounding clangs, a woman's face peered out from the drapes in the way Sally had predicted. We shared an anxious laugh. The door creaked open just enough for the woman to see us. "Yes?" Her hair was red and curly with more than enough frizz.

"Frau Buchler?" At the woman's hesitant nod, Sally said, "I'm Berta Kubek."

What would I have done if my long-lost daughter showed up at my doorstep? I would have taken her in my arms so she could feel the fullness of my heart beating against her. Romantic Katja. How often I have wished I could take the magic wand of fairy tales and give people the world of my dreams. But I couldn't do this for Sally, whose mother looked like a wild bird ready to bat against the bars of its cage.

"Come in," Frau Buchler said, less in welcome, I suspect, than in a desire to keep this meeting private. With jerky movements, she led us to the formal parlor. "Please sit down. Would you like some tea?"

We nodded in tandem.

While she rattled around out of sight, I examined the room. Drawn shades made the dark furnishings emerge from the dimness like monsters. The ornate antique furniture with its brocade upholstery and ball feet was evidently more for display than comfort (I would learn from Hans that it was called Rococo). I was nervous ahead of time about spilling tea on the Oriental rug, which was finely-woven in shades of gold and green that matched the upholstery.

Frau Buchler brought in a gilt-edged tray on which three porcelain tea cups were arranged with their saucers. She set the tray on the coffee table and motioned toward it with an open palm. As if to provide a model of the expected behavior, she took one of the cups between finger and thumb and perched on a side chair with the saucer on her knees. "So, Berta, what brings you to Germany?"

Sally's pose reminded me of a jointed doll whose head has been shoved too far in one direction. "Why, you, of course." she said. "I call myself Sally now, Sally Varsten, since I married. This is my stepdaughter, Katja."

I tried to smile. "Pleased to me you."

Frau Buchler barely glanced at me before addressing Sally again. "Where are you and your husband staying?"

"Andreas passed away. His mother is putting me up in Brühl."

Frau Buchler crossed her legs. "What can I do for you?"

"I, I thought…"

Did Frau Buchler have no heart? "Sally thought the two of you could get to know each other," I said.

"Oh?" The idea seemed novel to her.

"Are you happy, Mother?"

I hoped Sally didn't see Frau Buchler flinch at *mother.*

"Happy?" she repeated, as if pondering another new concept. I began to wonder if Frau Buchler had all of her wits, but when she continued, I knew intelligence wasn't the problem. "*Happy* is not a word Germans use these days. If you had asked that question five years ago, I would have said I was content. Now I look over my shoulder."

"It must be difficult," Sally said, "with your husband being Jewish."

Frau Buchler let out a strangled scream, as if Sally had reached over to choke her. "Whatever can you be talking about? Daniel is as Aryan as they come. Not a drop of Jewish blood."

"I don't understand. Before Father and I left Germany, he told me you were marrying a wealthy Jewish businessman—"

"Stop with your lies." In her haste to stand, Frau Buchler knocked her cup and saucer to the floor and spattered the rug with tea.

We heard the stairs creak and a gentleman in a pinstripe suit appeared, white-eyed. "What is it, Petra?" When he saw that we were not the Gestapo, he became brusque, maybe to cover his embarrassment. "What's the matter?" He stood with his hands in his pockets, revealing a gold watch chain that couldn't gleam as it would like, with so little light in the room.

"Nothing, nothing," Frau Buchler said. "Just clumsiness. I spilled my tea."

"My goodness, is that all?" He clucked. "And who are our guests?"

She panicked then and I hoped for her sake the Gestapo never did arrive at her door. "They, um, they—"

"I'm Katja Varsten and this is Sally Varsten. Sally is your stepdaughter from America come to reunite with her family."

Herr Buchler raised a neatly trimmed eyebrow. "*Sally?* Petra gave up her daughter *Berta* more than thirty years ago."

Sally stood to shake his hand. "I'm Berta, and I didn't give up my mother more than thirty years ago."

His hands remained in his pockets like gophers evading a mongoose.

"Such twists and turns life can bring." Frau Buchler twirled dry tufts of hair around her finger. A clump broke free and she stared at it.

I pointed to the spreading stain on the rug. "I'll help clean this up."

"No, thank you," Herr Buchler said, "that is the servant's job. At the risk of appearing rude, I must ask you to leave. Your visit is clearly distressing my wife."

Sally met his eyes without deference. "My arrival has been a shock, so I'll say goodbye for today. I will return, though, you can count on that. Here, Mother." She held out a slip of paper. "I wrote down where I'm staying in case you want to reach me."

Herr Buchler snatched the paper, ripped it in half and handed it back to Sally. "She won't be needing this."

Sally let the pieces float to the rug, where they landed on the spilled tea and gradually turned brown.

• • •

On the surface Ingrid's encounter with her mother had been pleasant enough. Ingrid said Nadine Oberlin was thrilled to see her though disappointed that her daughter wasn't prettier. Ingrid didn't seem to mind; she claimed to admire her mother's honesty and said she had no illusions about her own appearance. "Mother did compliment my womanly figure," she added, assuming the pose of a model.

Later, as we strolled through the garden collecting flowers for a bouquet, Grandma Rosa filled me in on the details that Ingrid missed or declined to share. Fraulein Oberlin lived at a "residential hotel" called the Peacock Club, which was really a brothel. It was popular with members of the SS, who never paid for the services they received. "The whores are allowed to stay alive," Grandma Rosa said, "that is their payment." She placed a sunflower in her basket. "Nadine Oberlin frolics like a dim-witted hare unmindful of the wolf's shadow. The SS tyrants don't care where they satisfy themselves, so it's of no importance whether the women are Jewish or not, but the Fuhrer could decide in an instant to rid Germany of her prostitutes and then Nadine would be doomed, for she is not just a prostitute. She is a *Jewish* prostitute."

I thought we had moved out of earshot, but Ingrid strode up gripping a bunch of chrysanthemums in one hand and tearing leaves from the stems with the other. "That's absurd. First of all, the Nuremberg laws forbid sex between Germans and Jews, and secondly, soldiers wouldn't behave in such a flagrant manner. You need to get your facts straight. My mother only introduces men to women. She doesn't sell her body, or give it away to pigs, for that matter."

Grandma Rosa waved her hand around to ward off a bumblebee. "You see Nadine as you want her to be, not for the person she is. Money wins her love over everything else, even common sense. It wouldn't surprise me if she turned in the SS soldiers because they didn't pay her."

"But why would the soldiers risk the Fuhrer's anger by breaking his law?" I asked.

Grandma Rosa patted me on the back as she would a little girl. "None of the laws apply to Hitler and his security forces. If the prostitutes were to complain, the soldiers would call them liars and order them put to death."

I felt as if I had been tripped and fell hard. "This is permitted in Germany?"

Her eyes seemed to lose color, right then, though I knew that was impossible. "This and much worse."

"Come back to America with us"—My heart beat faster as the dream took hold—"You can live with me."

She chuckled. "No, child. To hold you close whenever I please, this would bring me joy, but Germany is where I belong. If I were younger, I might be tempted, but I've lived too long as a German to desert my country. I'll stay and try to support those who are persecuted."

I sensed the peril. "How will you do that?"

She patted me again. "Best for you not to know."

"Come home with us," I whispered.

"I am home."

CHAPTER 20
HONOR THY FATHER AND THY MOTHER

A week passed and I was outside hanging clothes with my grandmother. Ingrid had just left to spend time with Nadine.

"I wish Henry would return." Grandma Rosa secured a blouse to the line with clothespins. "He needs to forbid these daily visits."

I shook a skirt out so it would hang properly, then fastened it to the clothesline. "Ingrid won't obey her husband. She came to Germany to see her mother."

"Nadine could call on Ingrid here, but rather than exert herself, the slattern puts her daughter in harm's way."

"How is Ingrid in danger?" I stooped to lift an apron from the basket.

"If she frequents the brothel, the Nazis will assume she is a prostitute. Even if not, sooner or later a soldier will ask for her services. And you don't refuse the SS."

"But when Ingrid explains—"

"What will she say? That she is the bastard child of a Jewish prostitute?" Grandma Rosa grabbed the apron from me, folded it over the line and jammed the clothespins on. "She may as well ask for lodging at a concentration camp."

I shuddered. "Then Henry and Hans must return soon."

• • •

As if granting my wish, the Spengler brothers arrived the next day, though they brought an unexpected guest with them. At the sound of voices, Ingrid and I peered down the steep staircase, but Henry appeared as if from nowhere and herded us into a bedroom.

"In minutes you will meet my father," he said, his eyes on Ingrid. "You are not to say a word about your heritage and before you call me anti-Semitic, listen. Herr Spengler is a Nazi. His conversation is liberally sprinkled with *Heil Hitlers*. Say nothing to imperil us. Do you both understand?"

I nodded, but he never looked at me.

He grasped Ingrid by the arms. "Do you understand?"

"You're scared out of your wits, that much I understand."

Hans had slipped into the room during this exchange. He addressed his brother. "Join Frau Varsten and Father."

Henry glanced at Ingrid.

"Go." Hans pushed him out the door, then closed it and faced Ingrid. "You understand nothing. Don't kill us all with your idiotic mockery. Father will hand us over to the SS without a qualm. It was not our choice to invite him here; this is no joyful family reunion. He insisted on meeting Henry's new wife, not to welcome her but to determine her *purity*. Germans who refuse to open their homes to visitors, he said, could have an 'unfortunate' fate. This was a thinly-veiled threat that we must take seriously."

Ingrid mulled over these words long enough to make Hans edgier than he already was. Finally she said, "Pretending to be Aryan will be part of my artillery in fighting the Nazis. I'll give them nothing to use against us."

"But how will we know what to say?" I asked Hans.

"When in doubt, play the part of an ignorant American."

Ingrid snickered. "That won't be hard for Katja."

"Don't underestimate your own ignorance, Ingrid." He kissed my forehead. "Ready?"

Herr Spengler was sitting in Grandfather Frank's chair, drawn by a malicious ghost, or so I conjectured. He stood when we entered the room. He was tall, with a swollen appearance that made him seem even bigger, a puffiness in his face and neck, a thickness to his body. His eyes, like Grandfather's, conceded nothing, saw no value in what they looked at unless it was useful in some way, as a hammer has use for pounding a nail. Eyes that weren't human. His lips, you could be certain, had never curled into a loving smile.

"My, what a pretty girl." He curled his imposter smile at me. "You are Henry's new wife?"

Something inside of me shriveled like a houseplant too close to a fire. "No, I'm his new sister-in-law." I held an arm out to my sister. "Ingrid is Henry's wife."

She was trying to smile, but her expression was puckered and wary, and then she curtseyed, which I'd never seen her do before. "Pleased to meet you," she said.

"Such dark features"—Herr Spengler appraised her as if she were an automobile offered for sale—"one would never guess you girls are related."

Henry put an arm around each of us. "But they are. Katja most resembles her mother, and Ingrid, her father. Both Germans."

"Really?" He raised an eyebrow. "I'd like to meet Herr and Frau Varsten."

Ingrid burst out sobbing. Here was another new behavior in her repertoire—fake tears, which I expect looked real enough to Herr Spengler. "I'm sorry to break down in front of you," she sputtered, "but this is still an open wound for me. Our parents died within a year of each other, back in America." She covered her face with her hands.

"There, there," he said woodenly. "Comfort your wife, Henry. Please accept my apologies for bringing up such a painful subject."

The tears put an end to Herr Spengler's questioning, but I had to wonder, did they prove she was German; did he think Jewish women don't cry?

Grandma Rosa had no choice but to invite Herr Spengler to supper. During the meal, he seemed drawn to Sally. I had cautioned her in advance to emphasize Ingrid's resemblance to Papa if the issue came up, but this advice turned out to be unnecessary because she diverted Herr Spengler's attention from any focus on Ingrid, or politics, for that matter. In fact, she chatted like a girl with this stern man. Being more than twenty years younger made her feel like a girl, I suppose. When she expressed interest in his trade as a cobbler, Herr Spengler bragged about the financial gains he achieved from expanding his business beyond his simple shop. Interspersed with this glowing account of affluence were disdainful comments about women who purchased shoes "too small for their duck feet," in contrast to "the beauties whose shapely legs taxed my restraint."

We listened politely and said nothing of importance. As the evening wore on we all felt the strain, especially since Herr Spengler extended his stay due to Sally's encouragement. When he described himself as "indulgent to a fault with my boys," I watched Henry and Hans struggle to harness their emotions. Only one son succeeded.

As Herr Spengler prepared to go, Hans said, "Whose childhood were you speaking of, Father? Certainly not ours, for Henry and I saw the back of your hand, not your open arms."

Herr Spengler's fury wrenched every feature of his face, but he gained control by making light of Hans' remark. "Children," he said to Sally, shaking his head. "They don't understand that discipline builds character."

"How did *this* build character?" Hans raised the back of his shirt to reveal purple scars running diagonally from shoulder to waist.

The fury leached out in what had to be The Gestapo Voice. "Put your shirt down."

The strange thing was that Hans immediately obeyed.

"Family business is private," Herr Spengler said, "and you deserved what you got."

He then behaved as if the scene with Hans had not occurred. He thanked Grandma Rosa for her sauerbraten ("delicious despite the paucity of meat"), said he was pleased to meet Ingrid and me, and told Sally he enjoyed her company. Before turning to leave, he gave the *Heil Hitler,* which we copied clumsily.

When the door closed, I brought my hand down as if it were a weapon, alien from me. We all looked at each other but remained quiet.

• • •

That evening, Hans and I sat on the hanging swing out on the porch. His first words dropped heavily. "I wish I weren't my father's son."

To hear a child speak against a parent makes me cringe, but I could come up with no defense for Herr Spengler. "He scares me."

"The perfect Nazi."

"Must you see him again?"

"I'm afraid so, though probably not often." Hans set the swing into motion. "He won't care about me, but he'll seek out Henry…and Sally."

"Why Henry?" I wanted to put off discussion of Sally.

"He'll try to convert him to the party."

I stopped the swing abruptly. "Henry has a Jewish wife. He wouldn't denounce her as less than a German, with no rights."

"Remember to keep your voice down outside."

I laughed. "Don't tell me you think your father is hiding in the bushes?"

Hans strode from one end of the porch to the other, scanning the area. "In these times, you can't be too cautious." He sat down. "Be on your guard and weigh your words carefully."

"Shall I stop confiding in you, then? In case you convert to Nazism?"

Hans sprang to his feet again, making the swing bob like a rowboat in a storm. I shrank from the fierceness of his bearing.

Whatever had possessed him just as swiftly retreated. He sunk down and guided the swing into a gentle swaying. "I'm sorry. My father's rage lives inside me like a bear in chains. But you and Ingrid *must* be made to understand the gravity of Nazism."

My breathing settled back to normal, but still I kept a distance from Hans. "Fear makes people joke about what's deadly serious," I said. "I'm confused. I boarded a ship to my homeland and ended up somewhere else. For years I've had the fantasy of moving back to Germany, but not this Germany, where a word can end up as a dagger aimed at yourself or someone you love. I would like nothing better than to sail back to America."

"I feel the same way, though I have to find my mother first. The only reason I agreed to see Father was to learn her whereabouts."

"She's alive?"

"Yes, in a mental institution in Frankfurt. Henry doesn't want to see her."

"I'll go with you."

He drew me close. "I was hoping you would offer."

• • •

Hans' mother was like the abused dogs I used to see pulling carts in Germany. They slunk, skittered, and avoided your eyes as you passed. If you approached directly, some would growl and lunge, others would put their tail between their legs and whimper for mercy. His mother was the second kind. Outwardly she didn't know Hans, but every once in a while I fancied I saw recognition in her eyes, though this could have been simply a response to kindness.

Frau Leonwell—she was registered under her maiden name—seemed petite at first, but she was actually of medium height, diminished by her bowed head and curved shoulders. Her hair was thin and nondescript. She had odd angles to her body plus two crooked fingers on one hand and an elbow that appeared misaligned.

She had no privacy at the institution. Her bed was one of many in a row, with no apparent grouping of patients by type of illness. The belligerent were mixed with the meek, and the smaller tortures that occurred were ignored by the staff in white coats. We took Frau Leonwell outside in a fenced area with only scraggly grass to look at and a path worn bare along the perimeter. Beyond the fence was the backside of a factory with its debris of rusted machinery and dumpsters.

"Mother," Hans said—I swear her eyes darted to him for a moment—"how do they treat you here?"

"Fine, fine, I like it here fine." Her head bobbed like a mechanical toy.

Hans looked at me.

"Are you happy?" I asked her.

She grabbed Hans in claw-like hands. "Take me with you."

Before he could respond, she released her grip and began rocking from side to side, hands flopping about like mittens pinned to the sleeves of a jacket. I took one hand and Hans, the other, and we walked slowly without asking her to talk. Her steps were regimented, each foot landing squarely on the path; any deviation would cause her to yank free and twirl her fingers in agitation. When Hans announced that it was time for us to leave, she had no reaction.

As we drove home in Grandfather Frank's automobile, we discussed Frau Leonwell.

"Could we take her back with us?" Hans asked.

I was already thinking along these lines. "From what Ingrid says, the Nazis are eager to rid Germany of anyone they consider inferior. People with mental illness or retardation are in that group. Your father would have to give permission since he's the one who institutionalized her."

"The biggest barrier will be Henry," Hans said.

• • •

In fairness, we should have discussed our idea with Henry in private. We chose to be unfair. We knew what Henry's answer would be if we asked him first, so we waited until his father invited himself to our house again.

Herr Spengler was eager to dispose of his wife. "Yes, yes, take Crystal to live in America. I understand they welcome mental defectives there."

Henry frowned at us. "Your motives are admirable, but we can't pay for her ticket." He turned to his father. "We had hoped to travel in the wave of tourists attending the Olympics, but it took two years to save the money for our passages. Hans and I obtained second jobs at the electric company—we are lucky Milwaukee provides such opportunities—and Ingrid worked as a waitress on evenings and weekends. Sally contributed the inheritance from her father's business and Katja took every babysitting job she could find. Even then, in order to afford passage we had to lower ourselves and pretend we were leaving for good. Those in charge of the less reputable ships will reduce fares in such cases and they don't bother to check on whether their passengers return by another ship. Apparently that rarely happens. So you see, if given half a chance, America will toss back her German immigrants."

Herr Spengler chuckled. "Such irony. They should be welcoming the superior race to improve their mongrel population. Ah, well, intelligence is inherited, too."

Henry laughed, but Ingrid regarded both men in stony silence. Hans and I exchanged worried glances. *Please, Ingrid. Please play along.*

Grandma Rosa came out of the kitchen with a plate. "Spritz cookies? I know they found favor with you last week."

Herr Spengler patted his stomach. "Yes, and here's the proof. At this rate I'll need to buy larger trousers."

"More tea?" Grandma Rosa refilled his cup. "Perhaps you can suggest how to finance your wife's passage. She must be quite a burden for you."

Herr Spengler blotted invisible crumbs from the corners of his mouth. "Crystal never was the wife I envisioned for myself, although she did produce two sons. Unfortunately, they suffered as a result of her inept mothering." He sipped his tea noisily. "As you can imagine, being associated with someone in a mental institution is an embarrassment. Worse yet, I'm certain Crystal is the reason I haven't been formally recognized for my efforts on the Fuhrer's behalf. I will gladly buy the ticket for her passage."

"Why doesn't she go by the name Spengler?" Hans asked.

"When I had her committed, I also divorced her, which meant she had no right to my name. She's not my responsibility any more, though I'm still willing to help her."

"How kind of you," Ingrid said dryly.

Hans shot her a pointed look and she added a smile to give the impression of sincerity.

"Thank you." Herr Spengler turned to Henry. "I know Katja and Hans are set on returning to America, but I intend to persuade you and your wife to remain."

"Why should we do that?" Ingrid asked.

He addressed everyone but her. "My eldest son has the discipline and strength of character to serve honorably in the SS."

"But he works for the railroad," Ingrid persisted. "He's no soldier."

"With training he will make an excellent soldier. Serving a railroad pales by comparison to helping Germany achieve greatness."

"Let me think about it," Henry said, and when Ingrid objected, he barked, "Quiet! This is my decision."

Herr Spengler nodded approvingly.

Ingrid tucked into herself so her face wasn't visible, but I feared her emotions would spew out if she had to contain them much longer.

Herr Spengler checked the time on the Grandfather clock and announced that he and Sally had to leave.

"Yes," Sally said, "we mustn't be late for the opera." She arched an eyebrow.

I pretended to be awestruck, saying, "Now I understand the reason for your lovely red silk dress and matching pumps."

The instant Herr Spengler's automobile pulled away from the curb, the shouting erupted, but it ended as quickly. Ingrid yelled that she would not be the wife of a Nazi and Henry yelled back that he had no intention of serving Hitler, that he loved his Jewish wife.

We stood absorbing the quietness like flowers in the sun, and I saw Ingrid look at Henry with something resembling love.

• • •

That summer was a time of defining ourselves: as individuals, as members of a family, and as citizens of a country. Before then, America was where I lived until I could go home. Now America *was* home. I only needed the rest of my family with me to be complete. Grandma Rosa was immovable, but Uncle Albert...

His face shone with longing as I described my freedoms in America—no limits on the books I read, the clothes I wore, the subjects I studied. My mail arrived unopened. I could attend movies, dances, and art exhibits as I pleased—so different from life in Germany under *The Decree of the Reich President for the Protection of the People and State.*

"Stop." Uncle Albert held up his hands. "You have me convinced, but I cannot leave Rosa. Since your grandfather's death, she has relied on me to manage the farm and supervise the youngsters who pick the apples. Though the bulk of our income is from the rental of farmland, taking our produce to market puts money in the kitty for harder times."

I didn't know how to overcome this obstacle. Grandma Rosa would not be able to run the farm alone.

In the end, Ingrid would provide a solution I had never dreamed of. Or desired.

CHAPTER 21
A PARTING OF THE WAYS

Grandma Rosa's uneasiness about Ingrid and her mother became Henry's obsession. Though he forbade Ingrid from visiting more than twice a week, she still went every day, which meant that upon her return, she would be subjected to Henry's rants about the perils of the SS. She would counter that it was worth the risk to finally get to know her mother. When these arguments escalated to the point where Ingrid threw a plate at Henry, Grandma Rosa stepped in and told them to curb their tempers or find another place to live.

Alone with me, Ingrid boasted that Nadine bought her fancy dresses and called her pet names. "I'm her Bunny Boo," she said, "but not in a baby way. We're more like girlfriends. We stay up late giggling over the muscles of young men at the club."

Yet at the peak of this turmoil in the Spengler marriage, the visits abruptly ceased and Henry had nothing to do with it; indeed, he was as puzzled as the rest of us. My sister's deepest darkness returned.

One muggy evening, Grandma Rosa and I were relaxing on the porch swing, admiring the sunset, when

Ingrid returned from one of her many solitary walks. Grandma Rosa patted the chair next to the swing and said, "Join us."

Ingrid plopped down, causing the wooden chair to creak.

"Tell us what's wrong, dear." It must have been the tenderness in Grandma Rosa's voice that coaxed Ingrid to confess.

"I thought Nadine was all lovey-dovey because she'd grown attached to me as her daughter"—Ingrid's words were cut short by a wheezing sob—"but she was only recruiting another prostitute for the brothel."

I felt sick to my stomach.

"Switch places with your sister," Grandma Rosa instructed me.

I stood up uncertainly and made way for Ingrid, who was immediately enfolded in Grandma Rosa's arms. I took the vacant chair that seemed miles away from them.

Grandma Rosa stroked Ingrid's hair. "I should have done this more often. Senta, too. I'm sorry we were so quick to raise a hand to you. We acted as if you were to blame for being Nadine's daughter."

With that, Ingrid bared her heart to Grandma Rosa even though all my life I had longed to be my sister's confidant.

Nadine had offered Ingrid an invitation of sorts. "You can come live with me under two conditions," she said. "Dump that stiff-backed husband and open your legs to men for money."

"Is that all?" Ingrid retorted. "Give up a good man to service tomcats? Leave a clean and roomy house for a filthy corner in a house of slobs? Such an irresistible proposal."

Fraulein Oberlin was unmoved. "All right then, live with your so-called good man—there is no such thing, by the way—and earn money at the Club on the side."

"And if I don't want to be a whore, what then?"

"Stop wasting my time. I'll begin courting another girl."

The full force of Nadine must have hit Ingrid then. "But I'm your flesh and blood," she said. "Don't you want me around for that reason alone?"

Nadine snorted so the beer she was drinking came out her nose. "I tried to get rid of you as a baby, but you're a boomerang come back to me. I never wanted you and neither did Andreas. I don't know what he told you, but he wouldn't have bothered except for your grandmother. She's the one who saved you. I didn't care then and I don't care now."

That was when Ingrid walked out on her mother.

Hearing this, Grandma Rosa smiled sadly. "The way you stood up for yourself makes me proud."

Ingrid met her gaze. For the first time, my sister and my grandmother took each other's measure and did not come up wanting. I found myself envying them both

• • •

Ingrid only returned to the brothel once, to deposit a pile of clothing in the doorway, everything Nadine had given her. But before she made her delivery, she inflicted damage—ripping a sleeve here, putting a handprint of grape jam there. She was systematic; I watched her gather the clothing together and ruin it piece by piece.

Despite the cruelty she had endured, my sister never lost her cunning. She informed Sally that Nadine was not her mother after all. Another prostitute had also been with Andreas, and when she gave birth to a child, so Ingrid's story went, Nadine pretended it was hers in an effort to ensnare Andreas Varsten in marriage. Thank god it didn't work, Ingrid added, and by the way, this mystery woman, who vanished after relinquishing the baby to Nadine, was Aryan.

Sally had no reason to doubt this tale of trickery and rejection, for she was not faring much better with her own mother. They met infrequently, always at Sally's insistence and when Herr Buchler was elsewhere. Maybe Ingrid's story unleashed Sally's true feelings, for she began making derogatory comments about Jews. She attributed Herr Buchler's coldness to the fact that he was Jewish and blamed him for her mother's disinterest. None of us disagreed with her outwardly, for we could not appear to be sympathetic to the plight of Jews.

• • •

In late July, Henry stomped into the kitchen where Grandma Rosa, Ingrid and I were chopping vegetables for soup.

"Is Sally home?" he asked.

"She went to Frankfurt with your father," Grandma Rosa said. "Their relationship vexes me. We should discuss it."

"Not now."

"What's wrong?" Ingrid asked.

He swerved in her direction. "Don't you know?"

Her face deepened to the color of anger. "What *is* it?"

"Join me in the living room so Hans can hear what I have to say."

Mirroring Grandma Rosa's actions, I untied my apron and set it on a kitchen chair. Ingrid was too intent on Henry to think about her apron.

Hans looked up from the book he was reading. Before anyone sat down, Henry said, "Nadine Oberlin has been arrested and herded to a labor camp with other Jews, charged with the crime of prostitution, though from what I hear only Jewish prostitutes were seized. Jewish businessmen from blocks away were also rounded up—what they are accused of, I can only imagine. The SS shut down the brothel and took over the building."

"Oh my god." Ingrid fell into the side chair, sending lace doilies floating from the arms like baroque snowflakes.

"Poor despicable Nadine." Grandma Rosa's words drifted out in a sigh.

"Taken over by the SS." Ingrid laughed hollowly. "That happened long before today."

Henry bent over her with his hands on either arm of the chair. "Was this your doing?"

Our eyes followed invisible arrows that pointed to Ingrid. One of these arrows, it seemed, had pierced her heart. "What do you mean?" she asked.

"Someone notified the SS by letter that Fraulein Oberlin was Jewish. Nazi soldiers don't care who they have carnal relations with, but they want the Fuhrer to think they care."

"You're accusing me of siccing those wolves on my own mother? I'll divorce you, Henry Spengler." Ingrid lurched from her chair, shoved him off balance, and headed for the door.

Grandma Rosa moved quickly to bar her way. Ingrid stood with her arms crossed, shifting from one foot to the other.

Grandma Rosa leaned to the side of Ingrid and confronted Henry. "Apologize for questioning your wife's integrity."

"I'm sorry." His eyes had a touch of desperation.

I couldn't blame him for his misgivings. We all knew Ingrid was capable of banning people from her life for good.

She did not acknowledge him.

Grandma Rosa rested against the closed door and contemplated Ingrid. "Accept his apology. You and Henry have not been married long enough to reach the depth of each other's souls. And your temper has no bounds. It was logical—though not proper—for your husband to suspect you."

Ingrid swung round to challenge him. "I would never turn in one of my own people—*never*—no matter how vile the person. I would *die* rather than conspire with the Nazis and you should know that. I accept your apology, but only because I've had similar doubts about you."

Henry sat on the sofa and crossed one leg over the other. "With Ingrid, even reconciling will contain a jab somewhere."

She offered a wry smile. "Yes."

We detested Nadine, but none of us wished for her imprisonment—or death, which Henry predicted. "Father mocks the naivety of Germans," he said. "They believe the word *camp* means a nice temporary place to stay when in reality it's a dungeon infused with death."

"I think many Germans convince themselves not to trust their senses," Grandma Rosa said. "They don't smell what is rotten or see what is hideous. They become deaf to the screams of their neighbors."

Ingrid had become increasingly agitated during this exchange. "It's time to share an idea that has taken hold of me," she said, quivering with excitement, "an inspiration, really. The injustice toward Nadine Oberlin clears the debris from the path ahead. The United States has many people defending women's rights, but Germany has few doing the same for Jews. I've decided to stay here with Grandma Rosa, if she's willing, and join this cause."

She couldn't be serious! We all began talking at once.

"Children, please." Grandma Rosa didn't need to raise her voice to command our attention. "Let me answer. I would welcome you, Ingrid, but if your intention is to hide Jews, you need to be aware that it's extremely dangerous."

Henry's mouth had dropped open and he had to marshal control over the muscles of his jaw in order to speak. "What about me? What about my job in America?"

This seemed a trivial concern to Ingrid. "Quit. Take up the cause."

Hans slapped his book down. "Not so fast. If your husband remains in Germany, how will he avoid being drafted into Hitler's Universal Military?"

"He can get a job based in Brühl," Ingrid said.

Hans shook his head. "Unemployment is rampant. Except for what Germany steals from Jews, it's an impoverished country. If by some miracle such a job were to become available, it would attract thousands of applicants. Germans may support Hitler, but they don't want to fight his war."

"There's another way." Ingrid curled a strand of hair around her finger. "Henry can claim physical disability."

Henry jumped up in alarm. "Ingrid—"

"A one-eyed man with a heart murmur does not a soldier make."

How could I could have missed a glass eye? Which one was it?

"Stop staring at me," Henry said in a growl.

I averted my eyes with the shame of a voyeur.

"The doctors couldn't save my left eye," he said flatly.

"Another outcome of that discipline Father boasted about," Hans said. "I can't wait to see his reaction when he learns his eldest son isn't fit for the SS because daddy punched him in the eye."

"The issue won't come up, since I have no intention of living in Germany," Henry said. "Everything I need is in America."

"Except your wife," Ingrid said.

"What did you do…" I asked haltingly, "…what did you do to aggravate your father?" I tilted my head toward Henry but directed my eyes elsewhere.

"I was thirteen and talked back to him. That's all I'll say. Ingrid should not be sharing what is personal."

"We're family," Grandma Rosa said.

Henry did not disagree and seemed mollified by her words. I thought Grandma Rosa was right, that we could honestly be called a family.

CHAPTER 22

OCEANS APART

Hans and I would be the only ones returning to America, though we would bring two new immigrants with us. Herr Spengler paid not only for Frau Leonwell's passage, but for Uncle Albert as her attendant. (We didn't exactly tell a fib, since Uncle was willing to assist with her care.) Even amid the atmosphere of oppression and fear mongering in Germany, Herr Spengler's many connections enabled him to cut through bureaucratic requirements and a multitude of forms to book four passages out of the country. He bribed Henry to remain by offering to pay the fare for Hans and me. Henry agreed to the deal—he had previously given in to Ingrid's ultimatum anyway—though he would not commit to military service, nor would he consent to stay beyond June of 1938. Clearly Herr Spengler expected to change his son's mind.

"My father's behavior is bizarre," Hans confided. "He's either forgotten Henry's visual impairment or he's ignoring its implications."

"Maybe disabilities don't count as much in this climate of madness," Ingrid said, "particularly those of an Aryan who could be used to the Fuhrer's advantage."

"Nonsense," Hans said. "Able-bodied men, that's what the SS is recruiting."

Grandma Rosa was the one who had persuaded Uncle Albert to join us in America, arguing that Henry could help oversee the farm. Uncle fretted over how she would cope when Henry departed, but she claimed to have a list of volunteers. I'm not sure this was true. I urged Henry to keep the money that had been allocated for our return passage, should they need emergency funds, but he insisted I take it to pay expenses while I searched for a job.

Henry wrote his employer that due to family matters he would not be returning as planned, but he would be grateful if the railroad would keep his records on file in case another position became available in a year. This was a sacrifice and to my way of thinking, more evidence of his love for Ingrid. Sally also decided to extend her stay in Germany and proposed that Uncle Albert help Hans run the apartment building in her absence, a satisfying arrangement for all. Hans would move into the larger apartment with his mother, Uncle Albert would take the efficiency, and I would stay at the Spengler apartment.

For those residing at the farmhouse in Germany, the question became what to do about Sally. Because Ingrid intended to provide hiding places in the attic and basement, Sally could not be trusted to live in the house, especially given her friendship with Herr Spengler, which raised another question: how to assist Jews under the nose of a Nazi. Ingrid saw it as a useful link, for as relatives of Herr Spengler, she and Grandma Rosa would be above suspicion, plus privy to information shared with Henry (although Henry said he would prefer not to have this advantage). Hans maintained that his father's visits to the farm would cease once he grasped that Henry was unfit for military service and, more importantly, when Sally no longer lived there.

"What could Sally possibly see in your father?" Grandma Rosa said. "A man in his sixties, a *Nazi*. Doesn't Sally understand the horror of that? After all, her mother is married to a Jewish man."

"We think Herr Buchler got a Befreiung," Ingrid said, "which reclassified him as Mischlinge—mixed race—or, if he was lucky, to the status of fully German. By knowing the right people, you can get a Befreiung if you fought in a war. Herr Buchler has a history of service to his country."

"But Sally knows he's Jewish, so how can she flirt with a Nazi? And what about Herr Spengler's violent nature, is she aware of that?"

"We warned her." Henry avoided Grandma Rosa's eyes. "In all honesty, she seemed to perceive this quality as..."

"Exciting," Hans said. "The more we talked about Father's cruelty, the greater her fascination."

The problem of Sally was solved without our intervention. She told us she had rented an apartment in Frankfurt to be closer to her mother, that she had sufficient savings to cover this expense.

The door had barely clicked shut upon her exit when Ingrid snorted and said, "Savings, my ass. Herr Spengler has set up his mistress."

• • •

A week before our ship was to sail, Ingrid and I traveled to Mannheim, retracing the route from Grandma Rosa's farm to the townhouse where we grew up. While I wouldn't dream of knocking on the door where strangers now lived, Ingrid had no such misgivings.

People were usually hesitant to answer for fear of encountering the SS on their doorstep, but the young couple who lived in the townhouse beamed at us, the woman with an infant son in tow and the man with a little girl clinging to his leg. They invited us in and encouraged our reminiscences. There was our old sideboard—*See the nick from the time Mama dropped her sewing shears?*—and there, the coal stove that shrieked when Papa opened the door. The man swung it open and we laughed to hear the sound.

The stairs creaked like they used to—how many times had I run up and down as they voiced their objections?—but seeing my bedroom brought on a jumbled mix of joy and anguish as I remembered Mama's tender ministrations. When Ingrid and I crossed the hall to the bedroom where our parents had slept, we stood transfixed. Was it ten years ago that they lived and breathed, here in this room? So long and yet not long at all. A glance at the attic window revealed the ghost of Mama airing feather beds.

"Time to go," Ingrid whispered.

I grasped the handrail, trying to steady myself as I descended the stairs for the last time.

As we stood on the porch steps to say our goodbyes, I asked the young woman if she kept chickens.

She smiled. "My Gretchen loves to tend the hens with me. Her first words were 'cluck-cluck.'"

I laughed. "Tell her you can find peace and quiet in a chicken coop."

The young woman smiled politely, thinking I wasn't quite right in the head, I suppose.

Once Ingrid and I were rattling along on the train again, seated off by ourselves, I asked how her allegiance with the Jewish people had formed. "We were brought up Christian," I said. "Surely that shaped the person you are now."

She held her ticket for the conductor to punch and remained silent until he strolled to the front of the train. "Faith is beside the point. Jews have been rejected and persecuted by non-Jews, as I've been rejected and perse-cuted by the people in my life."

My emotions must have registered on my face, for she chuckled and said, "You would do well to stand back from yourself, Katja. I'm not accusing you. I *am* accusing my grandparents, my parents—this includes Nadine Oberlin—and my teachers. I want to help those who are in a similar situation."

Ingrid helping people—this was a welcome change (though I thought the charges leveled against our family were unfair). "Mama and Papa would be proud," I said.

She was about to disagree, I could tell, but instead she sat back and watched the German countryside go by.

• • •

Four days before our ship would carry us to America, the SS arrested Herr and Frau Buchler. Sally did not hide the fact that she led the Nazis to them; on the contrary, she congratulated herself on this achievement. She then invited us to a goodbye tea at her apartment. I was the only one who accepted; the rest of my family made up excuses. Looking back, I believe I went in search of an explanation, a reason not to despise her.

After Sally bid the others a safe journey, she and I took the train to Frankfurt and then boarded a bus. "Herr Spengler says that those who put their country first, even over family, are the most exalted of Germans," Sally said. "I've emerged from my stepfather's Jew shadow to bask in the light of German purity."

I peered between the streaks of rain on the window, hoping to locate something pretty outside to distract me. But all I saw were umbrellas and newspapers held over people's heads on a dreary day, accompanied by the chant of Sally's dreary words. "Their Jewishness cannot taint me because I've proven my loyalty to the party."

I blinked at her. "You turned in your mother. Why? You could have let her go on with her life."

Sally's eyes widened to marbles set in ivory. "Heil Hitler!"

The people around us started as if a gun had gone off. One woman dropped a basket of apples that made plunk-plunk sounds of retaliation and then rolled down the aisle every which way. A man with furtive eyes and a snake tattoo raised his arm and mouthed Sally's words. She answered with a braying laugh.

After the woman had retrieved the apples and the other passengers were hunched forward again, Sally whispered, "To be frank, I couldn't care less about a person's religion, that's not why I exposed Herr and Frau Buchler. I did it because they made me feel worthless. To my mother, I was a nuisance, an object wedged between her and her lover. As for him, I gave him a real reason to wish I'd never been born."

I tried not to flinch when Sally put her arm around me, though I scrunched my nose at the sultry sweetness of her perfume. "I like you," she said. "I always have, except when Andreas favored you over me. At first I blamed you, but then I realized you weren't the guilty one. It was Andreas who rejected me. He was the guilty one."

I slipped out from under her arm. "What are you saying?"

"I'm only telling you how much I care, since we won't see each other for a long time, perhaps never."

"Papa's death was a suicide, wasn't it?" The question thrust its way out; I couldn't stop it.

She pulled back with a look of detached amusement. "What are *you* saying? That I murdered your father?" Her smile faded. "Only indirectly, by not being Senta."

"I'm sorry." I had to be careful. I couldn't make an enemy of Sally. Grandma Rosa and Ingrid must be protected.

"Yes, so am I."

We rode in silence except for the swash of tires plowing through water, until she said, "Herr Spengler will learn nothing of Ingrid and Nadine Oberlin from me. That much I owe you." The bus bumped to a stop. "This is where we get off." The instant the doors whooshed open she burst outside and hurried down the street.

I ran to catch up and said, between gasps of air, "Ingrid must have told you that Nadine Oberlin is not her mother."

Sally opened the door to a modern apartment building and wiped her feet on the inside mat. I did the same, then followed her down a hallway of plush carpeting to Number 115.

She pulled a key from her purse and looked at me. "That's what she told me." She smiled and said, "Come in."

When I caught sight of Sally's living room, I felt suddenly lightheaded. I managed to hold myself upright, though I teetered over the Oriental rug to avoid stepping on it. (I noticed the tea stain was permanent.) The room was filled with the Buchler's Rococo furniture.

"Please forgive me, Sally. I won't be able to stay after all. I've taken ill." I dashed from the apartment and ran across the street where a bus was pulling from the curb. I pounded at the door and was let in. I paid the fare and dropped into my seat, trying to breathe.

• • •

We stood on the dock beyond the silhouette cast by the ship. I tried to commit Grandma Rosa's face to memory: wisps of gray lashes accenting ocean blue eyes, rosebud lips turned up just so, and cheeks glowing light pink. Her body had nothing sharp, only a pleasant roundness, and she drew me to her bosom in a hug that was a perfect blend of firm and soft. I didn't want to let her go but when I did my reward was to look into her eyes again and catch that glint of violet.

"You will have a good life," she said. "You have equal weights on each side of your scale. You will meet an honorable man and marry without losing yourself. Senta and I did well raising you." She kissed one cheek, then the other.

"I'll treat my children the way you treated me." I kissed her in return. "I love you."

"I love you, too." It was the first time she had said this to me. German women rely on caretaking as their messenger and her words nourished a hunger I hadn't known existed.

I turned to Henry and shook his hand. "Take care of yourself, and my sister"—I glanced at Ingrid—"if she'll let you."

"I'll do my best on both counts." Henry tipped his hat, the one Ingrid had given him. "I expect to hear that you graduated top of your class in secretarial school. Your tuition is paid and you've got some money for rent until you find part-time work. When you get a real job, you'll teach those boys a thing or two about accounting."

"Thank you, Henry." I stood on my toes to kiss the side of his face, which made him blush.

Now it was time to leave my sister in Germany where she was adamant she belonged. "You can still change your mind," I told her. "Free-thinking women are more welcome in America than Germany."

Grandma Rosa put her hands on her hips. "If Germany loses women like Ingrid it will end up a nation of blowhard men and milk-toast girls."

We shared a hearty laugh at that.

I gazed at Ingrid. Her deep brown eyes were charged with energy, her mouth was moving as it did when thoughts raced through her head, and her hair was as unruly as ever. She had always been part of my life, a dark force that could also shine with goodness. Even after she married, I saw her almost every day. What would it be like to have her so far away, living in a country where war was imminent—a war against Jews, she a Jew. I grabbed her and held on tight despite her protests.

Ingrid's annoyance gave way to laughter. "My god, I didn't know you cared about losing your surly sister."

I let go and straightened her blouse where I had mashed it. "Really? You didn't know I cared?"

Ingrid's brows knit. "You do, don't you?"

I nodded, trying to keep my emotions from overflowing.

"And in my own way, I care about you, too."

I saw that she longed to be able to give more and I looked into her eyes and told her it was enough. And at that moment, for me, it was.

PART 4

AMERICA

1939–1955

CHAPTER 23
A BUSINESS AGREEMENT

One year turned into two and Henry came back without Ingrid. Staying in Germany would have required involvement in the war effort. Before Henry left, he excavated a small room adjacent to the basement in Grandma Rosa's house and concealed it with a false wall, a place for Jews to hide should Nazis storm the premises.

Henry arrived in Milwaukee in July of 1939. All he would say about Ingrid was that she had promised to follow within the year. In September, World War II was declared.

The United States had been in a recession, but the economy improved as orders poured in from overseas for items related to the war. The railroad transported materials, so Henry was able to get a better job than his previous one. He was fortunate to have his citizenship, since men with German accents were met with suspicion. The fact that his wife was still in Germany did raise eyebrows, though, and Henry purposefully gave the impression that he and Ingrid had parted because she wouldn't leave her frail grandmother. He did this to protect them both; he couldn't brand Ingrid as a traitor to Germany for fear of repercussions, though he planned to tell his coworkers the truth upon her return.

Hans and I celebrated Henry's homecoming by taking him out to a restaurant. Once the waitress had placed our meals on the table, Henry filled us in on life at the farm. "Ingrid and Rosa are tireless in smuggling provisions to Jews." He nudged his mashed potatoes with a fork to keep them untainted by meat juices. "Signs in stores forbid Jews from entering and many Jewish people are compelled to leave the country. Those who stay must go into hiding or face the possibility of a concentration camp. This past year the mood grew uglier, with Jews being arrested on a variety of trumped-up charges."

Hans and I ignored the food on our plates and leaned across the table to absorb Henry's every word.

"Ingrid is messenger as well as smuggler," he continued, "quick to act on hints from Father that the Gestapo is targeting a particular house. She arranges for the people to stay at the farm or somewhere else."

"What happens if the party learns that Germans are helping Jews?" I asked.

"Given that a German can be reported for spreading objectionable ideas, harboring Jews would mean certain arrest and probably death."

I expected this answer, yet hearing it was like taking a blow to the stomach.

Hans rubbed my back in gentle swirls. "Are Ingrid and Rosa careful?"

"Yes, yes, I made sure of that." Henry pressed his fingers against his temples. "They also have a vast chain of contacts who would know if an arrest was imminent. The Nazis in their arrogance underestimate the number of spies in their ranks, people pressed into the military who hate the Fuhrer and what he stands for."

"What has been Sally's fate?" Hans glanced up from mixing the ingredients of his salad with a fork. We had both begun eating at the same time, our appetites stimulated by the smell of meatloaf wafting from Henry's plate.

Henry frowned, deep furrows emphasizing the severity of his features. "To think I once admired that woman." He took a bite of meat (always a child's portion) and chewed methodically before swallowing. "Her name is Berta again, only now it's Berta Spengler." He wiped his mouth fervently with his napkin, as if the name were stained there and he wished to remove it.

Hans laughed. "That makes Sally-Berta our mother. And Katja, my sister."

I rubbed shoulders with him.

Henry scowled. "Only you could uncover humor in such a marriage."

"What else can I do? Here's a woman who hands her own mother over to the Gestapo and as if that weren't bad enough, she falls in love with a man who beat his children and drove his first wife crazy. Let them have each other." Hans stabbed at his salad, then jammed a clump of lettuce and cabbage in his mouth.

"What about the danger to Ingrid?" I asked Hans. "Remember my last conversation with Sally?"

He nodded, his cheeks bloated like a hamster storing food.

"Danger?" Henry held his fork and knife still.

When I told him about Sally's reference to Nadine Oberlin, he set his utensils down and folded his arms, mulling it over. Finally he said, "The Nazis would deem it peculiar if Sally were to reveal her knowledge of Fraulein Oberlin years later. She could be accused of withholding information valuable to the party. Besides, she can't prove anything. Nadine is undoubtedly dead and Ingrid's birth certificate lists Senta and Andreas Varsten as her parents."

"Are you sure?" My voice came out fluttery. "Have you seen it?"

"Calm down." He made pushing motions with his hands, as if closing a stuffed suitcase. "We had to present birth certificates to get our marriage license."

"Ingrid will be safe unless she makes Sally mad"—I was thinking out loud—"Sally isn't anti-Semitic as much as horribly vindictive, in my opinion."

Henry used his bread to sop up juice from the meat, apparently striving for a spotless plate. "Ingrid has developed caution. She playacts and does it well."

Hans bumped me lightly. "You've witnessed her skill at this."

"Yes, but how often is she put to the test? Are Sally and Herr Spengler regular visitors to the farmhouse?"

Henry signaled the waitress to bring more coffee and tapped his fingers on the table while she poured from a dented tin pot. After she returned to the kitchen, he said, "They hardly ever stopped by and only when I was there, too. Conversation was strained. Father rhapsodized about the Fuhrer, and at first Sally did, too, but with time she said less and less, until she didn't even bother to echo Father's fanaticism." He poured cream into his cup. "Eventually she stopped speaking altogether."

Hans and I looked at each other.

"Was he beating her?" Hans asked Henry.

"I didn't get the sense that he hit her; but browbeating, that he could be doing."

I ached for Sally and had to remind myself of her treachery. Rejected by her mother, like Ingrid, yet she took such a different path.

• • •

Henry reclaimed his apartment and since it would have been unseemly for single ladies to live with him—Doree was my roommate—we had to find a new place. By chance, a vacancy came up at the flat of another girl-friend and we moved into the bedroom we would share, joking that there would be space in the closet for two of my dresses after Doree hung up all of hers.

I expected Henry to offer to take in his mother but he did not. She continued to live with Hans, who arranged for Uncle Albert to watch over her in his absence. We hadn't lied to Herr Spengler after all.

Henry gave me a letter from Sally (none of us referred to her as Berta) in which I was instructed to put her jewelry and Hummel collection in storage until she could retrieve the items; I was to sell the rest. I spent weeks going through her possessions and when I came across a gift purchased by Papa, I put it in storage. I also admit to keeping a small jewelry box with a ballerina that twirled when you lifted the lid. Since I helped Papa select it, I knew its cost and included that amount in the money I deposited in Sally's bank account.

• • •

While Henry was in Germany, I had attended secretarial school, also working part-time as a maid at a local hotel. I graduated to find employment at *The Milwaukee Journal,* the city's major newspaper. My boss was editor of the features department and my responsibilities included answering the phone, taking shorthand, typing, and filing. I was not outstanding at this job. Although I was a decent typist, I became addled under pressure and made mistakes that required painstaking corrections with an eraser shaped like a flat wheel. I had to use enough force to remove the typo but not so much that I rubbed a hole in the paper; I then flicked off the debris with a little brush attached to the eraser. I was usually dissatisfied with the results and would retype the entire document at home.

The hubbub in a newspaper office overwhelmed me. People rushed here and there, bumping into desks, chairs, and each other. Work was dropped on my desk to be completed *ASAP,* or *yesterday,* as my boss liked to joke. The noise was inescapable; a cacophony of typewriters, adding machines, and loud voices that were usually arguing. At the end of the day, I would lug a heavy typewriter home in its case, my ears ringing and my head spinning. My boss was satisfied with his secretary, but I approached each day with dread, thankful the forty-hour work week had recently been established. I assumed the newspaper job was my destiny until Uncle Albert suggested otherwise.

Uncle and I frequented a large bookstore on Wisconsin Avenue with many nooks and crannies. Bookmarker carried new and used books as well as newspapers and periodicals. When no one was looking I would open a new book and stick my face in its pages, inhaling the faint scent of wood. I didn't mind that most books were published with thinner paper in an effort to conserve; capturing one of these pages between my fingers was like touching a hummingbird's wings. I never bought new books, though, and not because of my strict budget. I held used books dearer, for they seemed to have personalities beyond their stories and pictures. New books were like fashionable upper class people, admired for their clothes or hairstyles; used books were folks you invite to your house.

I also loved the quiet sounds of Bookmarker, the shuffling of feet as people moved from shelf to shelf in search of that special book, the plip-plip of pages being turned, and the whispered comments ("I couldn't put this one down" or "Mark Twain spins a yarn like nobody's business"). Ingrid would have ridiculed my romantic notions of "dusty old books," but Uncle Albert believed they held the key to my happiness. "You've attached yourself to the wrong kind of printed word," he said. "You need classics and romance, not murder exposés and advertisements for toothpaste."

One day he sidled up to me in the fiction section of Bookmarker and said, "Donald confided that the book store is becoming too much to run by himself. He stays open late two nights a week as a courtesy to the working person, but the long hours take a toll. He needs an assistant, someone who could be a partner in the business one day, someone like you."

He may as well have suggested I run for president. "Why, what a notion. I could never manage a business."

"Times like this I wish Ingrid were here to shout some sense into you. You would make a first-rate businesswoman. You have the knowledge of books and the accounting skill." He shook his head, adding a *tsk-tsk.* "Ah, well, that's down the road anyway."

My excitement grew with each word of encouragement, until reason intervened. Throwing away a year's worth of secretarial training to become a bookstore clerk would be foolhardy, especially considering the difference in pay. The newspaper paid more than the minimum wage; not much more, but every penny counted. "That settles it," I said, as if I had voiced my thoughts. "I can't afford to live on less."

Uncle Albert crossed his arms. "And what is it you spend money on?"

"Books," I said, breaking into a smile.

"Do what you love, even if it means less money."

"What's to say Mr. Kowalski would hire a girl?"

"Let's ask him." Uncle Albert pulled me to the bookstore owner's desk.

Donald Kowalski was well over six feet tall and everything about him was long and lean, including his ears and nose, though not so extreme that he was ugly or dour. He was a greyhound, not a bloodhound, with reddish brown hair in need of a trim. A genial, shy man, he appeared to be Henry's age, perhaps thirty. I had only spoken to Mr. Kowalski on the subject of books, about which he was well-informed and insightful.

Uncle Albert nudged me forward. "Don, meet your new bookstore clerk."

Mr. Kowalski reacted as if a white elephant stood before him swinging her trunk.

My embarrassment felt prickly as a rash. "You're a busy man. We shouldn't have interrupted." I turned to go.

"Wait." Mr. Kowalski's eyes met mine briefly, then focused on the papers littering his desk. "Have you quit your job at the *Journal?*"

I paused. How did he know where I worked? Uncle Albert, of course. "No, my uncle only just suggested it," I said. "He overstepped his bounds by promoting me for a job at Bookmarker."

"Not at all. I've talked with him about needing help. Would you be interested in the job?"

"I have a good salary where I work now—"

"I'll match your salary."

I thought I must have heard him wrong. "But I have no experience."

This was a man who smiled with his whole face. "You love books, you're well-read, and you have book-keeping training. Good thing your uncle promotes you. Listing the ways you aren't qualified is a poor strategy for landing a job."

"You're laughing at me."

"Only teasing. Here, I'll be serious. I'd be lucky to have you as a clerk. Keep your present job and work for me on Saturdays to see if the bookstore suits you."

My mind began adding and subtracting like the machines at the newspaper. "I'll work a month of Saturdays, but without pay, since you'll have to show me what to do. If we both think I'm qualified, I'll resign from my current position."

Mr. Kowalski grinned at Uncle. "She drives a hard bargain—free labor for a month." He bowed to me. "I accept."

"Let's shake on it, so it's a business agreement."

"Yes," he said, beaming, "a business agreement."

CHAPTER 24
MERRY CHRISTMAS, HAPPY NEW YEAR

I had my conversation with Donny in November and after only a couple of Saturdays, I gave my two week notice at *The Milwaukee Journal.* It seemed like forever, I was that eager to trade the indifferent and chaotic newsroom for the coziness of the bookstore. By December I was doing window displays, nestling beautiful editions of *The Night Before Christmas* and *The Littlest Angel* in cotton batting while Donny hummed Christmas carols.

On Sunday afternoons, when the bookstore was closed, Donny hosted our family songfest. We would take our places on the comfortable sofa and chairs of the *Reading Nook,* situated in front of the fireplace. Donny's voice was the cello in our orchestra, I was the flute, Uncle Albert, the clarinet, and Hans, the rich saxophone. Henry didn't sing, but got the embers of the fireplace glowing and kept an eye on his mother, who was soothed by our caroling.

Singing naturally led to visiting and refreshments. Donny would go to his upstairs apartment and make cocoa, then descend balancing cups on a tray. After I got to know him better, I joined him in the kitchen to bake Grandma Rosa's Spritz cookies, a perfect complement to the hot drinks.

Our conversation tended to center on Ingrid and Grandma Rosa. Communication from them was sporadic and letters were written in a code Henry had developed, which couldn't cover all situations. The letters did reveal that the farm house provided room and board for transient groups of people, usually three to four at a time. Guests rarely stayed more than a week before moving on to another house in a chain of hiding places. The owners of these homes were not acquainted with each other. The man who linked them alleged it was safer that way, since any host who was caught couldn't be coerced into identifying the others.

"That means those taken into custody could be tortured," I said.

"A risk that has to be taken," Henry replied, "or many more people would be killed."

I couldn't see beyond my concern for the safety of my sister and my grandmother and it bothered me that he could.

Grandma Rosa and Ingrid had the advantage of living on a farm, where fruit and vegetables could be canned to ensure food for the winter months. Although the pigs were long departed and the milk cow had gone dry, geese provided eggs and occasional meat, and Grandma Rosa still kept chickens. She also bartered her midwife services for food and supplies. Henry's helping hands were missed, but Jewish guests did the housework, freeing Ingrid and Grandma Rosa for the outside chores. Still, Grandma Rosa wrote: *We drop into our beds limp as rag dolls with no bones to support us, our brains made of loosely-woven cloth so that information passes through without sticking.*

I searched Ingrid's letters for a sign that she missed us but the only affectionate remarks came from my grandmother, her most recent letter closing with: *I have a favorite dream where all of us gather for a bountiful meal and eat until we pat our bellies and complain of being stuffed. Then we talk and laugh and share old stories. Our love, Grandma Rosa and Ingrid.*

There was never an intimate note from Ingrid to Henry, not even a comment directed specifically to him and I knew he didn't keep any part of the letters private. When curiosity got the better of me, I asked if Ingrid wrote any secret messages for him alone.

"Why would she do that?" he asked, his expression blank.

I shrugged. "No reason, I guess."

Donny fit in so well it seemed as if he had always been part of our lives. We were candid about the circumstances of Ingrid and Grandma Rosa, knowing he would understand, for his only living relative was a Polish aunt whose country had been invaded by Germany. Donny adopted our family, which is why Sunday get-togethers became a weekly event even after the holidays.

He wasn't like a brother or uncle, though; definitely not family in that way. I found myself attracted to him and dared to think he liked me, too, for I would catch him looking at me as I talked to a customer or shelved volumes at Bookmarker. Sometimes he glanced away to disguise his interest, other times he smiled in a most direct manner. When Hans told me Donny watched me with lovesick eyes, my cheeks grew hot and I became even more hopeful.

During my two Saturdays of learning the job, Donny had been a patient and indulgent teacher whose knowledge of books far exceeded mine. He taught me how to classify books for stacking in the correct section. In addition to numerous nonfiction categories, I decided whether a book should be filed under *Literature, Mysteries, Children's Fiction* and *Pulp Fiction* (he carried the last grudgingly, reasoning that at least it encouraged people to read).

On the other hand, Donny openly acknowledged his poor business skills. Although he kept a ledger where he entered titles of volumes purchased and what he paid for them, he failed to document when they sold and for what price. I told him this data was necessary to determine which books should be restocked; those that rested on the shelves for months and then had to be marked down did not fall in this category. Donny reacted as if this were the observation of a genius.

As the weeks passed, I also attended to the upkeep of the bookstore, though I didn't tell Donny for fear of offending him. I slowly replaced the cardboard signs that hung crookedly and were composed of oddly-shaped letters. I dusted, for who wants to page through a book that makes you cough and sneeze? When Hans whispered in my ear, "I see the merry housewife has been flitting about the shelves," I laughed and shoved him away, saying that only a perfectionist like him would notice my efforts.

I was wrong, for Donny was far from a perfectionist and he noticed. "Thanks to you, the store looks shipshape," he said, "but I didn't hire you as a maid. I deserve a kick in the seat of the pants for letting you take on this responsibility. I'll pay someone to do the cleaning."

"Please don't," I said. "I *like* caring for the book-store. Dusting the books and making the old wooden shelves gleam despite their nicks and scratches reminds me of taking care of a friend. I'm not expecting anything to look new, only well-worn and loved."

"Maybe you'll have the same expectation for me someday." He laughed, so I couldn't tell if he was serious underneath.

I said nothing, only laughed along with him.

• • •

The holidays filled us with joy one moment and plunged us into despair the next. On Christmas Eve we attended an evening service at church. After a sermon that Henry declared more political statement than reli-gious message, the choir sang carols that gave me goose bumps: *Silent Night; It Came Upon the Midnight Clear; Hark! The Herald Angels Sing;* one after another. When Hans did his solo, *O Tannenbaum,* I ignored the grum-bling behind us and savored his gift of Christmas-past in Germany. As we filed from the church afterward, I wiped at my eyes.

Donny put his arm around me, his big hand engulf-ing my shoulder so I felt grounded. "What is it, Katie? Did those people upset you?"

"Oh, no, I'm used to complaints about anything German. Hans' singing called up memories of my child-hood. How I long for Mama and Papa."

Donny drew me so close I felt his beating heart. "I'd do anything to erase the pain of losing your parents.

But I believe that when you lose people you love, others show up, not as replacements but to keep the love in your life constant."

I didn't ask if he was one of the people bringing this love, I only hoped that was what he meant. I would come to doubt it later, but Christmas Eve was full of promise.

We'd selected our Christmas tree earlier in the week and had quite a time of it. Henry and Hans would still be arguing over short versus long needles if not for Frau Leonwell. Usually she spouted nonsense, but on this day her meaning was clear: "Short needles will display the ornaments best." We all nodded, thrilled she had made sense (which happened more frequently now that she no longer took the strong medications prescribed in Germany). When another argument brewed over the height of the tree, Donny stated that the high ceilings of Bookmarker demanded the biggest tree we could find and that was that.

The huge noble fir we dragged from the lot was sparse on one side but we knew the gap could be filled with decorations. The ornaments placed so lovingly on the boughs consisted of a few hand blown glass pieces that somehow made it across the ocean unbroken, along with those we acquired in America or made ourselves. All had been stored in the box with Mama's money. (I had learned enough from my business classes to feel secure investing most of her nest egg, but I kept a hundred dollars in the ornament box out of respect for Mama, since like many others, she survived the depression vowing never to trust a bank again.) Along with the ornaments, we strung popcorn and hung tinsel and then stood back to admire our handiwork.

Frau Leonwell said, "The star on top is crooked."

We broke into laughter.

"Mother is starting to be herself again." Hans looked into her eyes, from which clouds had lifted, if only briefly, and said, "I'd like you to accept a lopsided star."

"No."

This unexpected boldness startled us.

"I can get the ladder," Donny said.

Hans was shaking his head. "Mother has to start accepting flaws. It was her husband's need for perfection that drove her mad and caused her boys to run away."

I asked, "Is Christmas Eve the time to teach such lessons?" I didn't disagree with Hans but wanted to acknowledge Donny's kindness.

Hans looked at his brother. "What do you think?"

"Christmas Eve is an *ideal* time. Mother, which would you prefer, a perfectly-straight star or sons who enjoy your company?"

Frau Leonwell's face contorted and she let her arms drop to her sides and hang there, as if the effort to communicate had sucked energy from her body to fuel her brain. "Fine. I just won't look at the star."

This was the start of my merriest Christmas in years.

We had waited until after the church service to open presents. My gift for Donny was a plaque to go above the door, crafted by an unemployed engraver willing to trade his labor for a typed resume. Etched into brass was *Donald Kowalski, Proprietor.*

Donny ran his hand over the letters reverently. "It's like giving Bookmarker finery to wear. I'm a true businessman now, owner of a distinguished bookstore."

He gave me a journal with *Katja's Musings* in gilt on a rich leather cover, accompanied by an elegant fountain pen. "Now you can write your thoughts and dreams in style," he said.

"But what if I make a mistake or splatter ink on the pages?"

"Don't give it a second thought. You can add and remove pages—see how they're tied? Your journal can become as thick as you like, that's why I chose it. You'll be able to put in everything you've written so far. Besides, you shouldn't worry about errors. Nothing in nature is perfect—the most symmetrical tree has a cock-eyed branch—so if your sentences contain cross-outs and ink spots, no harm done. Isn't this the lesson we're trying to teach Frau Leonwell?"

"Well, yes," I said, "but I'm still glad I can take out pages."

He tousled my hair. "You're impossible."

We saved the gifts from Germany for last. Because Grandma Rosa feared the package wouldn't reach us by Christmas, she had sent it far in advance, which meant I had been staring at the *Do Not Open Before Christmas Eve* tags for a month. Her gifts included a white vase with blue flowers, a music box of carved wood, and a porcelain doll from her childhood. Seeing her favorite items was bittersweet because I was certain she wanted me to have them in case something happened to her. I chuckled, reading the note attached to the doll:

I know you'll jump to the conclusion that I'm taking precautions should I become a casualty of war. No, Katja, I'm a survivor. What I'm not sure of is whether we will be permitted

*to keep possessions in the Germany fate decrees
for us. My goal is to see you again, cradling
these cherished objects in your hands.*
Merry Christmas from your loving
Grandma Rosa

Ingrid's gift to me was *A Vindication of the Rights
of Woman,* in English. She didn't know I was working at
a bookstore, but no matter, we didn't have this old book
(published in 1792) at Bookmarker. My heart did a little
leap when I saw Ingrid's script, which was awkward and
heavy because she pressed so hard: *For Katja, a book to
help you understand your sister, Ingrid.*

I held up the book for others to see.

"Ah," Donny said, "the feminist, Mary
Wollstonecraft—"

"What's wrong with her?" I demanded, set to defend an author I hadn't read and in so doing, my sister.

"Not a thing." He shifted away from me. "She's
a remarkable woman. It's a classic book and I've been
meaning to read it."

My stomach flip-flopped. "I'm sorry. I'm used to
men who mock women's rights and their defenders."

After giving this considerable thought—Donny
rarely acted on impulse—he offered a smile that danced
more in his eyes than on his lips. "Then you've been seeing the wrong men."

My stomach flipped over again, but for an entirely
different reason.

• • •

In the days that followed, Donny and I were busy with our After-Christmas Sale. This had been my idea and I had to convince him of its value. "It isn't prudent to store Christmas merchandise for a whole year," I said. "We can always pick up new books before the holidays. Besides, people who come in for the sale are likely to buy something else." And so I got him to run an ad in *The Milwaukee Journal* for December twenty-sixth.

At week's end, we lounged in overstuffed chairs in front of the fireplace, toasting our throbbing feet. "You were right," Donny said. "We did a brisk business. Usually the bookstore is dead after the holidays."

I loved my job and knowing that Donny was pleased with my work. In my good mood I blurted out an invitation I had been mulling over. "My roommates are planning a New Year's Eve party. Would you like to come? Hans will be there."

His face lit up. "Why, I'd be honored to finally meet Doree and Claire, though I'm useless when it comes to dancing. I've got two left feet."

"I wouldn't worry about that. Doree will make sure there's lots of food. You can stand around eating and avoid the dance floor."

"As long as you stand around with me."

"It's a deal." I held out my hand, but instead of shaking it, he gave it the world's softest kiss. I thought he might lean over and kiss my lips, but he released my hand and stood up.

I took this as my cue to leave. "Come at 8:00. Talk to Hans. You can ride over with him."

"I'll do that."

● ● ●

I didn't expect Hans to bring a friend. "Won't people ask questions?" I said.

"Because I'm with a man?" Hans laughed. "Not unless we perform the tango together. We'll play it as two gents going stag, actually three gents, since we're picking up Donny. Steve and I can dance with some girls to throw people off. Nobody will be the wiser. And since I'll be occupied with Steve, you can devote all your attention to your new beau." His eyes were full of mischief.

"Donny and I are just friends."

"Right. I've seen the way you look at each other."

I couldn't help smiling, couldn't hide my true feelings from my best friend. "I do really care about him. Wish me luck tonight."

Hans squeezed my hand. "You won't need it. All Donny-boy has to do is overcome his shyness and make a move."

"This is you talking? Hans Spengler rooting for a fellow to make a pass at me?"

"You're not a teenager anymore and Don's interest goes beyond your body."

● ● ●

Our flat was spacious, but you couldn't tell once it was packed with guests. Music blared from the phonograph and couples jammed onto the small dance floor created by clearing furniture from the dining room. Swing dancing was challenge enough in such cramped quarters, but when a couple tried the new Lambeth Walk, strutting with their arms linked, there were several collisions that dissolved into laughter.

Doree flounced around with her cheeks glowing. She did love throwing a party.

"You look beautiful," I told her. When I prepared to introduce Donny, my heart sunk. He obviously agreed.

Holding out his hand, he said, "You must be Doree. I've heard so much about you. I'm Donald Kowalski, Katja's...employee."

I stiffened.

"Pleased to meet you, Donald. I hope Miss Varsten has been getting to work on time"—Doree giggled—"Otherwise, you'll have to dock her pay."

"I'm very punctual." I drew my lips into a tight line.

Doree squinted at me, puzzled. "I was only teasing."

"Katja is a model employee." Donny smiled at her.

"Since you're talking about me like I'm not here, there's no sense staying." I turned my back on them, feeling their stares as I minced away.

From then on, I chatted with other young men to keep Donny from approaching me. Not that I expected him to do so.

Shortly before midnight, Hans took me aside and said in a growly voice, "What's wrong with you?"

"I don't know what you mean."

"Why have you been flirting shamelessly and ignoring Don? He's miserable."

I brightened a bit, then heard a familiar good-natured laugh and spotted Donny engrossed in a conversation with Doree. "Yes, I can see he's fighting tears."

"That's the first time I've heard him laugh all evening, and I say, good for him. About time he celebrated the new year."

"Nobody's stopping him."

I don't know where Donny was at midnight, but I was hiding in the bathroom. Over the noisemakers, I heard the strains of *Auld Lang Syne*. I sniffed loudly, picturing Donny kissing Doree. I had intended to stay put until the party was over, but someone knocked. I opened the door to a tomato-faced man named Ted who stunk of beer. To my astonishment, he embraced me, saying in a slur of words, "Wish me a Happy New Year, doll." He forced a kiss on me and when I struggled, he tightened his hold until I felt suffocated and queasy.

"Let her go." Donny's voice boomed. He grabbed Ted by the collar and wrenched him from me. I stumbled back into the bathroom. While Donny held him at arm's length, Ted feebly tried to swerve around and punch him. Then he bent over and threw up.

After Donny guided me out of the bathroom, I heard Doree yelp in disgust.

"I should help her," I said.

"No. You should dance with me." He pulled me to the dance floor.

"But I thought—"

He had me in his arms. "I can do a passable waltz."

"Why not ask Doree to be your partner?"

He drew back. "And why would I do that?"

I avoided his eyes. "I saw how you looked at her."

"Is that why you've been such a brat?"

"I'm not a brat." I could feel tears forming and this frustrated me. Weepy Katja.

"Katie, Katie, don't cry." He smoothed my hair. "Can it be you're jealous?"

"Go ahead and make fun," I mumbled into his jacket, an out-of-date scratchy tweed. His wardrobe needed a woman's touch.

"So you care a little for me?"

I would not say the three words before he did. "A little."

This didn't fool him, for he broke into his rich, full laugh. "I'm in love with you, Katja Varsten. Say you feel the same about me." He had stopped in the middle of the dance floor to gaze at me.

"I feel the same." I swallowed, then said, "I love you, too."

He kissed me with warm and gentle lips. I was in seventh heaven...until I heard the clapping. Our kiss ended. Hans and Doree came into focus. And a crowd of people around them.

Donny was blushing, and I'm sure I was, too. He said, "I didn't mean to be so public in declaring my affection."

"Everyone knew but Katja," Hans said, smirking.

So in at least one way, 1940 was a wonderful year.

CHAPTER 25
LOST IN THE STORM

On the second of January, 1940, I received a package. It was the one I had sent to the farm in Brühl, Germany before Christmas, and it was marked *Return to sender, no such person at this address.* My stomach cramped like it did the time I ate meat that had darkened too much. In this case the stabs of pain would torment me much longer.

I waited until Sunday's family gathering to break the news. Donny was generous with logs in the fireplace that afternoon, saying it would take more heat than usual to keep us warm.

Henry Spengler, normally a pillar of self-control, came as near to hysterical as I had ever seen him. He ripped into the package saying there must be a message inside, and when he found only the items exactly as we had wrapped them, he collapsed into a chair and buried his face in his hands. "Ingrid," he moaned. "Where is my Ingrid?"

When Hans crouched next to him, Henry looked over with a face red and puffy, as if he had been crying, but there were no tears.

Donny examined the package. "Someone sympathetic to Rosa and Ingrid must have returned it."

I peered up at him from where I sat cross-legged on the floor. "Yes?"

"Everything's here. The Nazis would have opened it and taken what they wanted, especially practical items like gloves and scarves, certainly the sugar and powdered milk. And they wouldn't have bothered to return anything."

This seemed true enough. "But then where are Grandma Rosa and Ingrid?" Panic shot through my body to my very fingertips.

In a flash Donny was at my side. "Don't assume the worst. They must be in hiding."

"I apologize," Henry said, "I should have held myself together for Katja's sake."

Hans sat on the arm of Henry's chair. "Emotion can get the best of people, even stoics like you."

"Is there someone you can contact," Donny asked, "a person who might know the whereabouts of Rosa and Ingrid?"

Hope blossomed in me. "Sally, maybe?"

"Or her husband," Hans said dryly.

"A moot point," Henry said. "Getting in touch with one will lead to the other."

The next day Henry sent a telegram to Herr Spengler.

• • •

Herr Spengler's response: *Ingrid Varsten and Rosa Varsten are traitors. I have no interest in what happens to them other than to wish them death in a concentration camp for harboring carriers of a plague to the Motherland—the Jews.*

• • •

We heard from this brutal man one more time. When we tried to contact Sally, Herr Spengler intervened, informing us that communication with Americans was forbidden. Our telegraphs to Grandma Rosa's neighbors went unanswered. As the months passed, Henry's frustration grew and he talked incessantly of returning to Germany to find Ingrid. The more Hans attempted to discourage him, the stronger his resolve, and this gave me another reason to toss and turn at night.

Daytime found me stumbling around in a haze of fatigue.

"You have to eat." Donny's voice was husky with concern. I was stacking books and he was scrutinizing me as he so often did now.

"You should be glad you don't have a fat fiancée," I said. "Better a stick than a marshmallow."

"I don't know about that. A marshmallow sounds cuddlier."

I blinked at him, hurt. Was I losing my attractiveness to him? I had not been attending to my appearance, allowing myself to become more haggard with each day.

The lines framing his eyes deepened. "If you love me, you'll take care of yourself. I'm beside myself with worry."

After that, I ate regular meals.

Hans helped bolster my spirits. "Trust in Donny's instincts that Rosa and Ingrid are in hiding. Hold fast to that belief."

"But why won't any of the neighbors answer our inquiries?"

"They're scared."

And so I did what I had done after the death of my mama and then my papa. I went on with life.

• • •

To fall in love in 1940 was to fear that your beloved would be snatched away. Only a fool could ignore what was going on in the world and the possibility of the United States entering the war. President Roosevelt had asked congress for money to mobilize a military defense; the Selective Service Act had been passed. Men from twenty-one to thirty-six years of age could be called up to defend our country. *Not my man!* I wanted to shout. *Please, please, don't take this gentle bookstore owner.* Donny could no more kill a person than I could, and we both knew it.

To keep me from dwelling on my fears, Donny made sure my mind was occupied with books and when I wasn't at Bookmarker he distracted me with outings. One spring day we went to the Washington Park Zoo, a favorite of mine. We stood before a cage admiring the male lion sprawled across the concrete, or at least I was admiring him.

Donny abruptly went down on one knee and took my hands in his. "Will you marry me?" he said.

"Yes."

The lion roared. It was as simple as that.

• • •

In May, I made a cake in honor of Ingrid's twenty-fifth birthday, persuading Frau Leonwell to help me. She stirred the frosting with a wooden spoon, more talkative than usual, perhaps because the attention was not focused on her. When the chocolate was as smooth as ice cream beginning to melt, she handed me the bowl and said, "Your sister was nice?"

I nearly laughed at this question, for *nice* would not be the first word that came to mind in describing Ingrid, and then I wanted to cry because Frau Leonwell had said *was,* as if my sister had died. But I kept these thoughts to myself so as not to discourage her from speaking. "Ingrid can be nice," I said, "but she has a temper." I applied swirls of frosting to the cake.

Frau Leonwell nodded knowingly. "Yes, my husband had a temper."

I pressed overly hard on the frosting and made a gash in the cake. "Ingrid is not like Herr Spengler. She lashes out with words, not fists." This wasn't entirely true, but my sister was no tyrant.

Crystal nodded again. "My husband hurt me with his fists and his words."

I spread frosting over the gash, then looked at her. "He can't hurt you anymore."

"No?" Her eyes widened as if she almost, but not quite, believed me.

"No. We won't let him." I handed her the bowl.

She took a big dollop of frosting and licked it from her finger (we'd had to teach her to do this), then said, "This will be the best cake ever."

• • •

We were celebrating Ingrid's birthday when Henry remarked, with no prior coaching from me, "Why, I do believe this is the best cake I've ever eaten."

I touched Frau Leonwell's hand. "It was made with love, that's why."

"Speaking of love"—Donny stood up—"Katie and I have an announcement."

"Hear! Hear!" Uncle Albert raised his hot cocoa in a toast.

"About time you got engaged." Hans clinked mugs with Uncle Albert. "Congratulations."

I stood next to Donny. "Would you kindly wait for us to make our announcement?"

Hans eyed us solemnly and Uncle Albert pinched his mouth into a pout using his thumb and forefinger.

I held in my laughter.

Donny cleared his throat. "Yes, well, we wanted to announce that Bookmarker was able to acquire the complete works of William Shakespeare at a cut-rate price." His face was grave.

"You aren't engaged?" Frau Leonwell asked in bewilderment.

Donny grinned. "I was only teasing. Katja has agreed to become my wife."

There were hugs and congratulations all around and for the briefest time we were able to forget that two people we loved were lost, maybe forever, and that others in the room could also be lost if our country went to war.

• • •

Planning a wedding was my escape. When an image of Donny in uniform popped into my head and set me to trembling, I grabbed the June issue of *Ladies Home Journal* devoted to brides. If I imagined new headstones next to those of Mama and Papa, I sidetracked myself by weighing the pros and cons of wearing a veil.

"I want Uncle Albert to give me away," I told Donny. We were strolling Mitchell Park, hand in hand, on a crisp October day, with cumulus clouds bulging above and leaves crunching beneath our feet, that time in Wisconsin when trees hold out their bare limbs to receive overcoats of snow.

"Hans will be my best man," Donny said.

I was pleased but wondered how Henry would react. I had a more pressing concern, though. "If I choose Doree for my maid of honor, you'll be looking at her instead of me."

Donny stepped in front of me and flopped his arms over my shoulders. "She's a pretty girl, but if the two of you were in a beauty contest, the crown would go on your head. I guarantee I won't even give her a passing glance at our wedding."

I ducked from under his arms and stood back from him. "But you were charmed by her."

"Whatever gave you that idea?"

I narrowed my eyes. "The New Year's Eve party. You and Doree couldn't get enough of each other."

He lifted his knit cap and scratched his head. "Women sure are perplexing." He pulled his cap back down so his hair stuck out in an uneven fringe across his forehead. "I was trying to impress your friend so she'd put in a good word for me. Doree's too bossy for my taste and sometimes her friendliness seems phony.

Besides, she has no interest in books. What would attract me to her?"

"When you put it that way, I can't remember," I said, loving him. "Did someone coach you on how to reassure your fiancée?"

"Katie, can't you tell that I'm totally, irrevocably smitten with you?" He cradled my hands in his.

We made our way back to the apartment swinging our arms and I wanted to hang onto this kind of love forever. I told myself that Donny's imperfections didn't matter. I would fight to make them not matter, for I didn't want to be like Mama in this respect, constantly finding fault with my husband.

CHAPTER 26

THREE WOMEN

Donny had just left when I answered a tap at my door, thinking he'd forgotten something. The thought of seeing him so soon was like expecting a candy dish to be empty and finding a bonbon. But it wasn't Donny standing in the doorway.

At the sight of the three women, I slowly sunk to the ground, vaguely aware that I was fainting.

I came to my senses on the sofa, with Grandma Rosa leaning over me. I brought my hands to her face like sepals encasing a flower bud. "I wasn't dreaming?" I said. "You're real?"

"Ja, your eyes don't play tricks on you."

She had lost a great deal of weight, which could be what had made her seem like a ghost in the doorway. "And Ingrid..." I sat up to study her. It was a curious phenomenon: while Grandma Rosa looked older and faded, Ingrid seemed younger and more vibrant.

"We were forced to flee Germany," Ingrid said. "We owe our lives to Sally Varsten." She gestured to the third woman, who I hadn't recognized. Sally was thin and pale in an olive green shift, her hair hanging straight and unwashed, her face without make-up.

I tried to keep my voice level, but it bit at her. "I thought you were called Frau Spengler."

She gazed at me dully.

"You'll hear the whole story soon enough," Ingrid said. "Please gather the family."

• • •

The *Reading Nook* was our meeting place.

An artist doing a portrait right then would paint the highlights in Henry's eyes and the warm colors in his face, capturing the happy twin of the Henry Spengler we had known for the past year. He sat next to Ingrid on the sofa with their shoulders touching, for him an act of great intimacy; she must have recognized this and placed her hand on his.

Donny escorted Grandma Rosa to one of the over-stuffed chairs, calling it the best seat in the house and fussing with the pillows so she wouldn't lack for cushioning. He paged through his German translation book constantly and because Grandma Rosa had acquired some English from Ingrid they were able to converse on a basic level. Donny offered Sally the other uphol-stered chair, but she insisted Frau Leonwell take it and chose a ladder-backed kitchen chair for herself. Uncle Albert and Hans pulled up chairs by Sally, but she slid backwards to keep separate. At my protest, Ingrid said, "Leave her be for now."

After the fire was sizzling and popping with pic-ture-perfect flames and everyone had a warm drink and a plate of cookies, Donny and I curled up on large floor cushions near the fireplace.

"Where shall we start?" Ingrid asked Grandma Rosa.

"The story begins with Sally."

We craned our necks to look at Sally, who stared at the bookshelves.

Ingrid spoke softly to her. "Please."

Sally writhed in her chair, her face contorted like a person drowning. "I was supposed to die in the gas chambers, I deserve to die." She dug the nails of her right hand into the left, where many marks already existed.

None of us knew what to do except Ingrid. She helped Sally to her feet and guided her into our half-circle while dragging her chair along. As soon as Ingrid set the chair next to the sofa, Sally sat docilely. She sniffled and wiped her nose on the back of her hand.

Ingrid snapped her fingers in quick succession. "Henry, your hanky."

Looking none too pleased, he produced a bright white, carefully pressed handkerchief.

Ingrid gave it to Sally, saying, "We owe our lives to this woman. Within hours of learning the farm was scheduled for a raid, she got us into hiding and arranged transportation out of Germany, providing us with new identities and fake paperwork. She had the money and the connections because of Herr Spengler. More importantly, she had a vast warehouse of knowledge—far more than he suspected—through years of listening in on conversations and rummaging through files. Herr Spengler was a staunch believer in the inferiority of the female sex and that was his downfall; he never gave women credit for cleverness and intelligence. He also thought he had Sally under his thumb.

"I asked Sally to obtain three tickets, saying we had another female to take with us. I didn't let on that *she* was this third person. I knew she wouldn't come willingly, yet staying would have meant certain arrest."

"But that's what I wanted," Sally said, "to suffer the same destiny as my mother and her husband."

"You were wrong to turn them in, but naive about their fate," Grandma Rosa said with the weariness of repetition. "You thought they would be imprisoned with other Jews, which is ghastly, but not the atrocity of a death camp."

"Another failing of your father"—Sally glanced from Henry to Hans—"is that he talks too much. Months after my mother and Herr Buchler were taken away, he bragged that he personally saw to their deaths in the ovens. He expected me to celebrate." Sally's face reminded me of newsprint gone brittle and about to disintegrate. But she held herself together and continued. "At that instant, I slid out from under Herr Spengler's thumb. I realized he had twisted my hurt into hatred, that my petty revenge led to horrible deaths for the woman who bore me and the man she loved. I must do a fitting penance to gain God's forgiveness. I should suffer the same death as the Buchlers."

"How could another death please God?" I said. "You saved two lives by risking your own. This seems a fair penance."

Grandma Rosa took a sip of hot cocoa. "We tell her this over and over, but our lives don't seem to count for much."

This lit a faint flame in Sally. "The opposite is true," she said. "Herr Spengler's cruelty taught me that I'd been loyal to the wrong people. You and Ingrid are heroines. I had to keep you safe."

Grandma Rosa grasped her cup in both hands, as if to draw the right words from its warmth. "If you harm yourself, you drop a yoke of guilt on our shoulders. You *must* choose a different penance than death."

In the silence that followed, the fire sputtered and a log broke with a snap. Finally Sally said, "Since you cared enough to smuggle me out of Germany, maybe God's will is that I do some good in America. I'll seek His guidance on this."

We all breathed easier then, but I couldn't help adding, "If you're tempted to act rashly, remember how Papa's suicide devastated us."

Sally met my eyes for the first time. "I don't want to hurt anyone else, ever."

"I have a question," Hans said to Ingrid. "How did you get Sally aboard the ship against her will?"

Ingrid laughed. "Ask Grandma Rosa."

When we all looked at her, she said, "I'm due for some more hot cocoa."

I smiled sweetly. "No stalling."

"Such disrespect." She made a clucking noise. "As a midwife, I could obtain medicine—"

"You slipped her a mickey?" I said, marveling at the complexity of people.

"Who is this *Mickey?*"

Hans grinned. "It means adding drugs to a drink."

Grandma Rosa touched the edge of her cup to her chin. "That is exactly what I did. Enough to make her appear drunk, but not cause unconsciousness. This put the spotlight on us as we boarded the ship, didn't it?" She smiled at her coconspirator.

"Oh, yes..." Ingrid stretched her arms above her head. "When I announced that Sally was distraught at leaving Germany, the gawkers stopped acting so damned self-righteous."

I took Grandma Rosa's cup from her. "I'll refill this. You've earned your hot cocoa."

Donny motioned for me to sit down, then gathered the empty cups on a tray. He returned with them filled and while he served us, Henry paced in front of the fireplace.

He stopped by Sally and said, "I hate to spoil the cheerful mood"—To me, he seemed bent on doing exactly that—"but how will you get a divorce from Father?"

"That won't be necessary. We never married."

My cup stopped midway to my lips.

"Herr Spengler promised we would wed some-day, but it seems the time was never right." She sniffled loudly. "Finally he admitted that my connection to the Buchlers would reflect badly on him politically, that his previous wife's insanity had taught him to be cautious." Her eyes darted to Frau Leonwell. "By then I was used to having nice things. Besides, I had nowhere to go."

Hans readjusted the logs in the fireplace with a poker. "Our father was such an ass." He said it so mat-ter-of-factly even Sally managed a smile.

"It goes to show that good can come from a bad situation," Ingrid said.

Henry glowered at the fire. "What good can come of a woman being a whore?" The flames seemed to glower back, illuminating his profile and giving him a menacing appearance.

I recoiled at his language, but Sally didn't so much as flinch. It was clear she had been called that and worse.

Grandma Rosa stood and tapped Henry on the shoulder. "You."

He raised an eyebrow.

"Fight the part of your father that has lodged in your heart and hardened it."

Henry shrank from her but said nothing.

"For Sally to live in the United States, she is better off not married to a Nazi," Ingrid said, "that much should be obvious. It's the good I was talking about."

"We would be wise not to mention her relationship to Herr Spengler in public," Grandma Rosa added.

"What about having a father who's a Nazi?" Hans said. "How will that reflect on his sons?"

"You both cut off contact with him and reunited with those who harbored Jews," Ingrid said. "Those actions show where you stand."

I munched the edges of a raisin cookie, then brushed crumbs from my lap. With a sidelong glance at Sally, I said, "You did call your husband by his first name, didn't you?" It seemed a ridiculous question, yet...

"He insisted on Herr Spengler." Her lips moved when she said this, but her face revealed no emotion of any kind.

Hans rolled his eyes. "I rest my case about the word *ass,* though no one raised an objection."

"You're well rid of him," I told Sally, then turned to Grandma Rosa. "Life in Germany before you left, what was it like?"

She sighed heavily.

An onlooker until now, Donny spoke up. "Our new arrivals need time to rest from their ordeal."

Ingrid translated and Grandma Rosa gave him an appreciative look. In German, she said, "Do not let this one get away, Katja. He's a gem."

Donny waited expectantly for a translation.

"Don't you dare," I warned Ingrid. "He'll be unbearable."

She laughed. "Grandma Rosa was telling Katja she hit the jackpot and should hang onto you."

"Though of course I already know that." I expected his eyes to light up, and they did.

• • •

For the first time, I looked forward to leaving Bookmarker early. I was eager to have Grandma Rosa to myself, though she would only stay a night before moving into Hans' old room at the Spengler apartment. Doree volunteered to sleep on the couch so that my grandmother and I could each occupy a twin bed and have privacy. After I tucked Grandma Rosa in as she used to do for me, I chuckled to myself, thinking about my understanding boss. Donny had said, "Don't come in tomorrow. Spend the day with your grandmother." I gazed into his eyes with their feathered lines at each corner and said, "I do love you." He replied, "And I, you." I thought my life as rich and full as it had been in the days of growing up in Germany.

But Grandma Rosa was not the same woman in America that she had been in Germany. Like the sunfish of my childhood plopped into an aquarium, everything was foreign and she kept hitting against the glass of language and culture. No chickens to tend, no homegrown vegetables to can, no fields to stroll. Donny and I took her to the parks and lakes of Wisconsin, but memories of Germany clouded her vision so she couldn't see our Midwestern beauty. She became snappish and difficult to please.

"Give your grandmother time," Donny would say in response to my grumbling. "This is a whole new country, an adjustment for someone her age."

It was Uncle Albert, not I, who would serve as the bridge between Germany and America. He asked Grandma Rosa to lend a hand with the preparations for our Thanksgiving feast, beginning with shopping. He spoke English well and through his translating she was able to interact with others. Being with him had the additional advantage of reminding her of home. I was too Americanized.

Albert also invited her along on his daily errands, hoping that together they would bring about a change in Frau Leonwell, who followed him mindlessly, showing no interest in the goings-on. My uncle was a wise man, for not only did Grandma Rosa coax Crystal out of the crazy behavior she sought as refuge, but Grandmother herself found new meaning in her life.

The women had much in common: a husband with an angry heart (or, as Hans maintained, no heart at all), sons who flamed the heat of that anger, and love for the homeland intertwined with shame. And more. Theirs was a generation whose high standards wounded children; while Grandma Rosa had not been as extreme as Frau Leonwell in her discipline, her treatment of Papa and Ingrid was severe. Yes, the two women had much to link them.

Grandma Rosa wasn't alone in needing a purpose.

"After two years of risking everything to save others," Ingrid confided to me, "my life as a housewife is making me dull-witted."

Henry assumed that his wife's craving for excitement had been sated in Germany, that she would welcome a calmer life in America. He should have known his wife better, though at least for a while circumstances gave him what he wanted.

CHAPTER 27
NEW LIVES

Christmas 1940 had little to do with gifts of a material nature. Our gifts were the company of each other, though I did receive a present that combined both features. After the midnight Christmas Eve service, Donny asked me to join him at Bookmarker, "to share a moment between the two of us." Something important was about to occur, this much I knew from the special day and early hour. Donny settled me on the sofa with a blanket to warm my lap and a crackling fire for the rest of me. He hemmed and hawed and then handed me a small package. Nestled inside a worn velvet box was a ring, a diamond encircled by a filigree of small rubies.

"I hope you won't think I'm penny-pinching by offering a family heirloom rather than a store-bought gift," Donny said. "This was my mother's engagement ring. I have a photograph taken right after my father gave it to her."

He handed me an ornately-framed portrait, one I hadn't seen before. The woman had a quiet elegance, her plain features made pretty by the warmth of her expression; her husband grinned as if he had a secret he couldn't wait to tell. Contemplating the two of them was bittersweet, for like me, Donny had lost his parents when he was young, another way in which we were bound together.

"You and my parents would have adored each other," Donny said. "Mom was the epitome of all a mother should be, and all a wife should be, too, judging by the way Dad chased her around and made her blush. He wasn't the same without her and I bet he wouldn't have succumbed to pneumonia if she had been at his bedside. Love gives you the strength to fight illness." He wiped away a tear. "It would mean the world to me if you allow this symbol of their love to become a symbol of ours."

"Why, Donald Kowalski, you speak like a poet." I extended my left hand and he slipped on the ring. "I'll cherish it."

To me, the ring had an extra dose of love attached because of the connection with his parents, and it also seemed to give me their blessings.

My sister was less impressed. When I displayed my ring that evening, she said I deserved a new ring of modern type.

"You make fun of the 'mindless sheep' who embrace every fad," I scolded, "yet you criticize me for not following fashion?"

"Do what you want then," she said with a shrug, her way of conceding the point.

• • •

On the first of February, 1941, Ingrid told me she was three months pregnant, stating this news as if it were a condition like diabetes to which she must adjust. "It's my punishment for giving in to passion and not taking proper precautions," she said, giving more information than I wanted, as usual. "Both Henry and I were starved for sex. I didn't have the time or desire in Germany, what with my rescue activities, though there was this Jewish man"—her tone became wistful—"What I would give to know that Mathias survived."

"Please stop." Daydreaming about infidelity while carrying Henry's child struck me as obscene.

"You want us to be close, or so you say, but then you censor me." She stalked from the room.

Did Ingrid really care about closeness? I doubt it, for she chose topics that would upset me and thus keep me at a distance.

Though Ingrid was blasé about the upcoming birth, the rest of us could hardly contain our excitement. We proposed names, agonized over the right bassinet or high chair, and debated the merits of girl versus boy. (I fancied a niece, but except for Grandma Rosa, who wished for "a healthy baby," everyone else agreed the first child should be a boy.)

In May, when Ingrid turned twenty-six, Grandma Rosa commented that her best present was wrapped within her body. Ingrid replied, "I'd rather have a string of pearls, thank you." We all laughed in an effort to convince Henry—and ourselves—that she was joking.

I held out hope that my sister would take on the glow attributed to expectant mothers, but instead her complaining expanded in proportion to her belly. "Oh, how I ache," she moaned. "The weight of the baby will make me sway-backed, I swear." Once, she fell onto the sofa like a fat doll whose knees won't bend, saying, "My legs, they're swollen to the size of rolled-up sleeping bags." Another time she chose supper to announce that "the gas will cause me to explode and send the baby into outer space."

We were stuck with the misery of her company and the best we could do was make light of it. At one point Hans asked Henry to consider having only one child so we would be spared from enduring Ingrid's bellyaching again. He and I laughed at his pun, but Henry sighed and said, "Perhaps the second child will be easier." In my opinion, both men were optimistic to assume that Ingrid would entertain the notion of another baby.

The subject of children came up one morning when Donny and I were working in the store before it opened. I was going through a stack of books brought in by an elderly woman, setting aside those I envisioned reading to my future niece or nephew. At his desk, Donny was checking off the contents of a box of new books. He looked at me over his reading glasses. "Remember those books we ordered on how to be a good parent? They're here."

"Now if we can just persuade Ingrid to read them."

"Henry could use instructions, too."

"You'll get no argument from me on that." I held up an especially nice edition of *Gulliver's Travels*. "Should we save this for little Emma or Roy?"

"A bit advanced, don't you think?"

"Surely the child will be precocious." I added the book to the pile that would be offered for sale. The bookstore did need to make a profit, after all.

"So," Donny said nonchalantly, "you like children, do you?"

"Hard to believe there are people who don't." I riffled through a new edition of *Tortilla Flat* and wondered how it ended up among the dusty old volumes.

"So...will you want children of your own someday?"

I closed the book to give him my full attention. "Of course. Why do you ask?" My stomach twisted into a knot. Had I taken too much for granted?

He examined a tear on the dust jacket of a cookbook. "Because I want children someday and I thought it was a subject we should agree on."

"Oh?" Naturally this was what I hoped to hear, that he saw children in our future, yet I found myself bristling. "Are you making conditions on getting married? If I wanted to remain childless, would you take back your proposal?"

"Easy, Katie. I'd be disappointed—and surprised, to be honest—but not enough to live without you. I proposed without any conditions except that you love me and I love you."

How sweet he was, what a shrew I was. "Donald Kowalski, I will be honored to be your wife and the mother of your children."

He came to me and kissed me until I was breathless. Then he backed away, stumbling over a stack of books. His face was flushed. "Let's not wait too long to take our vows."

I touched my own cheeks, which were radiating heat. "No, let's not wait too long."

"How about setting a date?"

I felt a quickening inside, as if I were a runner at the start of a race. "It will have to be after Ingrid's baby is born so we don't outshine that event."

"I've always liked fall."

In October I would be a married woman of twenty-two.

• • •

The anniversary of my parents' deaths in August came and went, yet for two weeks afterward I asked Donny to take me to the cemetery. My grief was like trudging up a steep hill and never getting to the top, as one event or another—this time my future marriage—caused me to lose ground. There would be no Mama to fasten the back buttons of my wedding dress and no Papa to give my hand to Donny. What finally drew me away from this fixation on death was my sister's contribution to life.

After spending a Sunday afternoon at the gravesites, Donny and I arrived at the apartment building to find my family in turmoil.

"Thank goodness you're here," Grandma Rosa said. "Henry called. Ingrid's having labor pains. I'm on my way."

Ingrid's insistence on Grandma Rosa as midwife had provoked many quarrels with Henry, though our grandmother had delivered hundreds of babies. When Ingrid asked me to assist, I said that my experiences as a little girl hardly qualified me for the job. She reluctantly agreed to let Henry hire a registered nurse, but turned a deaf ear to his pleas for a doctor. Henry had a physician standing by anyway—he didn't tell Ingrid this, but I knew and didn't object, being well aware of the complications that can arise during birth.

Ingrid screamed with the best of them; indeed, I can't recall any woman making a greater fuss. Her shrieks were more like the bark of a wild animal and seemed less from pain than anger at the pain. Fortunately the labor lasted only a few hours, for as Grandma Rosa would say later, Ingrid *ejected* her baby.

The boy was long in body as Henry must have been at birth, pale and slightly underweight. He didn't cry at first and when he did it was a whimper. I had the uncharitable thought that he was relieved to escape my sister's womb. The outside world had to seem peaceful by comparison.

While Grandma Rosa washed the baby, I cleaned up Ingrid, who yelped and squawked that I was being too rough. I wiped the sweat from her brow and ran a comb through her hair, then let her rest while I changed the linens.

"We'll bring Henry in when you're ready," I said, when I saw her stirring. "Would you like to put on lipstick?"

Ingrid's eyes opened in tiny slits. "Why would I care how I look? I want him to know how much I've suffered so he doesn't ask me to do this again. Let's delay telling him—that way he'll think I had a longer labor. I can start screaming again to convince him; believe me, I'll have no trouble screaming. It's all I feel like doing."

"Stop this nonsense," Grandma Rosa said. She finished dressing the infant in the new white gown she had sewn for him, then cradled him in her arms. "It's time you acted like a proper wife and mother. Take your newborn so your husband can see you together." She held the baby out to Ingrid.

"No." Ingrid raised her arms to hide her face. "If you won't let me scream, I'll go to sleep." She turned on her side and scrunched her eyes shut.

Grandma Rosa was agitated. She and I had witnessed women rejecting infants before, but not our own flesh and blood, and that was different. I touched her arm lightly and said, "Best to leave Ingrid alone for a bit. Let her get used to the idea of being a mother. We can care for the baby."

"But he should be with his mother, and if he'll nurse, that would be best for him."

I sat on the edge of the bed. "Ingrid, if you'll nurse the baby, we'll keep Henry away for a few hours."

Ingrid propped herself up with a pillow and flung open her gown to expose her breasts. "Give him to me."

"His name..." Grandma Rosa eyed Ingrid as she would a stranger beating a dog. "Have you and Henry chosen one?"

"As long as it's not *Henry, Frank,* or *Andreas,* I don't care. Let Henry decide."

Grandma Rosa and I turned away from the sight of the infant suckling while Ingrid stared off into space.

"Mother and baby boy are doing well," I said to Henry, closing the door behind me. "Give them time to get acquainted."

"Ingrid said she would be pleased if you chose the name," Grandma Rosa added.

Henry grinned. "Then he shall be Stefan Spengler. A good German name." He hooked his thumbs to his suspenders and rocked on his heels. "My son, Stefan."

I nodded. "I like that." The name fit the baby well enough—a soft name for a quiet child. And though

Ingrid's indifference was troubling, Stefan had a large family to make up for it. We already loved him.

• • •

At six weeks of age, Stefan attended his first wedding. The ceremony was held at our church on an overcast day. Leaves were falling and winter was coming and Donny appreciated the beauty in this. "We get to grab onto the tail feathers of autumn before it takes flight," my poet was heard to remark.

Ingrid led the procession as matron of honor, with bridesmaid Doree next in line. Both wore pastel blue gowns sewn by Grandma Rosa. I followed on Uncle Albert's arm, comfortable with him as a stand-in for Papa, but pretending that Mama's face smiled at me from the first pew. She would have loved the white satin dress Grandma Rosa made for me, with intricate lace added by Frau Leonwell.

Halfway up the aisle I stopped thinking about the family I had come from and concentrated on the family Donny and I would become. He was handsome in his dark gray suit, beaming as if I were an angel beckoning him to heaven. As soon as the priest pronounced us man and wife, my new husband kissed me, then lifted me off my feet and swung me around. We ran down the aisle laughing.

Standing in the receiving line, I anticipated a snide comment from Ingrid, but she surprised me by whispering, "That's the way it should be done."

I kissed each cheek. "Thank you, sister."

The reception was held at a local German tavern, with sausage and sauerkraut served family style on long tables. Sally had labored over the wedding cake, an elegant three-tiered affair with frosted silver bows and a gazebo to protect the miniature bride and groom. Donny fed me cake in small amounts, carefully removing any dots of frosting left on my lips. "I was going to lick it off," he told me, "but I'd hate to shock your grandmother."

I giggled. "A wise decision."

We danced every waltz, holding each other tight, and for my sake Donny tried the spirited polka. After stomping on my toes repeatedly, he turned me over to Uncle Albert, but appeared at my side the instant the lively tempo faded. Yet as the hours passed, my light-heartedness gave way to anxiety over the intimate act that would be expected of me that night. Sally had explained the sexual act years ago, but I was concerned that I wouldn't be able to bear the pain of the first time and that my body wouldn't respond as it should.

Ingrid's boisterous laughter interrupted my thoughts. She was getting louder, which had to mean she was drinking too much. Since I didn't want to witness a scene on my wedding day, I asked Donny when he wanted to leave.

"Hours ago." He nuzzled my ear, his thoughts having nothing to do with Ingrid. "I'm wild to have you all to myself."

Before we could slip away, Ingrid pulled me into the ladies' room, snapping, "Get moving!" at the waitress who was washing her hands.

After the girl scurried past, Ingrid said, "I know you're frightened and nervous, so I'm offering you advice, take it or leave it. Think about nothing else but giving Donny pleasure and enjoying the pleasure he gives you. Nothing else, do you hear? If you do as I say, you'll find sex natural and right."

She was serious, I could tell, and sober. "Thank you," I said. "I'll take your advice."

Her smile was guarded, probably to discourage a hug or kiss, for Ingrid could only absorb so much affection. She said, "You married for love, you lucky girl."

"Yes, but love can also grow once you're married. Look closely at Henry and you'll see much to love." At her unyielding expression, I added, "Did you know he planned to travel to Germany and find you, without regard for the danger to himself?"

She looked almost pained at this revelation.

"Your Henry is a prince who would slay dragons to rescue his princess," I said.

Ingrid would normally respond with sarcasm, but she must have thought better of it. "You listened to my advice, so it's only fair I listen to yours. I'll look more closely at Henry."

And then I was whisked away by my prince.

● ● ●

My family had bought us a night at the Pfister Hotel, where movie stars and rich people stay when they come to Milwaukee. A valet parked Donny's car, an old Chevrolet four-door that seemed dilapidated next to the others even though Henry had washed and waxed it for the occasion. A man in a burgundy uniform with gold epaulets took the luggage to our room, freeing Donny to carry me across the threshold. Even after he set me down, my feet barely touched the ground, for I was transformed into the waif from a Dickens' novel who suddenly learns she is royalty. I glided through the sitting area with its gold brocade drapes and tufted love seat and stopped to gawk at the four-poster bed with sheer curtains.

"Care for a drink?"

My husband was hovering over a skirted table with glass top. A bottle of champagne chilled in an ice bucket next to an array of cheese and fruit.

"Oh, my." My hand went to my heart. "This is far too rich for me."

"We deserve a night of luxury. Who can tell where I'll be in a few months, maybe a trench in Europe. In that case, I'll survive hell by picturing heaven—my beautiful wife in surroundings worthy of her."

At first I was upset that he brought up the war, but then I recalled Ingrid's counsel and knew that I had to grab each moment of joy (strange to have this advice come from my sister).

Donny popped the cork on the champagne, eager to toast our new life together. I thought my aversion to beer would carry over to any liquor and I prepared to tolerate a glass for his sake. Instead I loved the sweetness and the bubbles, and I also discovered that drinking two glasses of champagne made my anxiety disappear.

Donny kissed my neck and shoulders so that I tingled inside and when he touched me through my clothes, the feeling intensified until I knew the meaning of bliss. We undressed each other slowly, stopping to kiss again and again. As I grew more excited, my brain stopped analyzing and my passion took over and all I could do was give in to the pleasure. There was pain, but Donny was so gentle it hurt only briefly and then the pleasure returned.

Afterward, I lay gazing at my husband's face, his features showing his good nature even in slumber. I could imagine nothing better than lying cozy with him in a feather bed of finest down, lovers sleeping on a cloud. I was Katja Kowalski now, an honest name. I was where I should be.

• • •

I reflect on my wedding night often, how I was able to feel everything that was right in my life without fretting over what could go wrong. I'll always be grateful I had this respite and couldn't conjure up anything as terrifying as an attack on Pearl Harbor.

CHAPTER 28
LIVES FOREVER CHANGED

Ithought I was marrying a bookstore owner, but it turned out I married a soldier. In contrast to many new wives, I was blessed to have ten weeks with Donny before he shipped out. Yet how could I celebrate the New Year knowing that a few days into 1942 my husband would be gone?

After the attack on Pearl Harbor, Donny and I listened to the radio in Bookmarker with growing dread. Fear was like poison ingested in small amounts, making me sicker each day. "I won't let them take you," I said, raising my voice over the frightening drone of the radio. "You can hide. I'll tell the draft board you hated being married and ran away."

Donny looked up from the stack of books on his desk. "Don't talk crazy. I need to support our country. Think about all the innocent people who died at Pearl Harbor and the terrifying reach of Hitler. I have to serve, but I'll come back to you."

I clutched a picture book to my chest. "No, you won't. I lose every person I love."

• • •

My husband's leave-taking was traumatic for everyone because of me. Against a backdrop of Ingrid's disgust and Henry's tight-lipped embarrassment, Hans pried my hands from Donny so he could board the U.S. Army bus. Grandma Rosa was occupied with calming Frau Leonwell, whose agitation increased in proportion to my own. Sally stood motionless, eyes vacant.

In the months that followed, I let the bookstore consume me. I kept it open ten hours a day; before and after business hours, I stocked shelves and did the bookkeeping. At day's end, I trudged upstairs, but once in bed minus the distraction of work, I was flooded with images of my husband bloody in a foxhole, emaciated in a prison camp, tortured by Nazis (Germans, the horror of that). I lay awake each night in torment.

One snowy morning, shortly after I opened Bookmarker, the bells on the door jingled. I peered around the cash register to see Hans shut the door and flip the *Open* sign to *Closed*.

"Don't do that," I said. "I can't turn away customers."

"Yes, I see they're coming in droves." He gestured at the empty store. "You don't need to be open at eight in the morning."

"But those are my posted hours."

"Change them. It can't be producing much extra income. Most businesses have cut their hours."

I didn't want to discuss the real reason for staying open, so I changed the subject. "What are you doing here this early?"

"I'm worried about the both of us."

The quiver in his voice might have been a car screeching to a halt, so effectively did it capture my attention. I was instantly aware of the dark circles under his eyes, the haggard set of his mouth, his torment. I came out from behind the counter. "What's wrong?"

He picked up a volume at random and paged through it. "I've been asked to report for a physical"—he slid the book back on the shelf—"to determine my fitness for military service."

I closed my eyes in an effort to absorb this information. With my focus on Donny, the possibility of Hans being called up hadn't entered my mind, I suppose because it would be like sending a lamb to battle. I forced myself to look at him. "You can get out of this."

"I'd be branded a coward for trying."

"Let's build a fire to keep us warm while we talk." I led him to the hearth.

"You should save the wood for when you really need it."

"I really need it now."

He lit a match to a pile of kindling, then placed a small log on top. We sat close together on the sofa, listening to the whoosh of fire discovering wood.

"It *is* soothing," he said finally.

"Let them call you a coward. You don't have the temperament for combat."

He snorted. "You're saying I'm poor soldier material because I'm homosexual?"

Now *I* was annoyed. "You'd make a poor soldier because you're you."

He sighed and rested his head on my shoulder. "I'd make a damn poor soldier."

We talked for most of the morning. Hans had come seeking permission to speak about the unspeakable— how to dodge the draft. I gave permission willingly and in the privacy of the bookstore we were free to discuss paying a doctor to label him unfit for duty.

"He'd have to make up a disease," Hans said, "since I don't have a heart murmur, like Henry, and damn it, Father didn't cause me to lose an eye." He laughed harshly.

"What if you nurtured a condition a doctor could diagnose honestly? You could irritate your skin and bring back your eczema, or fake an illness that suggests a more serious problem. Complain of dizziness, for instance." I went so far as to propose he use his homo-sexuality to avoid soldiering. "I think it's considered a perversion," I said. "They might not want you because of it."

"Yes, and then my status as a pervert would be broadcast to the neighborhood and I'd be assaulted or worse. Not only that, Jazzman would fire me."

As we stared at the embers in silence, I replayed a painful conversation in which I told Donny I had inves-tigated how to sidestep military service, so he needn't risk his life. He was shocked. "Your love is making you selfish," he said. "What if everyone tried to avoid serving their country? Tyrants would rule. Don't bring this up again."

Donny's usual displays of affection stopped in the ensuing days, and one morning, when he was standing at the bathroom sink shaving, I asked if he still loved me. He grabbed a towel and wiped shaving cream from his chin, then turned to face me. "I love you with all of my heart." He stroked my cheek. "Love means taking the good with the bad."

I shied away from his touch. "The bad?"

"If you're honest, you'll admit there are things about me you'd like to change." I opened my mouth to object, but he put a finger to my lips. "Listen. No one loves everything about another person. If they say they do, they're either lying or deluded—they love someone who doesn't exist. I love you, but not some of your near-sighted views. You only seem to care about those who are close to you."

His words sucked the oxygen from the air.

"I won't lie to you," he continued, "and you shouldn't lie to yourself. Consider whether you'd be a better person for looking beyond your family to your neighbors, and further to the people of the world. If you can't see that far, it's all right because I love you for so many other reasons we can disagree on this point."

Only after Donny left for the war did I realize that loving a person "warts and all," as Hans put it, is to love more truly and I became secure again in Donny's love for me. He would have to accept the wart of nearsightedness, though, for I would never willingly sacrifice my family and friends to a greater good and I saw nothing wrong in this.

And so I connived to keep Hans in my world by whatever means.

"You can declare yourself a conscientious objector," I told him. "Refuse to serve in the armed forces on moral or religious grounds." I had memorized the correct terms to use for purposes of persuasion.

He flopped to the corner of the sofa and extended his arms to either side. "But here's my dilemma—I genuinely support the war effort. I just can't *kill* anyone. Isn't there a way to defend the cause but avoid battle?"

Of course there was. He could be a conscientious objector who refuses to bear arms and serves in some other capacity. But must I share this information with my beloved Hans? If he believed the only way out was to decline service altogether, life would go on as normal, with Hans visiting me at the bookstore during the day and singing at Jazzman at night. Donny would be ashamed of me for having these thoughts, but then I had no intention of sharing them.

It wasn't for humanitarian motives that I ended up telling Hans the truth. I told him because he was my best friend and he needed to make his own decisions.

He decided. Uncle Albert would manage the apartment on his own while Hans went off to war as a sailor in the Navy. He did not declare himself a conscientious objector and when I demanded to know why, he replied that he had to make the same commitment to his adopted country as those who were born here, for only then would he be a true American. I suspect his real reasons were buried too deep for him to acknowledge and had to do with his fear of being perceived as weak or effeminate; he had equated the inability to kill (for a just cause) with cowardice, a legacy from his father.

• • •

In the meantime, Ingrid grew increasingly restless and unhappy. As we stood outside Bookmarker on a breezy March morning, she adjusted the awning on Stefan's stroller and complained that her life lacked purpose.

"But you're raising a son." I gave Stefan my hand to grasp and marveled at the long fingers with their delicate nails. I smiled and received the slightest smile in return. At seven months old, he had the tentativeness of a wild bunny.

Ingrid rolled her eyes. "There are millions of mommies raising kiddies. It's a self-indulgent act. The world doesn't need more people and there are plenty of orphans to adopt."

I picked up Stefan. "Don't talk like that in front of him."

She laughed. "I know you think he's a gifted child, but he doesn't understand what I'm saying."

I shook my head. "Look in his eyes. He understands the message beneath your words."

She looked at me instead. "Can you watch him while I run an errand?"

Ingrid often left Stefan with me or Grandma Rosa at the last minute. This was in addition to the times she asked us in advance. She probably spent a couple of hours with her son in the morning and a few minutes putting him to bed at night. Henry cared for him after supper, at Ingrid's insistence; she reminded him that having a baby had been his idea.

I kissed Stefan on the forehead. "Sure, I'd love to take care of this sweet boy." He was better off with the rest of his family; we all gave him more love than his mother did. "Come inside and set the playpen up next to the counter."

"You're a doll." Ingrid was all business and eager to be on her way. She unfolded the playpen I had bought secondhand for Stefan's visits and said, "I'll see you in a few hours." I knew this meant all day, that she would return just in time to greet Henry at the door.

I watched in alarm as she walked away. "Ingrid," I called.

She looked over her shoulder, frowning.

"Say goodbye to Stefan."

"Oh, yes. Bye-bye," she said, without warmth, then blew him a kiss.

"Mama," he said, his arms open in a flaccid manner. At least that's what I thought he said. If I was right, it was his first word.

His mother was already out the door and didn't hear him.

• • •

Though I would have done anything to keep Donny and Hans out of the military, I supported the war effort in my own small way, starting with a display of books in the window of Bookmarker. Since most of my customers were women, I placed *The Navy Wife, How to Dress at Wartime,* and *So Your Husband's Gone to the War* in prominent positions, but I also added books about battle strategies and politics for the older men and those of draft age who were not able-bodied, like Henry.

Instead of keeping the bookstore open for long hours, I volunteered with the Salvation Army. Not only did we assist people struggling in this time of rationing, we also gathered warm clothing to send to our men overseas. At night I wrote newsy letters to servicemen, despite the objections of Grandma Crystal (which is what we had come to call Frau Leonwell). "Men will think you are flirting," she warned, "a married woman without morals."

"Don't be silly," I said. "My letters contain news of Milwaukee and cards from school children addressed to *Our Heroes in Uniform*. There's never anything of a personal nature."

I didn't allude to Les, the lonesome soul who had begged me for a photo—which I didn't send—and then promised that once released from duty he would give me a better life than my husband ever could. I answered that I loved my husband and knew the right girl would come along for every soldier, including Les. I closed by saying I would not write to him again. When another letter was delivered, I marked it *Return to Sender* and popped it back in the mail.

I wrote to Donny every day. At week's end, I tied the letters with a ribbon and sent the packet out the following Monday. I reported on my daily activities like entries in a diary, to create the illusion of living together despite the huge distance between us. Once, on an impulse, I reread my letters before corralling them with ribbon and was embarrassed by their mundaneness. I added a postscript to Sunday's letter, asking Donny if my correspondence bored him. His reply was emphatic:

My Dearest Katie,
Your letters are anything but boring! They transport me to a better world. Never stop telling me the details of your life, how you paint a line on your stockings to give the appearance of seams, clever girl, or how you reuse fabric from our old clothes to make Stefan's shirts. These stories are reminders of sweetness for

those of us whose ears ring with bomb blasts
and human screams.
   Your Loving Husband, Donny

Donny sent a letter each week and I came to rely on this regular communication. A larger gap in time would cause my mind to flip through each possible scenario—wounded or captured or dead—like previews for a war movie. Donny would write of his buddies, the friendships formed lying in a foxhole or shivering in a tent. He spoke of Ron and Pete and Oscar with such affection I grew attached to them. But there was a price to pay. Pete was the first to be killed, leaping from a foxhole to help a man who had fallen. The war years were like that: we shed tears for people we had never met.

• • •

I was hosting a birthday breakfast in Ingrid's honor, with the whole family present, including Stefan in his high chair, when she announced that she had joined the Women's Army Corps.

After a moment of stunned silence, Henry slapped his napkin on the table and stood up. "I forbid it." He sat down again and carefully arranged the napkin on his lap as if that settled the matter.

As if anything with Ingrid was ever settled.

"It's done. If you try to prevent me from going, I'll file for divorce."

Poor Henry, forced to handle this news with an audience. I couldn't bear it. "What about Stefan?" I said from across the table, trying desperately to keep my voice level so as not to alarm my nephew. "You would leave your child motherless, a boy not yet one?"

Ingrid leaned forward just enough to jut her face into mine, the bully of childhood. "He'll always have a mother, but she'll be away for a while. He'll be fine. After all, I've managed without a mother for most of my twenty-six years."

"Yes," Grandma Rosa muttered, "and look how you turned out."

"No small thanks to you."

"Katja makes an important point." Henry's voice was shaky. "Who will care for Stefan?"

"You're his father," Ingrid said. "You can assume some responsibility."

"He has a job," Grandma Crystal said.

"So he does." Ingrid glanced at her, then at Grandma Rosa. "I see plenty of freeloaders who can babysit during the day."

Why must Ingrid heap hurt upon hurt? "Shame on you." I said. "You elevate your selfish needs over those of your son, then speak to your elders with disrespect when they protest. I say goodbye and good riddance." In a ludicrous gesture, I clattered down the stairs and collapsed into a chair by the fireplace, leaving my guests to fend for themselves.

It wasn't long before Henry descended the staircase with barely a creak and aligned himself on the sofa. He had taken to smoking a pipe and lit it now, staring into the fireplace that of course had no fire on this May morning. Perhaps he imagined one, or maybe the gloomy cavern fit his mood.

"I'll help watch over Stefan," I said. "He can come to the bookstore with me."

"Thank you." He cleared his throat. "I'll never divorce Ingrid."

"I know that."

We sat lost in our own thoughts.

Eventually, Grandma Crystal clumped down the stairs. Grandma Rosa followed, rocking Stefan in her arms. "I couldn't talk any sense into your sister," she said with a shake of her head.

An hour or so later, Uncle Albert appeared with Ingrid. I had a flicker of hope until I read their faces and saw that my sister's resolve was all the stronger for our efforts to discourage it.

Ingrid faced the fireplace, then spun round to confront us. She was the fire. "I'll be leaving in September," she said, "the day after Stefan's birthday. I expected congratulations for making this sacrifice, but you're all too rigid in your thinking." Her eyes landed on me. "Katja speaks with Senta Varsten's disapproving tone. She cannot see beyond her tidy bookstore. I'll not stand by while Hitler destroys my people and takes over the world."

Right then I hated her. "You and your self-righteousness. *I* can't see beyond *my*self? You don't care about the Jewish people. You're using them to get revenge for all the wrongs done to you. This is for you, not them."

She glared at me. "Who would have thought milquetoast Katja could express an opinion? The problem is, you think your opinion matters to me. Well, it doesn't." She turned away. "Henry, will you take me home or shall I walk?"

He was pathetically eager. "I'll take you. Let me get Stefan."

"Happy birthday, Ingrid," I said, with mockery that was ugly to my own ears. These were the last words I spoke to my sister before she left to join the war effort.

• • •

Ingrid had crossed some line, or maybe she hadn't. Maybe she was the same old Ingrid and I was the one who did the crossing. I alone refused to have anything to do with her. Grandma Rosa knit her a scarf and mittens. Grandma Crystal embroidered *Ingrid* on a set of hankies. Uncle Albert treated her to a hamburger at Moser's. Henry took her dancing, and even Sally baked her cookies. They weren't condoning what Ingrid had done. She was family and they were afraid she wouldn't come back. The difference was, I never wanted to see her again; whether she came back or not was irrelevant to me.

On the eve of Ingrid's departure, Grandma Rosa approached as I dusted Bookmarker's shelves. She grabbed a feather duster for herself and began working beside me. "Ingrid is your sister—"

"No sister of mine abandons her husband and child."

She used a step stool to reach a higher shelf. "In her mind, she isn't deserting them anymore than Donny deserted you."

I let out a puff of air. "How dare you compare her to Donny."

"Katja"—Grandma Rosa waited for me to look up at her—"Ingrid confided that Stefan was better off without her, that she doesn't have what it takes to mother a child and she might do more harm than good."

"She was certainly right about that."

Grandma Rosa flicked the duster across the books, then stepped down so she was level with me. "What if Ingrid doesn't return? You'll regret not saying goodbye."

"I'll have no regrets." I knew this wasn't true. Even so, I would not speak to my sister.

• • •

How naive I had been to marry only two months after the anniversary of Mama and Papa's deaths, as if I could buck the trend of loss. First Donny, then two more were gone, just like that— my brother-in-law (brother, really, as I thought of Hans) and my sister. Mama used to say her girls were opposites and that I was the one who looked on the bright side. She would have been disappointed that this was no longer true. I stopped singing. I didn't listen to music on the radio, only reports of the fighting. Any reading I did was the newspaper. I had trouble getting up in the morning and so I delayed the opening of Bookmarker to eleven o'clock most days. I closed at five and went to bed early. I slept as if drugged and I slept a lot.

Weeks into this routine, I shuffled downstairs and was surprised to see my family bustling about. The store looked different. I gaped at Grandma Rosa in her apron and jumped when Grandma Crystal scurried by with a mop. I squinted in the intense light. "Someone cleaned the windows."

Hands on her hips, Grandma Rosa looked me up and down. "About time. No wonder you open the store so late. With the grime on those panes, you couldn't tell it was daytime."

Her intent was to shame me, but I felt nothing.

"Speaking of grime…" Grandma Crystal pointed a finger at me.

"What?"

She fluttered her hand. "The mirror. Go look."

I shrugged. "Not interested."

Grandma Rosa slapped me on the behind. "Get upstairs." It didn't occur to me to disobey and she hurried me along with little shoves.

She pulled me into the bathroom and flicked on the light. "Look at yourself."

I studied the stranger in the mirror.

Grandma Rosa held up a strand of my hair and let it fall back in a clump. "When was the last time you washed your hair?"

"Uh"—My brain was still sluggish—"now that you mention it, I don't know."

"Katja."

Something in her voice broke through my stupor. I looked at her beloved face in the mirror and saw that it was puckered with anxiety. She said, "Remember your father, how he stopped caring…"

I rubbed my knuckles in a way that had become such a habit the skin was raw. "But I can't keep caring. The war kills more people every day. The next will be Donald Kowalski or Hans Spengler or Ingrid Spengler. Fear is poisoning me."

Grandma Rosa turned me so we were eye to eye. "You have the strength to bear whatever life gives you. I've seen people undergo much worse. The Jewish people we harbored, my god, they had seen their loved ones dragged off to death camps. Those dear to you have a fighting chance, and they're all fighters." The violet glint of her eyes seemed too vivid for me, like looking into the sun. "And remember, you aren't alone. We're here, your family."

• • •

Donny expressed his concern loud and clear through V-Mail. His message arrived soon after I had written one paragraph for the entire week. I had no need of ribbon since there was just the single page. I listed the customers who visited the store and their purchases, and then I described my loneliness. I told him there was nothing else to write. He set me straight:

Dearest Katie,

How is our nephew, Stefan? Is he walking? What books does Henry read to him? Does Uncle Albert continue his whittling? He was turning into quite the craftsman before I left. I'd like a collie—has he tried to carve any dogs yet? Be sure to ask him. Tell Sally my mouth waters when I think of the strawberry tarts she bakes. I can't wait to gorge myself on tasty food after these bland rations. Let Grandma Crystal know that I never go anywhere without one of her hankies in my pocket. Besides its obvious usefulness—my nose runs constantly in this damp British climate—the fancy embroidered initials will ensure its return if I lose it! Tell Grandma Rosa I miss her and I've come to appreciate her nursing skills, for a good nurse makes all the difference in the recovery of our wounded.

And you, dearest, must go on with LIFE. In time, your family will be reunited and before you know it we'll all be getting on your nerves again. In the meantime, regain your sunny disposition. Read the comics. Go see a Marx Brothers movie. Eat ice cream sundaes! I dream of doing these things, but most of all I dream of being with you, showing you how very much I care.

Your loved ones are miles away in other lands, not six feet underground. Stop mourning us before our time.

Your Loving Husband, Donny.

I was bent over the dark chasm of hopelessness and my family pulled me back before I toppled in.

CHAPTER 29
KEEPER OF SECRETS
1946

I was cuddling my infant girl, Elisabeth, in the apartment above Bookmarker. Donny had made a rocking chair for us—such an unexpected bonus, this practical skill. He complained that the chair creaked but I told him this was its way of conversing with me.

Donny had been released soon after the war's end in 1945. (Many servicemen were not so lucky and had to wait until well into the next year.) For once, September was a time of reunion rather than parting. Beth was conceived the day after he came home, in a midday tryst, my boldness a shock to both Donny and me.

Yet when I first saw Donny, I drew him to me like a mother instead of a wife, for he was weary and forlorn despite our joyous reunion. He had not killed anyone in his service to our country, thank God, but he witnessed the results of killing and maiming by others. Due to his emotional state after the death of his friend Oscar, he was reassigned to a medical unit. He traveled in the ambulance, bringing injured soldiers from the battlefield on stretchers and completing paperwork to keep them at the hospital or send them back to the mainland. In the months after Donny's return, I coaxed him out of his blue moods by focusing on our life together and the blessed event in our future.

On this June afternoon, my husband was working downstairs and I was watching my daughter's eyelids flutter as she drifted into sleep. A knock at the door startled me. "Come in," I called, expecting Hans. He had returned in December, my best Christmas present ever, and often stopped by on his way to work.

But it wasn't Hans.

Ingrid stood in the doorway. She looked older— after all, she was thirty now—but prettier. And stylish. She wore pleated slacks and a sweater with pearl buttons. Yet something was different beyond these superficial changes. What was it? The lines in her face had relaxed, the angry discontent was gone.

"This is my niece?" She approached the rocker.

I nodded and pulled back the blanket to reveal my baby's face. "Elisabeth Senta Kowalski."

Ingrid folded her arms and surveyed us. "Mother and daughter are beautiful and serene."

"Thank you." I had nothing to say, though I hadn't seen my sister in years. She had arrived home a few weeks ago, but no one in my family could persuade me to visit her, not even Donny, who said it was time to forgive. I thought maybe I had forgiven Ingrid, but I couldn't forget. It wasn't that I was mad; I just didn't care to know her anymore. Sometimes people stray too far from what is right and we must let them go.

Ingrid swayed almost imperceptibly, as if adjusting to a force I couldn't see. "I know the welcome mat isn't out for me," she said, "but may I talk to you?"

"Yes, certainly." I wasn't interested in Ingrid, but I loved Stefan. After being abandoned by the most important people in our lives, my nephew and I naturally gravitated toward each other. In the years I cared for him, we became close, especially since Donny had insisted on waiting until war's end to start a family. Always the optimist, Donny assumed he would survive and he didn't want me to be alone while expecting a baby.

"Is Elisabeth asleep?" Ingrid asked. "Would she be more content in her crib?"

"Her eyes are closed, so the logical conclusion is that she's sleeping. Do I need my hands free to talk?"

Ingrid smiled. "Only to strangle me. I just don't want any distractions. Would you mind?"

"Yes, I do mind. Speak softly so as not to wake her. If my attention wanders, you'll have to be patient until it returns to you." I breathed in Beth's sweet baby smell and it was like a tonic, calming my nerves.

The rocking chair was a friend, an ally, but when it creaked, I held still to silence it.

Ingrid seated herself on our plaid sofa, a second-hand piece whose shabbiness embarrassed me. She ran her fingers across the nubby fabric. "Has Henry told you anything about my life with the WACs?"

He had, though I never asked. "He said you nursed soldiers injured on the front. That must have been difficult since you once said you couldn't stand being around sick people."

Ingrid laughed. "Katja never forgets anything that offends her, even after more than a decade. Has it ever dawned on you that people can change?"

I sniffed. "Am I to be insulted, then?"

She slouched as if she'd tried to lift a heavy object and failed. "No, but please be open to what I have to say."

"Then say it."

"Your words, the last time I saw you, they stayed with me."

"Which, in particular?" I had worked to blot that day from my memory.

"You said I joined the WACs for selfish reasons, not to help the Jewish people."

I still thought this.

"You were right at the time, but I want you to know I'm different now."

You can't change your personality.

She tilted her head back and smoothed her hair, which had auburn highlights and fell in soft waves. "You don't believe me." Her eyes met mine again. "Your judgments harden with time, it seems. When I joined the WACs, I received on-the-spot training because of the shortage of nurses and tremendous need. You can't imagine the state soldiers would arrive in—"

"I can. Donny helped at the hospitals—"

"Yes, he and I have spent many hours trading experiences. He needs to unburden himself. Encourage him in this. It isn't healthy for a man to keep his suffering bottled up inside to avoid upsetting his wife."

Donny had confided in Ingrid? If he tried to talk to me about the war, I switched topics. Otherwise I seemed to say the wrong thing. When he expressed horror at the bombings of Hiroshima and Nagasaki, I said that our country needed to do whatever it took to protect our freedom. "The Japanese are *people*," he retorted, "not vermin to exterminate. How are we any better than the

Nazis when we decide it's acceptable to murder women and children, whole families, along with the soldiers?" I accused him of being un-American and stormed from the room.

Mulling over the conversation later, I was upset with myself for parroting words I'd heard on a radio broadcast, about issues I should have more carefully considered. Yet I didn't express these regrets to Donny, and I realized now that this incident marked the last time he talked to me about what he called "the nightmare I never wake up from." He had found a more sympathetic listener in Ingrid.

"What goes on between husband and wife is none of your business," I told her.

"Of course you would say that. I'll set his story aside, then, and continue with my own." She crossed one leg over the other like a man.

"Let me put Elisabeth in her crib." I was suddenly protective of my daughter's innocence, as if she could absorb whatever Ingrid had to say.

When I returned, Ingrid said, "Did she wake up?"

"Not really." I smiled, thinking of Beth's gurgling as she adjusted her arms and legs and snuggled back into sleep.

Ingrid seemed to be waiting for a cue from me. "I'm ready," I said.

She held onto the edge of the sofa, as if bracing herself. "Tending the wounded, I tried to get used to the blood, the screaming, the hideous injuries. I thought I was tough enough to withstand the violence of war, but the truth is, the brutality softened me. I began to feel people's pain. All that time in Brühl hiding Jews was more about getting back at Germany than helping real people. I've always felt separate from others. I broke through this, just a little, when I met Mathias. Somehow he got to me. But he was gone in a flash. Another man, John Aaron, lingered."

I put my hands over my ears. "I won't hear that you were unfaithful to Henry."

Ingrid uncrossed her legs so both feet rested on the ground, then gripped her knees. "You're twenty-six years old, not a child anymore. Stop acting like one." She curled and uncurled her fingers, finally resting her hands in her lap. "People have complicated reasons for doing what they do and you shouldn't be so high and mighty. You never know how you'll react unless you're actually in a situation. What happened between John and me will help my relationship with Henry. All I ask is that you hear me out. Can you do that?"

"All right," I said in a clipped voice, my insides tangled like cats in a fight.

Ingrid kicked off her shoes and brought her legs up next to her body. "This sofa is so comfortable," she said, patting it. She smiled crookedly and began her story.

"I'd been working for two years in England when they carried John into our field hospital. By then I was good at assisting the doctors. John was conscious, talking, though not always making sense. He had a sturdy face, strong and handsome, and being from Boston, a fetching accent. His hair was curled back from the sweat and grit of battle, and later, when I washed it for him, I discovered it was a rich dark brown. But oh, his eyes...I knew straight away he was a person of substance. The color didn't even register at first because it was as if I looked directly through his eyes to *him*. I believe I fell in love the first time our eyes met. Don't set your jaw, Katja, you can't make me feel guilty. This was no act of will.

"He'd been shot in three places and was in agony, though he tried not to show it." Her voice swelled with pride. "I was so relieved when the morphine took effect and he could escape the pain, at least for a while. I assisted the doctors as they stabilized him, then stayed at his side while he rested from these efforts. Nurses often did this with the seriously injured, trusting that the presence of a caring person helped pull them through."

Ingrid put a hand under each armpit, as if warming herself against a frigid wind. "John suffered terribly. He was sent by ambulance to the closest hospital; he needed emergency surgery to amputate his leg from the knee down. He requested me as his nurse—he said I was a tender and gentle angel sent to heal him. Can you imagine anyone saying that about me?" She laughed. "No, I see you can't." She nodded as if to herself and went on. "I'd been at our makeshift hospital for months and was due to leave anyway, so they reassigned me. Fate intervened." She searched her pockets and pulled out a handkerchief—Henry's, I saw by the initials—then dabbed at her eyes. Following my gaze, she folded the letters inside the cloth.

"During his six months at the hospital, John learned to get around on crutches. I'd sit outside with him during my break or come to his room after my shift. We talked about our hopes and dreams. He was a photojournalist in civilian life and he continued taking pictures while serving his country, recording his sentence in hell, he said. He gave me his camera and photos for safekeeping. I treasure them." She clasped her hands together like a young girl, the young girl she never was. "We were soul mates."

It seemed that every muscle in my body tightened. *Sometimes people stray too far from what is right.* "You didn't let on that you were married?" This voice of mine was brick hard.

Her hands dropped to her lap, palms up, lifeless. "No. I pretended Henry didn't exist, not only with John, but in my own mind." She stared past me and at that moment I saw on her face what she would have seen on mine when we were children, if she had looked: the desperate need to be *understood*. A weight lifted, so real I swear my shoulders relaxed with its removal.

My words came out wobbly, for I was forming thoughts as well as trying to scale the barrier of Mama's morality. "I think you wanted to start over, do it right and fall in love instead of merely accepting a man as a companion. You didn't mean to be unkind or disloyal to Henry."

Ingrid's face took on the glow of light filtered through stained glass. "Yes, that's it," she said. "My marriage never came up. I didn't wear my rings because they were a nuisance when we had to scrub up or put on gloves. Besides, most WACs were unmarried and John made that assumption about me."

"Where is he now?" My stomach churned at the notion of a divorce in the family, its effect on Stefan, on Henry.

Her face lost its glow, replaced by a haunting desolation. "He's been dead almost two months. They let me come home because I was so distraught."

"Ingrid." I went to her side and held her. "I'm sorry." We stayed together as sisters for longer than we ever had. Then she took a breath and continued.

"An infection coursed through his body, a complication of the original surgery. Nothing would halt it—John compared it to Hitler's invasion—and he lost weight, grew weaker. At some point I realized I was losing him.

"One evening I was sitting next to his bed, staying the night as I usually did, dozing on and off. When the hospital had settled into quiet moans, doors closing here and there, I felt John's hand on mine, warm with fever, I thought. But it was the heat radiating from his heart, or I like to think so, anyway. He said the pain had subsided and there were three things he knew for sure—that it would be back, that he was dying, and that he wanted to make love to me before he left the world. He apologized for not making an honest woman of me." Ingrid smiled. "When I told him we were married in spirit, his eyes filled with relief. 'We are,' he said. 'I love you.' I told him I loved him too, then slid under the covers. Though we had sex it wasn't about sex but love and I've never felt anything like it."

"Yes, that's how it is with Donny."

She touched my knee. "Cherish him." Her hand fell to her lap again. "We were together on a Tuesday and John died on Friday. She looked away. Far away. "That's not the end of my tale, there's something no one knows, something you probably won't accept."

Ingrid said this with such dignity that my answer had no accusation. "You're going to have a baby?"

She was not surprised that I had guessed. "I need your advice. Should I tell Henry?"

I overcame my modesty to ask if she had been intimate with him since her return.

"The very night. I'm no fool."

I flinched. Still Ingrid. "Who else knows about your love affair? Did you tell anyone in England, any of your fellow WACs?"

She hung her head. "No one."

"Then it should remain secret."

"You, of all people, are advising me to live a lie?" She looked sideways at me.

"There's no reason to hurt Henry. You would break his heart."

"Yes," she said distractedly, "there's that. But in fact I debated hiding the truth for my child's sake."

"Oh?"

"I grew up with a mother who resented me and a father who was afraid to show affection. The same forces would effect this baby, only it would be his father resenting him—I'm sure it's a *him*—the difference being that I wouldn't hide my love."

I felt disheartened that she hadn't mentioned Stefan, that she wasn't aware of her resentment toward him.

Ingrid patted her stomach. "I don't want this child to feel like an outcast. Think how that affected us as sisters."

I pondered this. "If you had been kept in the dark about Nadine Oberlin, your life would have been better."

Ingrid shook her head. "Mama wasn't capable of ignoring the truth and hiding her feelings."

I conceded this, but couldn't help reflecting on what might have been. "Let's say you could go backwards in time and a magic wand could make Mama believe you were her child. Would you choose such a life?"

"I would be a different person in that case. John loved me for the person I am. If this *better* life meant never knowing John, I would take my life as I have lived it."

The light instead of the shadows. Ingrid truly had changed.

• • •

I traded secrets with my sister.

I expected her to fly into a rage when she heard about Mama's house money, but she said I did the right thing, that if she had known years ago she would have demanded cash and frittered it away. Now she *wanted* a house. "I'm not searching anymore," she explained. "My life is with Henry and our children."

That summer of 1946, Ingrid and I bought a small farm outside of Milwaukee. According to the law, the property probably belonged to our husbands, but no matter; we agreed that what was ours was theirs anyway. We just liked the idea of women having property in their names, and our husbands had no objections. The farmhouse, outbuildings and barn sat on forty acres of land, most of which we rented to a neighboring farmer for growing corn and tomatoes. Grandmothers Rosa and Crystal made themselves at home in what had been a cottage for the hired help. I smartened up the kitchen with gingham curtains and a matching tablecloth. Ingrid gave the outside a fresh coat of white paint and redid the green shutters. Pregnancy did not slow her down.

Henry and Ingrid moved into the main farmhouse with Stefan, anticipating the birth of their second child. Although I was an owner of the farm, I didn't live there, which goes to show the unexpected curves the road of life will take. I continued my career as a businesswoman at Bookmarker, with my home in the upstairs apartment. Donny and I owned the building, which might not qualify as a house by Mama's standards, but then again I was learning to live by my own standards now. At Ingrid's insistence, part of Mama's money was used for necessary repairs. Donny and I loved Bookmarker and agreed that raising children among books was at least as good as surrounding them with farmland. Besides, every other Sunday the entire family gathered at the farm. It reminded me of childhood summers in Brühl and I took pleasure in creating these new memories for Beth.

Uncle Albert moved into an upstairs room in the farmhouse, but Hans stayed on at the Cherry Street apartment building. Though he had given up his dream of being "discovered," he had regular engagements in nightclubs and at special events like weddings. His pianist of many years joined him to co-manage the building. They pretended Steve lived in the efficiency, but I knew the truth. Oftentimes Hans and Steve went on "double dates" with the same two woman and these odd couples served as covers for each other. When people teased Hans about marrying, he would laugh and say he was a confirmed bachelor who enjoyed playing the field. Strange how I became the keeper of secrets.

When the shop next to Bookmarker became vacant, Donny and I convinced Sally to rent it and establish a bakery and coffeehouse. We put tables outside our businesses to encourage people to savor German pastry with coffee and a good book. Sally lived in a small room in the back of her shop. As penance, she devoted her free time to volunteer work for her church, mostly raising money for the poor. I'd like to say these charitable acts quelled her unrest, but they merely kept her alive. Suicide was a sin in the Catholic Church and thankfully she no longer contemplated the act, but she remained a tormented soul. I persuaded her that a mopey, sullen baker would be bad for business, so while she was working, she gave herself permission to liberate the animated and outgoing Sally of the past.

Ingrid's baby was born on the second day of the New Year, 1947. As Henry had hoped, his wife dealt with this pregnancy better than the first; in fact, she was a different woman. She had the glow that was absent when she carried Stefan and for the first time, she seemed happy. I remembered something Papa once said, that happiness comes from feeling loved. He was almost right. I believe you must feel loved *by someone you love*. For Ingrid, that someone was John. Poor Henry had been powerless to make her happy.

Although Ingrid uttered the same ungodly screams during delivery, once the baby was born, she opened her arms to receive him. "Welcome, Adam John Spengler," she said, nuzzling his puffy cheeks. (She told Henry it was her turn to choose the name.) Grandma Rosa was relieved but I was watchful, and in the coming months I would remind Ingrid to be fair in managing her boys. Although she had become more affectionate toward Stefan, only through vigilance could she keep favoritism from creeping in. I also trusted that she would learn to love Henry. Learn to love your own husband? I had to wonder how Mama would cope with these newfangled ideas, along with other twists and turns in the lives of her daughters—from my career to Hans' homosexuality to Ingrid's child by a soldier. Not well, I would wager, but beneath her outrage she would have loved us anyway, as she did Ingrid, and oh, wouldn't Papa have made a fine grandfather?

Adam was an adorable child. While Stefan accepted displays of affection on his own terms, Adam clamored to be gathered in our arms so he could shower us with kisses. *Charmed,* Grandma Crystal would say of him. Henry was nonplussed by this smiling, cooing, precocious son. "How in the world did two such Gloomy Guses produce a ray of sunshine?" he asked. We all laughed.

That same night Donny commented that "Adam could have been adopted, so little does he resemble his parents in looks or spirit." I knew Adam favored John but I replied that if you looked closely you would find Ingrid's brown eyes and dark lashes. You wouldn't think so at first because Adam's eyes shone with goodwill, but close scrutiny revealed the mother in the son.

"Yes," Donny said, "I see what you mean."

When Adam was only a few months old, Ingrid informed me that she intended to raise him in the Jewish faith, since that was the heritage of his parents. How would it appear to others, I said, to have one child Jewish and the other not? She considered this, then said, "You're right. I'll raise both boys Jewish. After all, Hitler would have declared Stefan a Jew." She went on to point out that many in Milwaukee were of the Jewish faith.

I sighed. "But Henry isn't Jewish, and he might like a say in the decision."

Ingrid was constantly shaking up Henry's world, yet I'd come to the conclusion that he was attracted to this quality in her. Maybe she expressed some Bohemian part of himself, though it was hard to imagine him having such a side. In any case, they would have to work it out between them, as they always did. As for me, I would concentrate on making Stefan feel loved in spite of his mother's distance. Would the love of auntie, brother and stoic father be enough? But he also had grandmothers who had softened in their lifetimes, as well as an uncle and great uncle. Besides, Stefan was more independent than Adam, less needy when it came to affection. Could I be worrying about the wrong child?

I knew only too well the cost of being dependent on people.

CHAPTER 30
SISTERS AND BROTHERS
Summer 1955

I sat on the steps, watching my girls play hopscotch in front of Bookmarker and trying to figure out where I went wrong. Elisabeth was nine and had Donny's auburn hair, though curly and thick like mine. Anna was five, with light brown hair straight and coarse as fishing line. I was an experienced parent of thirty-five, yet how poorly my first child had prepared me for my second! Beth had never been anything but quiet, loving, and obedient. She slept through the night after only a few months and adapted to changes in her schedule with hardly more than a startled look. Terrible twos? If denied something, Beth pouted but soon forgot about it, so eager was she to please her Mama and Papa. I used to wonder what all the fuss was about in raising children. With the birth of our second, I understood.

Anna cried in a way that set me on edge, a shrill, relentless agitation that would not be comforted, so unlike Beth, whose whimpers moved me to nestle her on my lap. Anna's first year exhausted Donny and me, for she woke up often in the night. We tried holding her, feeding her, ignoring her, but nothing worked. It seemed she had to screech her displeasure until she spent herself. And then she slept. Usually by this point my nerves were so frayed I would rise and get the percolator going to provide a soothing cup of coffee while I waited for the sun to rise.

As a toddler, Anna had difficulty sharing, but people told me this was normal. I wanted to ask, is it normal for her to push her big sister hard enough to knock her over? And Anna never seemed to rest; if I turned my back for an instant, I would find her ripping pages from a book or scrambling up the stairs with a scissors.

Donny and I had a business to run. This had not been a problem when Beth was little, for she was content in her playpen and soon could be trusted to totter about between the shelves. It took one lesson for her to learn to hold books in the highest regard. When she chewed on the corner of *Alice in Wonderland*, my *No!* so upset her she never mistreated another book. Anna, in contrast, wanted to destroy books because she resented being told she couldn't, or maybe she was jealous of our love for them. If we put her in a playpen she banged against the bars like a lion cub snatched from its mother, her shrieks clearing customers from the store. We had to take turns watching her upstairs, a strain during busy times when the store needed two people. Sometimes Grandma Rosa cared for Anna, but this meant trips back and forth to the farm, which wasn't practical on a regular basis. Anna worshiped her Great Uncle Albert, and he was devoted to her, but that didn't mean she minded him and I couldn't ask him to chase after the girl and risk aggravating his arthritis. Hans offered to babysit in a pinch, but Sally said she couldn't manage our youngest. So the burden of Anna fell on her beleaguered parents.

Kindergarten loomed in the near future, casting an ominous shadow. Donny and I agonized over how such a headstrong girl would adjust to school. Overhearing one of our many conversations, Grandma Rosa admonished us yet again to be firmer in our discipline; her shadow, Grandma Crystal, stood in the background bobbing her head. Punishing Anna only made her resist us more. Nor was it good for us. Once, after she climbed onto Donny's desk and scribbled all over his papers, he gave her a spank on the bottom. She didn't cry and the minute he released her, she grabbed a book from the shelf and flung it at him. He was shaken by having taken his hand to her and simply picked up the book. We both felt hopelessly inadequate.

• • •

On a Sunday in July, I sat at the picnic table with the women in my family, watching the cousins play hide-and-seek in the large backyard of the farmhouse. One result of Adam's good nature was that he followed Stefan around with adoration written on his cupid face. Stefan for his part was protective and nurturing of his little brother, so when Anna demanded to be *It* again, he told her it was Adam's turn.

She had a fit. With a familiar heaviness in my stomach, I got up to intervene knowing I would trigger a full-blown temper tantrum and a barrage of advice about the proper management of Anna.

Ingrid touched my shoulder. "Mind if I try?"

"I can handle my own—"

She squeezed lightly. "Anna is like I was, don't you see it?"

Yes, I did, and I was terrified. Was Anna's temperament some cruel joke played on me by God? I had to face the truth—I could *not* handle my own child. "Do what you can," I said, sitting down again, holding back tears.

Ingrid walked up to the children, crooking a finger at Anna. If I had done this, my daughter would have taken off in the opposite direction, but she approached her auntie with an open and curious expression. Ingrid put a hand on Anna's back and called the others together. She stooped to be at eye level with the children and asked Anna to explain why she was upset. I rolled my eyes. What was the point? She would demand to be the seeker. Which is exactly what she did. I looked over at Grandma Rosa knowingly, but her eyes were fixed on Ingrid.

"Why should you get two turns in a row?" Ingrid asked matter-of-factly. "That doesn't seem fair."

"I'm the best *It*. They're slowpokes."

"They probably take longer to find you because you pick such good hiding places. Now Anna, here are your choices. You can take turns, which means you hide from Adam, and after that, from Stefan and then Beth. You and I can hide together, if you like—"

Anna perked up and to my shame, my heart sunk, for if Ingrid succeeded, it would shine a light on my failure. I told myself that what counted was helping Anna.

"—but if you can't accept these rules, you may stand with me and watch the others play."

Anna shook her head back and forth vehemently.

"There's one more choice. You can do something else, like draw a picture or sit at the table with the grown-ups."

"Hide with me." Anna beseeched Ingrid not just with her voice, but her eyes. She had never looked at me that way.

Ingrid took her by the hand and they scurried off while Adam counted.

The grandmothers were well into their discussion of how children are pampered nowadays when Ingrid joined us at the table. "All's forgiven," she said. "They're friends again."

I swallowed my pride. "Thank you."

"You're welcome. And now I'll add my two cents worth to the advice the older generation has been heaping on you."

"Well!" Grandma Rosa folded her arms. Crystal followed suit.

"Oh, come on, you take pleasure in telling us how to raise our kids. Sometimes we accept your guidance, sometimes not. But let's face it, no one understands a strong-willed girl better than I do."

"No one would argue with that." A smile played on Grandma Rosa's lips despite her effort to be stern.

Ingrid turned to me. "Take a hint from Uncle Albert's handling of a similar girl many years ago. Give Anna some control over what happens to her. Butting heads only makes matters worse. She's stubborn."

"As a mule. We know." Using more force than was necessary, I tapped the salt shaker against the picnic table to free up the contents.

"And let me offer the same advice you gave me—"

I stopped my tapping, certain I wouldn't like what was coming.

"Don't favor one child over the other."

My grip tightened around the shaker, which was a tin replica of a milk can. The little handles cut into my palm. "How dare you point a finger at me! I love both my girls."

"No one's questioning your love," Ingrid said. "If you take an honest look at your family, though, you'll see that Beth is the *good* girl and Anna is the *bad* girl"— she waved her hands to dismiss my objections—"You can be sure they know how you feel. Kids pick up on such things."

I let the shaker roll on its side; salt spilled out in a mound. "Who are you, to pass judgment? I'm waiting for your apology."

Ingrid snorted. "You've got a long wait." She sauntered off.

I set the milk can upright. "The nerve of her." Hot with anger, I brushed the spilled salt onto the ground and then rubbed my hands together to remove the excess.

"Ingrid is worth listening to in this," Grandma Rosa said.

"Stop saying I'm a bad mother!" In my haste to get away, I slammed my knee into the bench, but I made sure to run to the farmhouse without limping so they wouldn't have another reason to criticize me. I shut myself inside the guest bedroom and broke into tears.

Nearly an hour had passed when Donny peeked in to tell me lunch was being served.

"I'm not speaking to any female member of my family," I said.

He sat on the bed, where I lay with a cold wash-cloth on my forehead. "Headache?"

"Ingrid-induced."

"What did she do now?" He put the washcloth aside and gently rubbed my temples.

I described the incident with righteous indignation.

Donny continued massaging in silence. Finally he said, "I never thought about it before, but we don't treat Anna the same as Beth."

I pushed his hands away. "You can't mean that. We love them equally."

"Relax, Katie." His sweet smile eased my tension, but only a little. And then not at all. "Ingrid upset you because her words rang true," he said. "Of course we love both girls, but maybe not with matching love. Face it, they're poles apart and we gravitate toward Beth."

"I won't face a lie." I turned into the pillow and murmured, "Go away."

He moved in closer. "What did you say, sweet-heart?"

I wrenched my head free to shout, "Go away!"

He recoiled as if he'd bent to smell a rose and got stung by a bee. I squeezed my eyes shut but the expression on his face remained in my mind's eye.

The click of the door signaled that I was alone.

• • •

A month later, Anna sought me out in the kitchen to ask if she could spend a week at the farm.

"I'm sorry," I said, "your father and I can't leave the bookstore for that long."

Her brows knit. "No. Auntie Ingrid said just me."

"She invited you for a week?" I looked askance at her. "Is this one of your stories?"

She crossed her arms and puckered her lips. "Auntie asked me 'specially."

"Let me call her, then." I expected Anna to stop me. She didn't.

After getting Ingrid on the line and discussing Anna's request, I held my hand over the receiver. "Auntie says she did invite you to the farm, but she didn't talk about how long you could stay."

Anna looked like she was about to cry and I felt small inside.

"You can begin your visit this Sunday," I said. "The rest of us will go home, but you can stay the week."

Her grin took over her face. She jumped up and down, clapping her hands, then raced around the kitchen table.

Anna's emotions had a wildness that unnerved me. "Enough," I said.

Anna stopped in her tracks, her face tense with the concentration it took to keep still.

"Go and play."

She skipped from the room and I made the arrangements with Ingrid, keeping my tone businesslike. I hadn't received an apology yet.

When I hung up the phone, I was startled to find Beth staring at me. "Anna bragged that she's going to the farm for a week."

I nodded.

"Can I go, too?"

"*May* I go. No, you'll stay with us."

"Why, Mama?" She lowered her eyes as if she were being punished.

It hadn't occurred to me to include Beth in the visit and I searched for an explanation. "This is something Aunt Ingrid wants to do with Anna." Then it hit me. The reason I wanted Beth home had nothing to do with Ingrid. The truth was, I looked forward to a week without Anna, but I couldn't bear for Beth to be gone that long. I would miss her too much.

I sunk into one of the vinyl-covered kitchen chairs and rested my arms on the table.

"It's okay, Mama. I'll stay here if you need me."

"Let me think about it, okay? If this time is for Anna, we can arrange another time for you." I was trying to speak like a normal mother, not a bad mother who favors one daughter over the other. "Run along now. I need to speak with your papa."

She shuffled from the room, turning repeatedly to check on me.

I'd brought up Donny as an excuse. What I wanted was to be alone, to get my thoughts together, but first I would check on Anna.

Beth was already at her desk, immersed in a book, and didn't notice me passing by. I found Anna in her room jumping on her bed.

"Stop that right now," I said. "If you want to go to Aunt Ingrid's you'll have to be good."

She plunked herself down at the foot of the bed. "Then I won't get to go." She said this with such conviction my heart ached. I grabbed her in my arms and held tight. "Oh, sweetheart, you *are* good."

Though she resisted at first, her body gradually lost its tautness and her breathing slowed. When I released her, she was peaceful, a flag that drifted in the breeze instead of flapping about and fighting the pole.

• • •

In the end, shared secrets and a shared curse brought Ingrid and me together. We learned to laugh about our preference for one child over the other and joked that we should exchange kids, Stefan for Anna. We had an unspoken pact: each of us would try to make up for what the other couldn't give. I understood Stefan's unassuming and sensitive nature. "He'll be a great scientist or engineer," I told Ingrid. "Adam can introduce him to girls." We both laughed at this.

As far as Anna was concerned, Ingrid knew how it was to bump against the world, though she noted an important difference between herself and my daughter. Anna's boldness arose from self-confidence rather than from a need to prove herself. "This girl will go far, you watch," Ingrid said. "She'll become a politician or filmmaker, someone flamboyant who leaves a mark. In the meantime she can vent her energy on the farm. She wants to ride. Let her have a pony."

We became optimistic that despite our failings, our children would develop into adults who always, always, felt loved. Papa was so right about the importance of that.

Ingrid and I didn't stop arguing (A pony? Who would take care of it?), but we forced each other to see our children, our motherhood—ourselves—from another point of view. And in the process we finally began to know and appreciate each other.

What I mean to say is, the half sisters became whole.

ACKNOWLEDGEMENTS

I am indebted to my mother, Emilie Cywinski, for all the reasons a daughter is indebted to her kind and virtuous mother, but in this particular case for her willingness to share—by means of an old-fashioned tape recorder—the details of her childhood in Germany, her immigration to the United States, and her experiences growing into adulthood during the Great Depression and World War II. Although *Chasing My Sister's Shadow* is not Emilie's story, aspects of her life are woven throughout and give the novel its heartbeat.

My dear friend and critique buddy, Sarah Jo Smith, has my deep appreciation for reading this novel several times and offering invaluable feedback. Not only did her insights and editing skills improve my novel, but Sally has the ability to infuse her critiques with praise and encouragement that invariably lifts my spirit. Our faith in each other as writers helps keep us on-track.

Another dear friend, Andrea Taylor, deserves heaps of gratitude (and chocolate) for reading through my novel more than once and offering an astute commentary that had me rethinking critical passages. Andrea always seeks to understand the underlying themes of a story in an intelligent and thought-provoking manner. What interesting discussions we've had!

Thanks also to Kathryn Briggs, a valued friend who I have come to know through the amazing Albany Historic Carousel & Museum. Kathryn is an excellent proof-reader, fast and thorough in spotting errors and making corrections, plus an avid reader who loves books.

Mary Undlin and the members of Club Read gave me important input on a much earlier version of this novel and I will always remember their enthusiastic support. Mary has never stopped encouraging me in my writing pursuits and is a treasured longtime friend.

Rebecca Swift's creativity and talent were instrumental in translating my artistic vision into a top notch book cover that showcased my paintings, plus collaborating with her is so much fun! Thank you also to the folks at 52 Novels, for helping me navigate the technical aspects of book production and for always being willing to answer a seemingly endless barrage of questions.

And finally, I'm grateful to my husband, Allan Haight, not only for applauding my hard work, but for reminding me to enjoy the process. As in other aspects of life, he keeps me grounded, while at the same time urging me to take flights of fancy. Life is about balance and he lives accordingly.

• • •

READING GROUP GUIDE
Chasing My Sister's Shadow

1. If the Varstens had remained in Germany, how would their lives have been different?
2. What factors precipitated the discord between Senta and Andreas?
3. Andreas believed that he loved Senta more than she loved him. Do you think this was true? If so, did Senta's feelings have anything to do with Ingrid? Do you think a similar imbalance exists in most relationships?
4. What factors drove Andreas Varsten to commit suicide? Could his suicide have been prevented?
5. Were there any negative effects on Katja as a result of being the favored child?
6. In what ways had Katja changed by the end of the story?
7. Would Ingrid have been better off if Senta and Andreas had given her up for adoption?
8. Was Ingrid likeable? Explain why or why not.
9. Why did Ingrid become interested in women's rights? What about her personality and/or background made her sensitive to gender bias? How did Katja evolve with respect to women's rights?

10. In what ways had Ingrid changed by the end of the story?
11. Is *Chasing My Sister's Shadow* Ingrid or Katja's story?
12. If you had the same history with Sally as the Varstens did, would you have accepted her back into the family despite her actions in Germany?
13. If the episode between Ingrid and John hadn't taken place, do you think Katja would have reconciled with Ingrid?
14. According to Katja, "Sometimes people stray too far from what is right and we must let them go." Have you ever let a beloved person go because he or she did something morally unacceptable? If so, did you ever regret your decision?
15. In your own life, what key events changed you for the better (or worse)? Think about what your life might have been like without the occurrence of these events.

ABOUT THE AUTHOR

Lena Lingemann holds a Ph.D. from the University of Wisconsin at Madison and worked as a school psychologist for many years. In addition to her middle grade novel, *Promise of Wings,* she has had two children's picture books published (under the name Linda Lingemann). Lena lives in Oregon's Willamette Valley with her husband and always at least one Bouvier des Flandres. You can contact her through Facebook and www.lenalingemann.com.

www.ingramcontent.com/pod-product-compliance
Lightning Source LLC
Chambersburg PA
CBHW020226180626
46810CB00006B/2067